G.I. JOE

SIERRA MUERTE

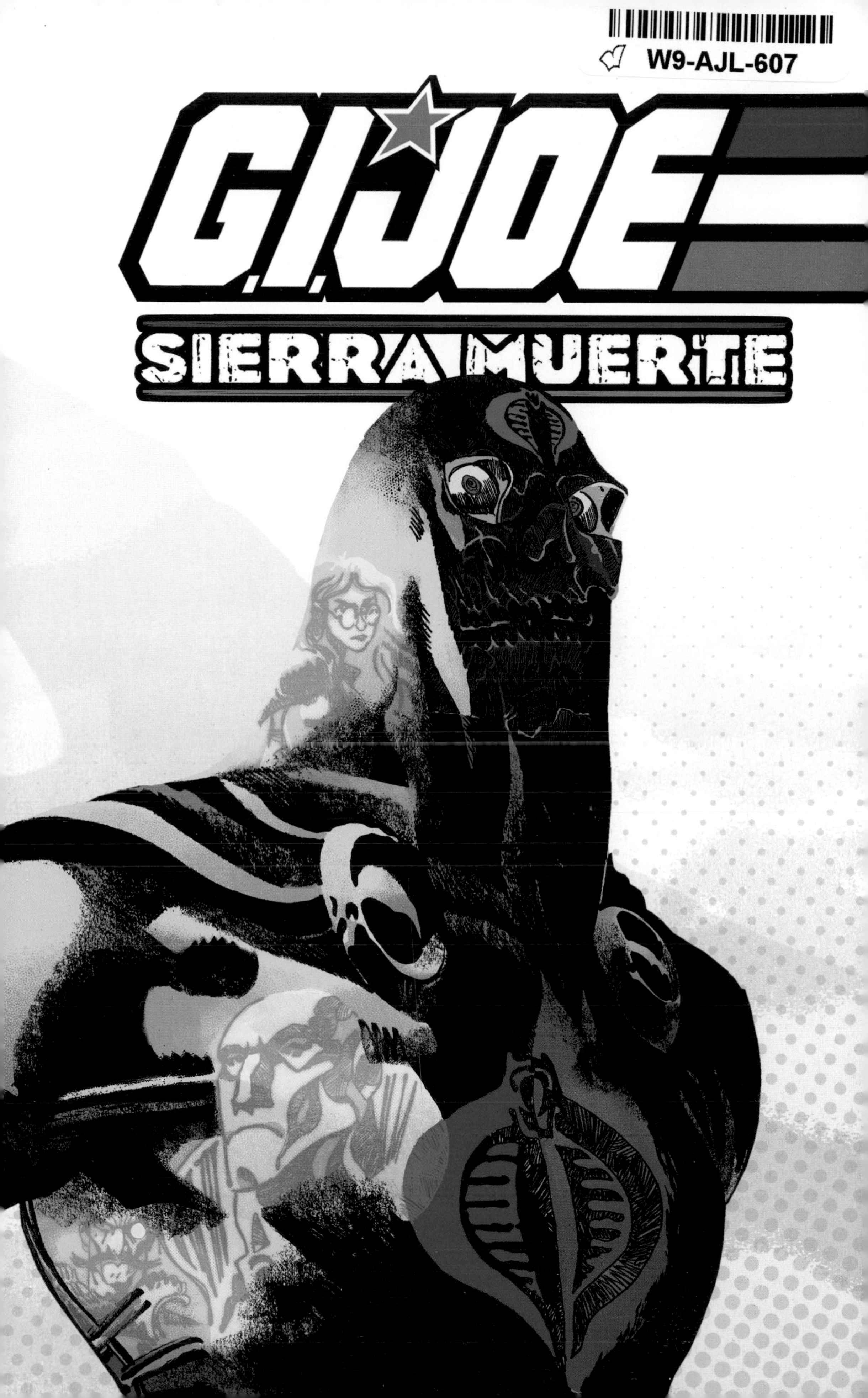

Become our fan on Facebook **facebook.com/idwpublishing**
Follow us on Twitter **@idwpublishing**
Subscribe to us on YouTube **youtube.com/idwpublishing**
See what's new on Tumblr **tumblr.idwpublishing.com**
Check us out on Instagram **instagram.com/idwpublishing**

IDW
www.IDWPUBLISHING.com

Licensed By:

COVER ARTIST
MICHEL FIFFE

COLLECTION EDITORS
JUSTIN EISINGER
AND **ALONZO SIMON**

COLLECTION DESIGNER
CLAUDIA CHONG

Chris Ryall, President, Publisher, & CCO
John Barber, Editor-In-Chief
Cara Morrison, Chief Financial Officer
Matt Ruzicka, Chief Accounting Officer
David Hedgecock, Associate Publisher
Jerry Bennington, VP of New Product Development
Lorelei Bunjes, VP of Digital Services
Justin Eisinger, Editorial Director, Graphic Novels & Collections
Eric Moss, Senior Director, Licensing and Business Development

Ted Adams and Robbie Robbins, IDW Founders

ISBN: 978-1-68405-524-1   22 21 20 19   1 2 3 4

Originally published as G.I. JOE: SIERRA MUERTE issues #1–3.

Special thanks to Hasbro's Ed Lane, Beth Artale, and Michael Kelly for their
invaluable assistance.

For international rights, contact licensing@idwpublishing.com

ART & STORY
MICHEL FIFFE

SERIES ASSISTANT EDITOR
MEGAN BROWN

SERIES EDITOR
DAVID HEDGECOCK

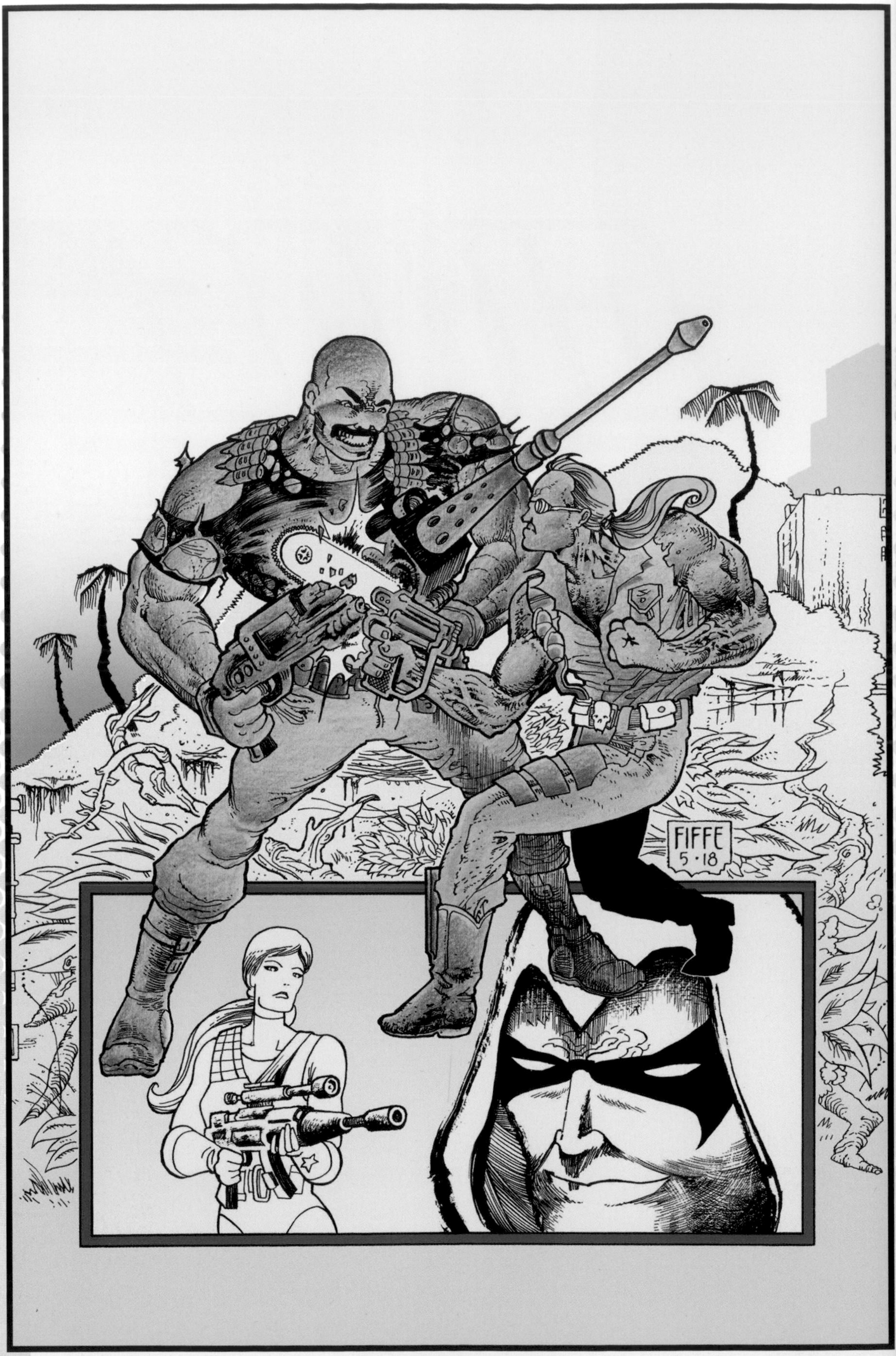
FIFFE
5·18

ART BY **MICHEL FIFFE**

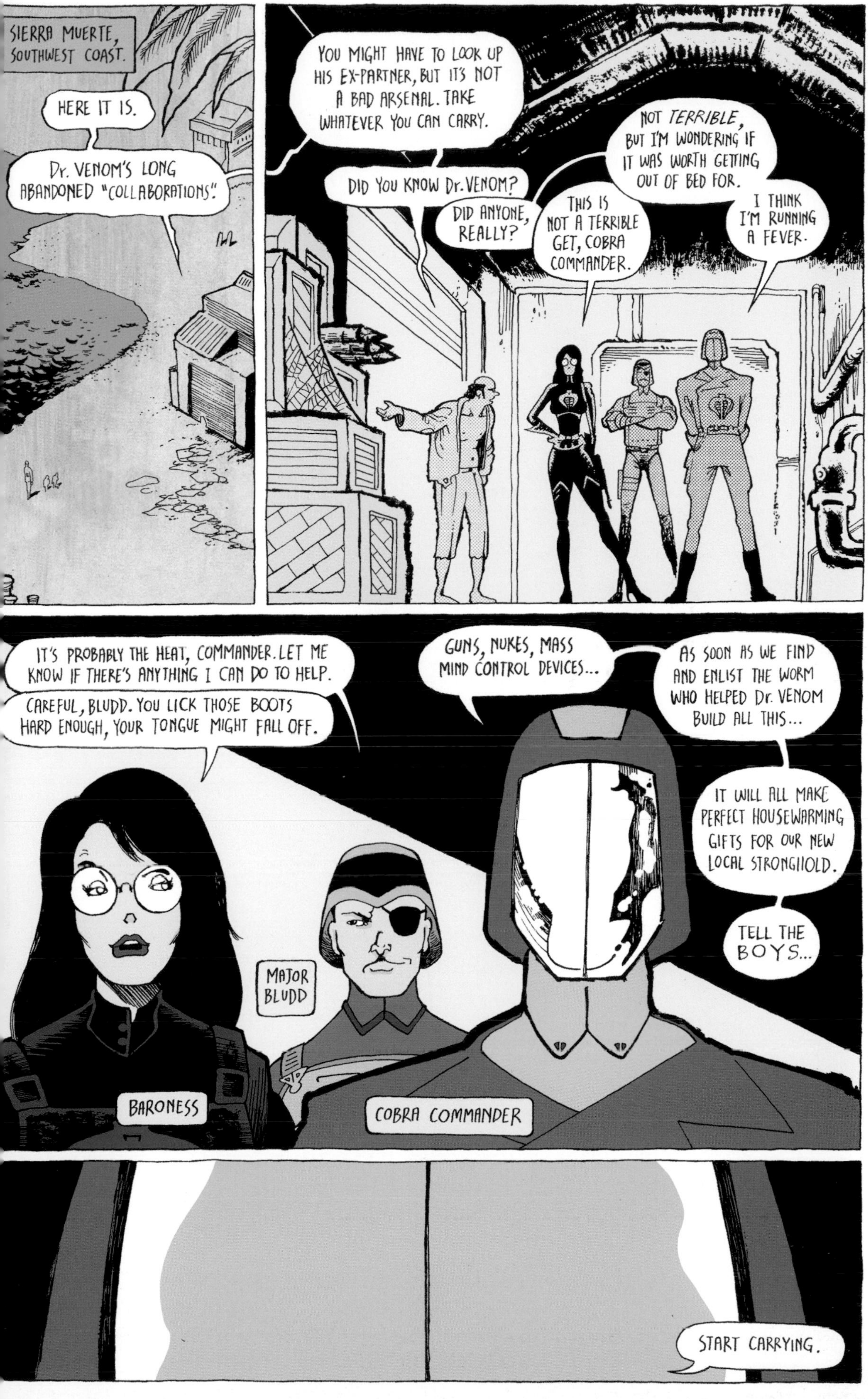
SIERRA MUERTE, SOUTHWEST COAST.
HERE IT IS.
Dr. VENOM'S LONG ABANDONED "COLLABORATIONS."
YOU MIGHT HAVE TO LOOK UP HIS EX-PARTNER, BUT IT'S NOT A BAD ARSENAL. TAKE WHATEVER YOU CAN CARRY.
DID YOU KNOW Dr. VENOM?
DID ANYONE, REALLY?
THIS IS NOT A TERRIBLE GET, COBRA COMMANDER.
NOT TERRIBLE, BUT I'M WONDERING IF IT WAS WORTH GETTING OUT OF BED FOR.
I THINK I'M RUNNING A FEVER.
IT'S PROBABLY THE HEAT, COMMANDER. LET ME KNOW IF THERE'S ANYTHING I CAN DO TO HELP.
CAREFUL, BLUDD. YOU LICK THOSE BOOTS HARD ENOUGH, YOUR TONGUE MIGHT FALL OFF.
GUNS, NUKES, MASS MIND CONTROL DEVICES...
AS SOON AS WE FIND AND ENLIST THE WORM WHO HELPED Dr. VENOM BUILD ALL THIS...
IT WILL ALL MAKE PERFECT HOUSEWARMING GIFTS FOR OUR NEW LOCAL STRONGHOLD.
TELL THE BOYS...
MAJOR BLUDD
BARONESS
COBRA COMMANDER
START CARRYING.

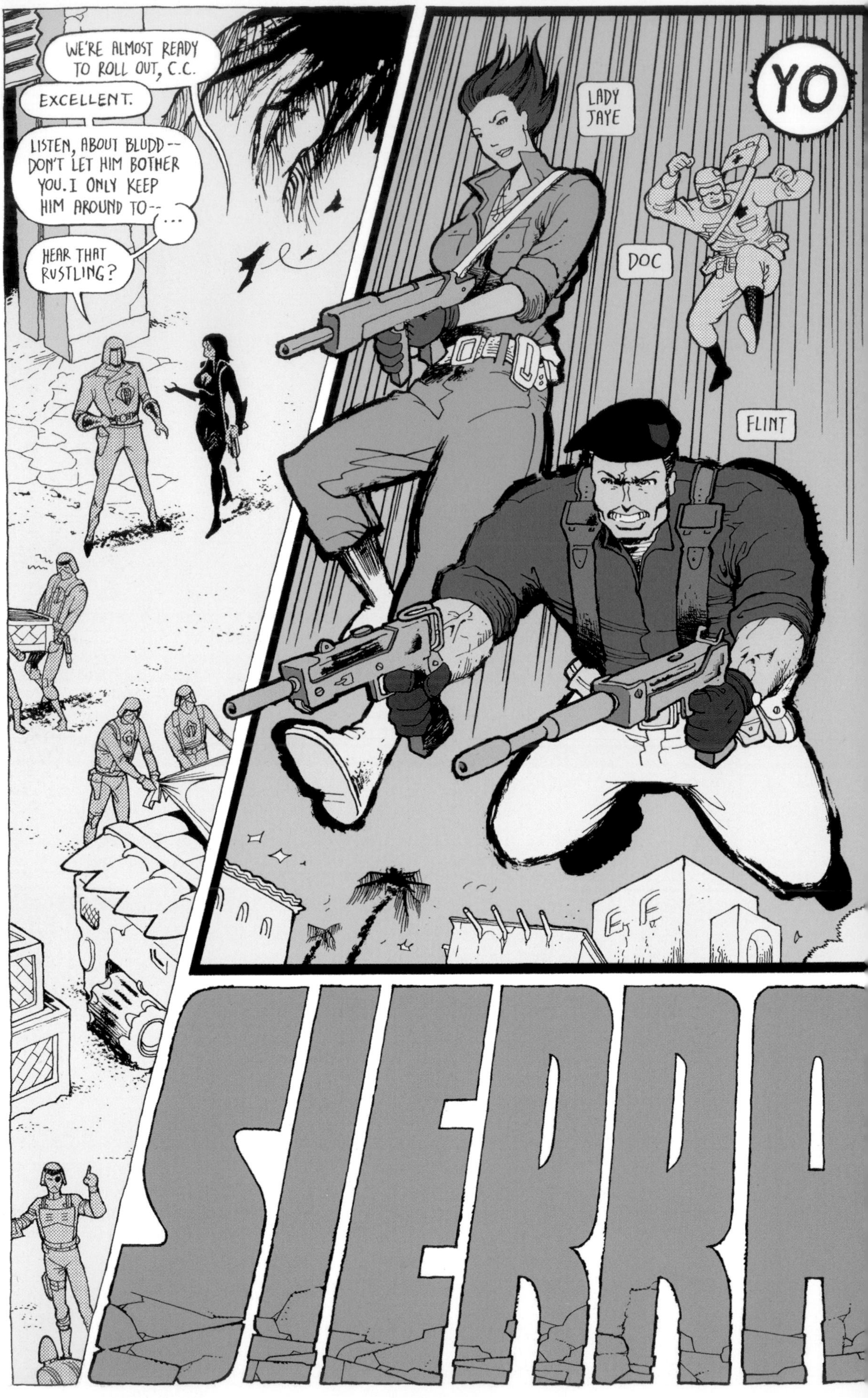
WE'RE ALMOST READY TO ROLL OUT, C.C.
EXCELLENT.
LISTEN, ABOUT BLUDD -- DON'T LET HIM BOTHER YOU. I ONLY KEEP HIM AROUND TO--
...
HEAR THAT RUSTLING?
YO
LADY JAYE
DOC
FLINT
SIERRA

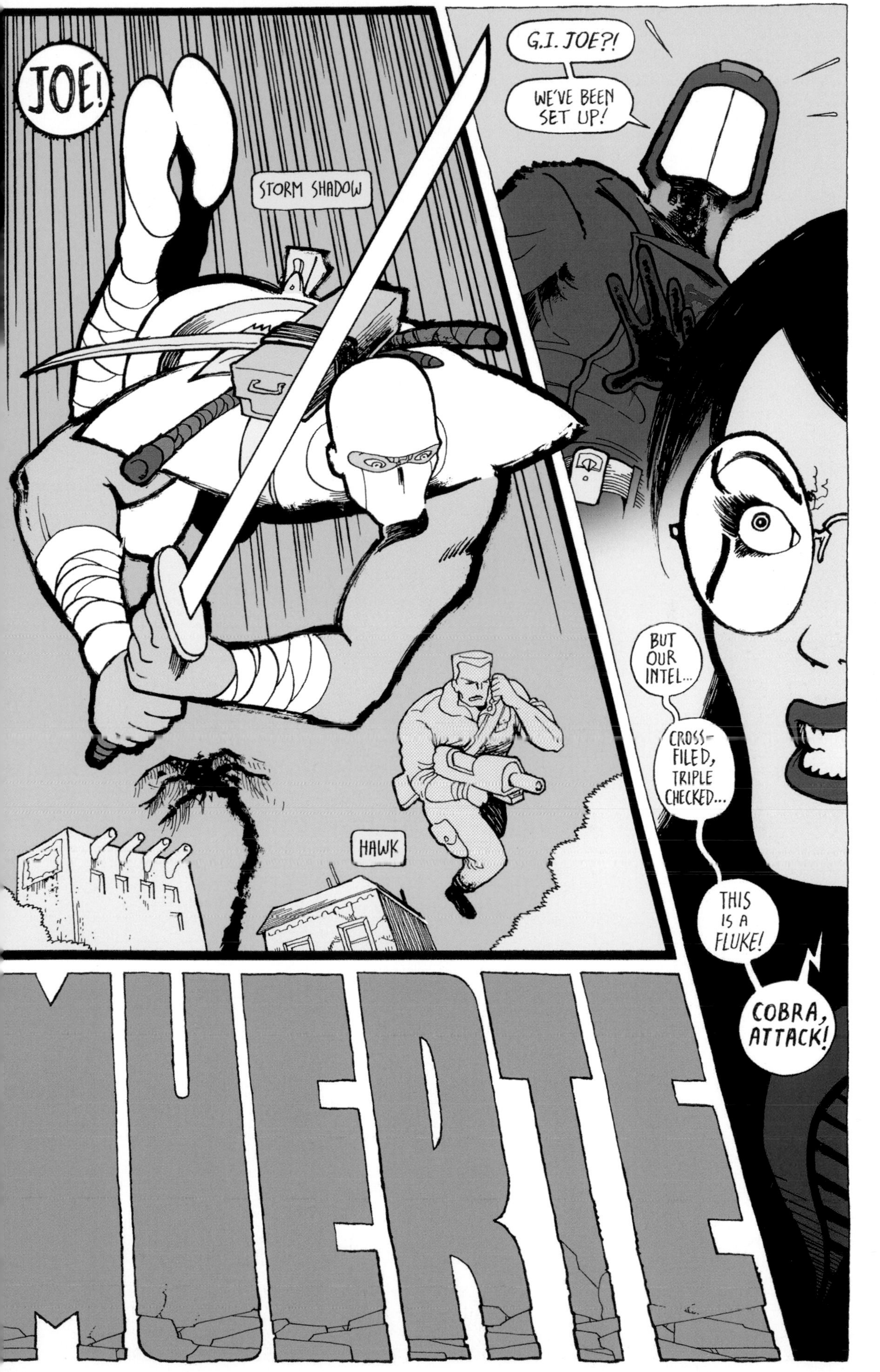
JOE!
STORM SHADOW
G.I. JOE?!
WE'VE BEEN SET UP!
HAWK
BUT OUR INTEL...
CROSS-FILED, TRIPLE CHECKED...
THIS IS A FLUKE!
COBRA, ATTACK!
MUERTE

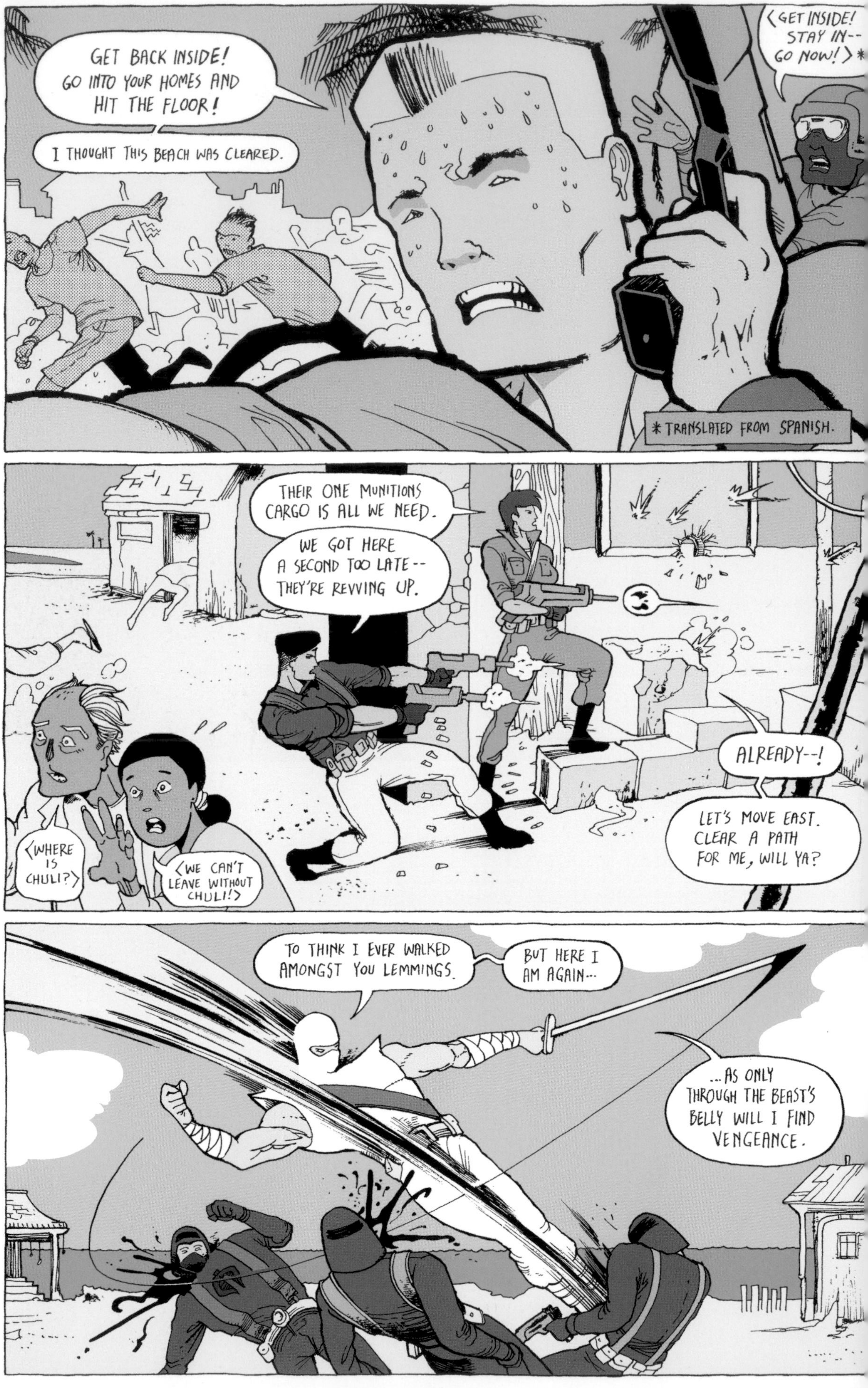
GET BACK INSIDE! GO INTO YOUR HOMES AND HIT THE FLOOR!
I THOUGHT THIS BEACH WAS CLEARED.
<GET INSIDE! STAY IN-- GO NOW!>*
*TRANSLATED FROM SPANISH.
THEIR ONE MUNITIONS CARGO IS ALL WE NEED.
WE GOT HERE A SECOND TOO LATE-- THEY'RE REVVING UP.
ALREADY--!
LET'S MOVE EAST. CLEAR A PATH FOR ME, WILL YA?
<WHERE IS CHULI?>
<WE CAN'T LEAVE WITHOUT CHULI!>
TO THINK I EVER WALKED AMONGST YOU LEMMINGS.
BUT HERE I AM AGAIN...
...AS ONLY THROUGH THE BEAST'S BELLY WILL I FIND VENGEANCE.

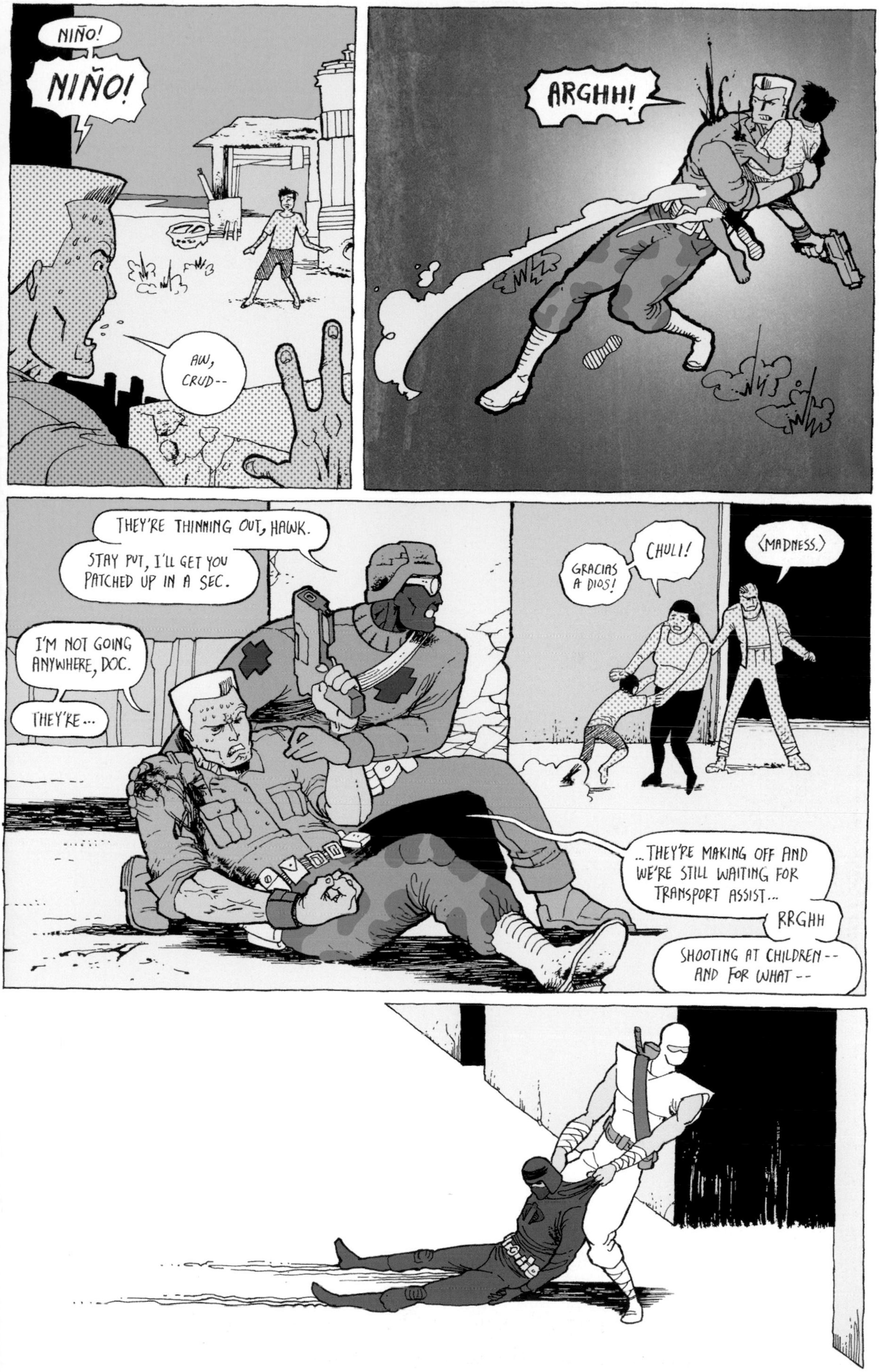
NIÑO!
NIÑO!
AW, CRUD--
ARGHH!
THEY'RE THINNING OUT, HAWK.
STAY PUT, I'LL GET YOU PATCHED UP IN A SEC.
I'M NOT GOING ANYWHERE, DOC.
THEY'RE...
GRACIAS A DIOS!
CHULI!
⟨MADNESS.⟩
...THEY'RE MAKING OFF AND WE'RE STILL WAITING FOR TRANSPORT ASSIST...
RRGHH
SHOOTING AT CHILDREN-- AND FOR WHAT--

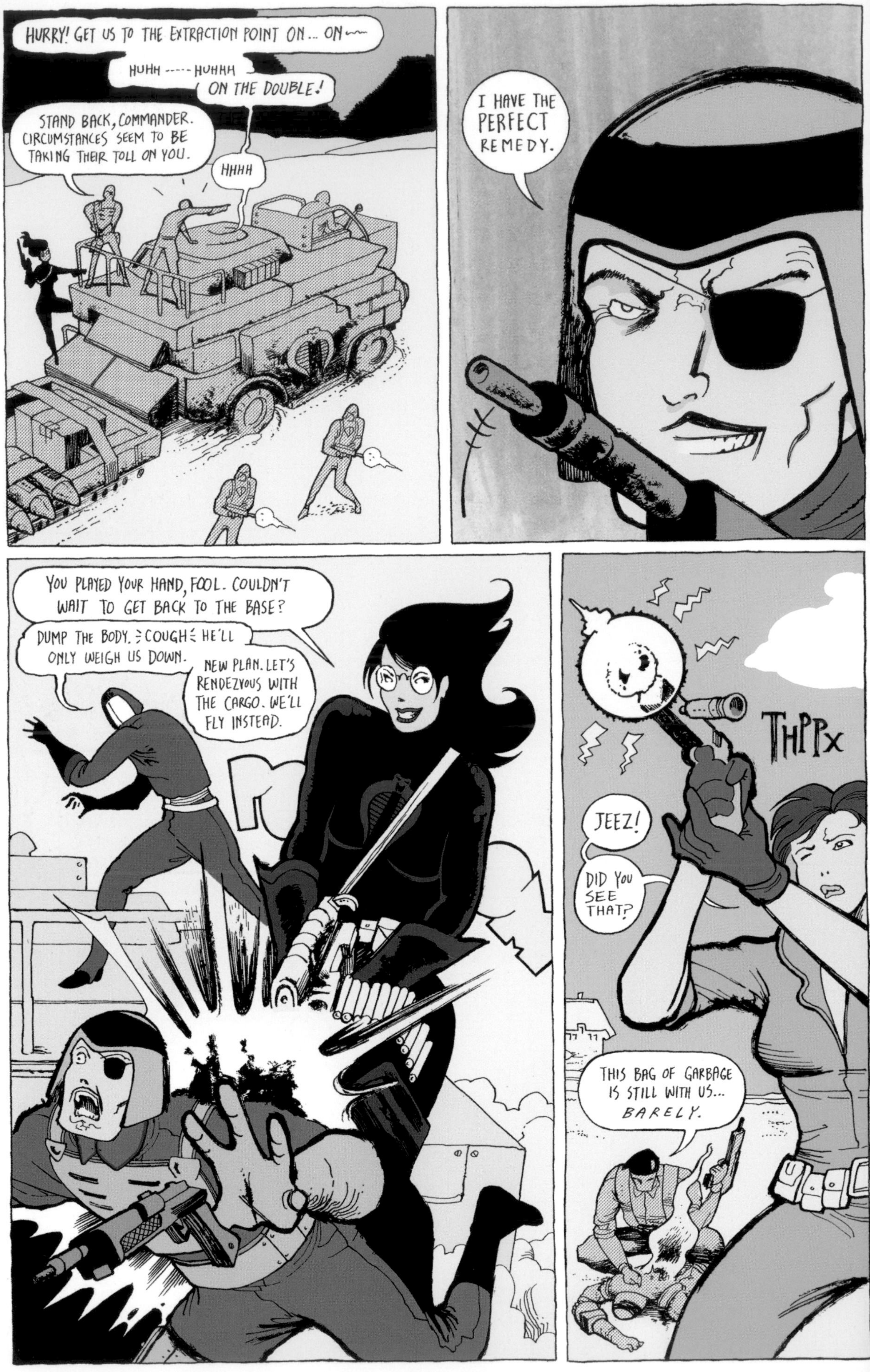
HURRY! GET US TO THE EXTRACTION POINT ON... ON~
HUHH ----- HUHHH
ON THE DOUBLE!
STAND BACK, COMMANDER. CIRCUMSTANCES SEEM TO BE TAKING THEIR TOLL ON YOU.
HHHH
I HAVE THE PERFECT REMEDY.
YOU PLAYED YOUR HAND, FOOL. COULDN'T WAIT TO GET BACK TO THE BASE?
DUMP THE BODY. COUGH HE'LL ONLY WEIGH US DOWN.
NEW PLAN. LET'S RENDEZVOUS WITH THE CARGO. WE'LL FLY INSTEAD.
THPPx
JEEZ!
DID YOU SEE THAT?
THIS BAG OF GARBAGE IS STILL WITH US... BARELY.

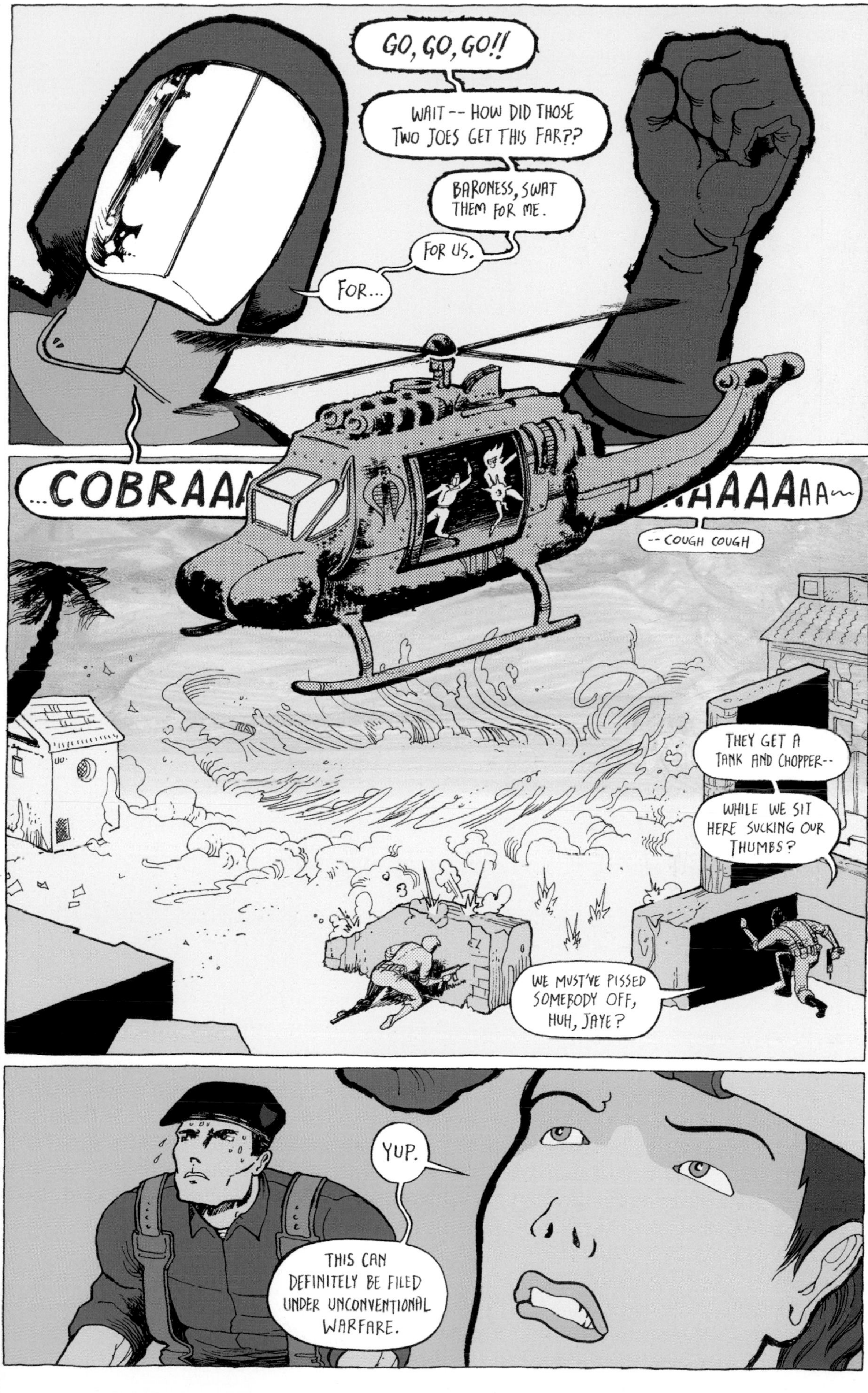
GO, GO, GO!!
WAIT -- HOW DID THOSE TWO JOES GET THIS FAR??
BARONESS, SWAT THEM FOR ME.
FOR US.
FOR...
...COBRAA
AAAAAA~
-- COUGH COUGH
THEY GET A TANK AND CHOPPER--
WHILE WE SIT HERE SUCKING OUR THUMBS?
WE MUST'VE PISSED SOMEBODY OFF, HUH, JAYE?
YUP.
THIS CAN DEFINITELY BE FILED UNDER UNCONVENTIONAL WARFARE.

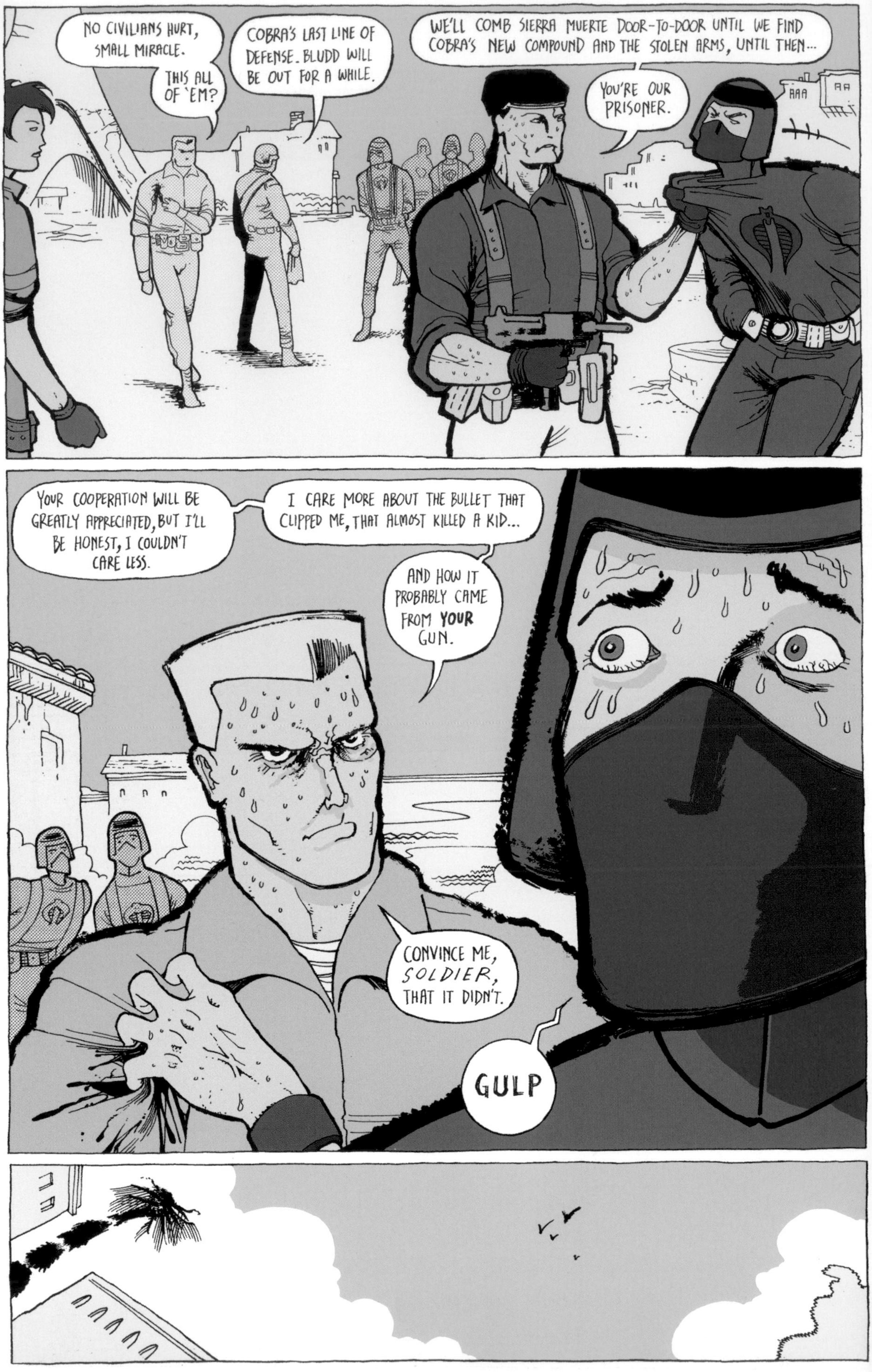
NO CIVILIANS HURT, SMALL MIRACLE.
THIS ALL OF 'EM?
COBRA'S LAST LINE OF DEFENSE. BLUDD WILL BE OUT FOR A WHILE.
WE'LL COMB SIERRA MUERTE DOOR-TO-DOOR UNTIL WE FIND COBRA'S NEW COMPOUND AND THE STOLEN ARMS, UNTIL THEN...
YOU'RE OUR PRISONER.
YOUR COOPERATION WILL BE GREATLY APPRECIATED, BUT I'LL BE HONEST, I COULDN'T CARE LESS.
I CARE MORE ABOUT THE BULLET THAT CLIPPED ME, THAT ALMOST KILLED A KID...
AND HOW IT PROBABLY CAME FROM **YOUR** GUN.
CONVINCE ME, *SOLDIER*, THAT IT DIDN'T.
GULP

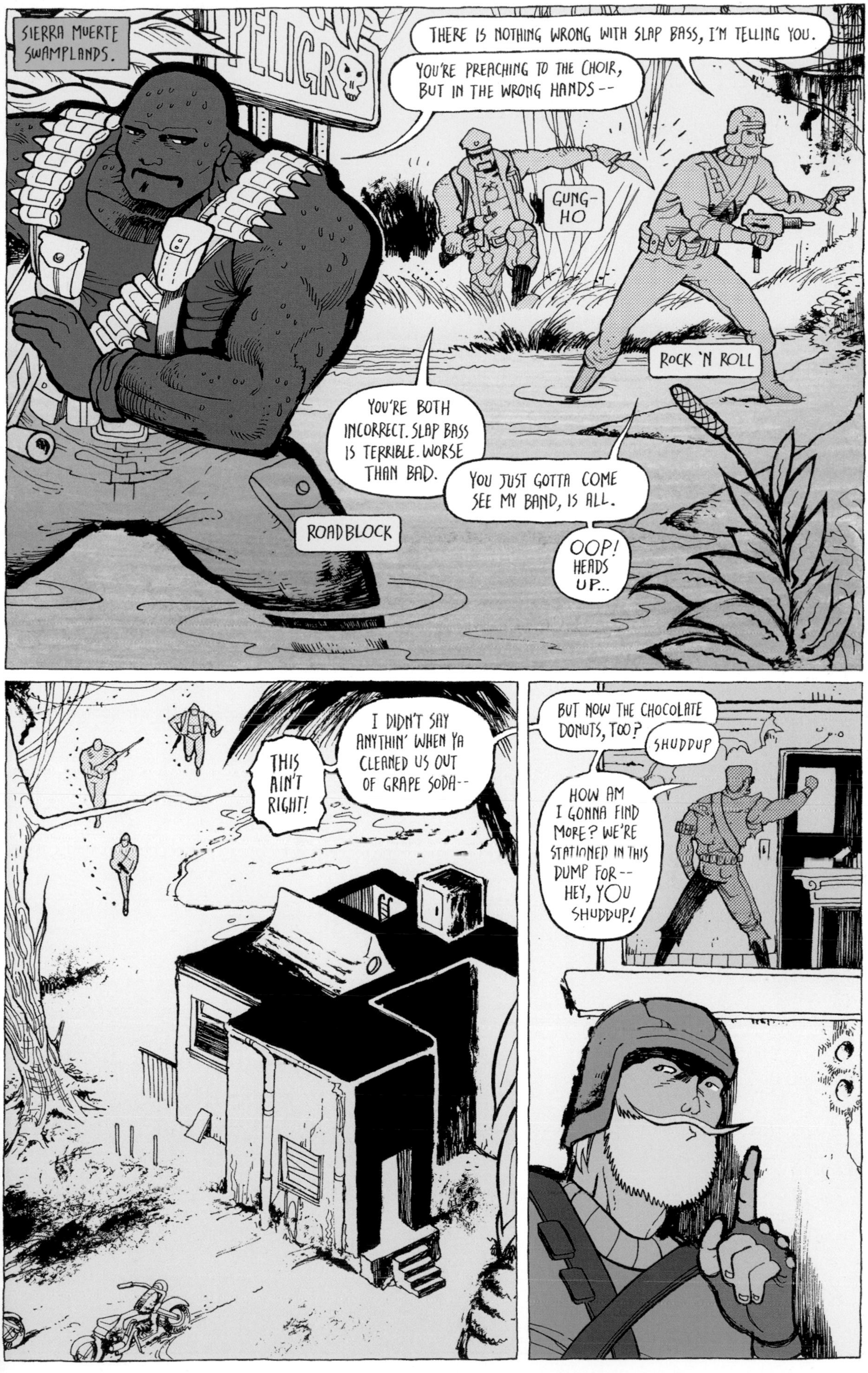
SIERRA MUERTE SWAMPLANDS.
PELIGRO
THERE IS NOTHING WRONG WITH SLAP BASS, I'M TELLING YOU.
YOU'RE PREACHING TO THE CHOIR, BUT IN THE WRONG HANDS--
GUNG-HO
ROCK 'N ROLL
YOU'RE BOTH INCORRECT. SLAP BASS IS TERRIBLE. WORSE THAN BAD.
YOU JUST GOTTA COME SEE MY BAND, IS ALL.
ROADBLOCK
OOP! HEADS UP...
THIS AIN'T RIGHT!
I DIDN'T SAY ANYTHIN' WHEN YA CLEANED US OUT OF GRAPE SODA--
BUT NOW THE CHOCOLATE DONUTS, TOO?
SHUDDUP
HOW AM I GONNA FIND MORE? WE'RE STATIONED IN THIS DUMP FOR-- HEY, YOU SHUDDUP!

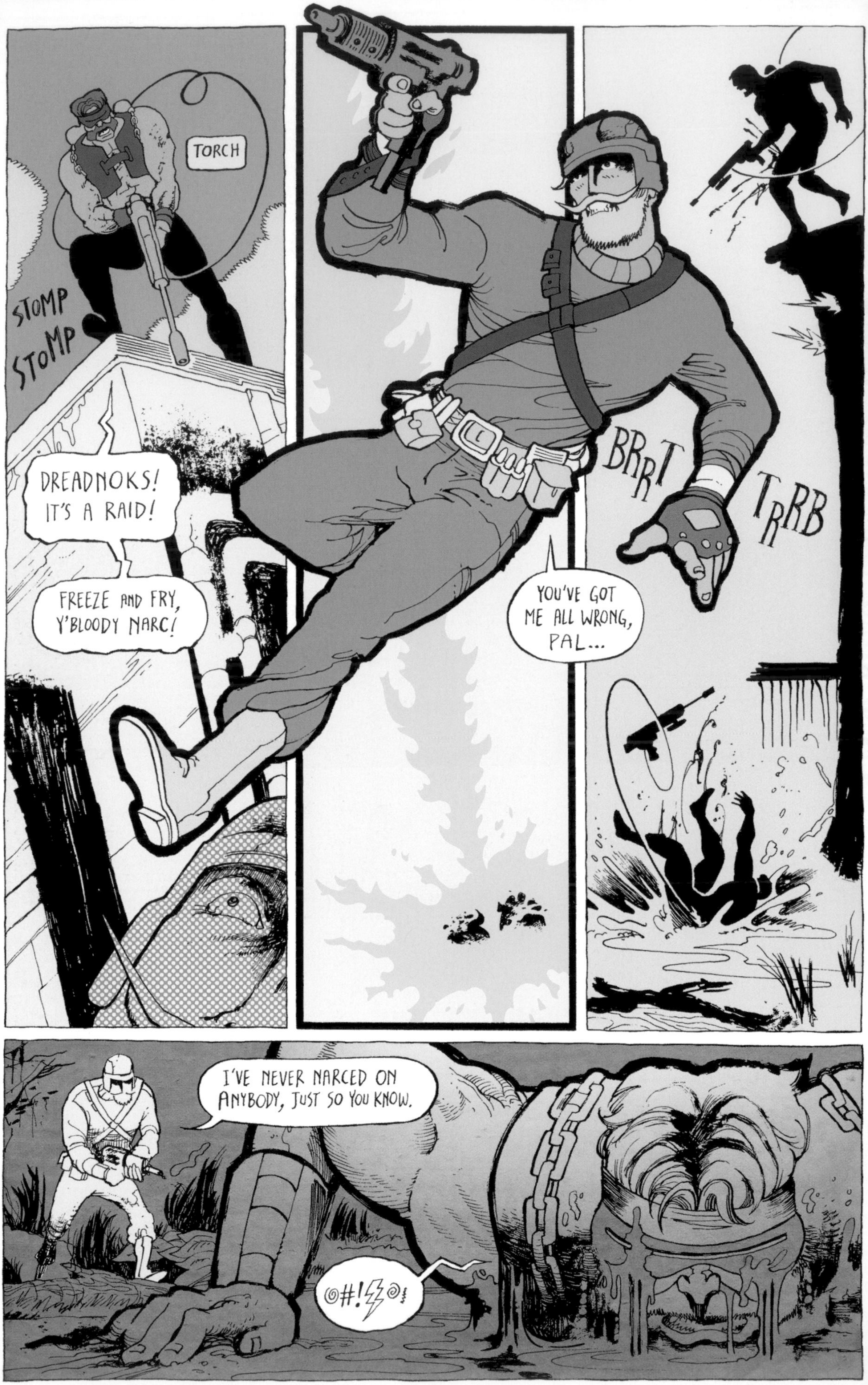
TORCH
STOMP
STOMP
DREADNOKS! IT'S A RAID!
FREEZE AND FRY, Y'BLOODY NARC!
YOU'VE GOT ME ALL WRONG, PAL...
BRRRT
TRRB
I'VE NEVER NARCED ON ANYBODY, JUST SO YOU KNOW.
@#!

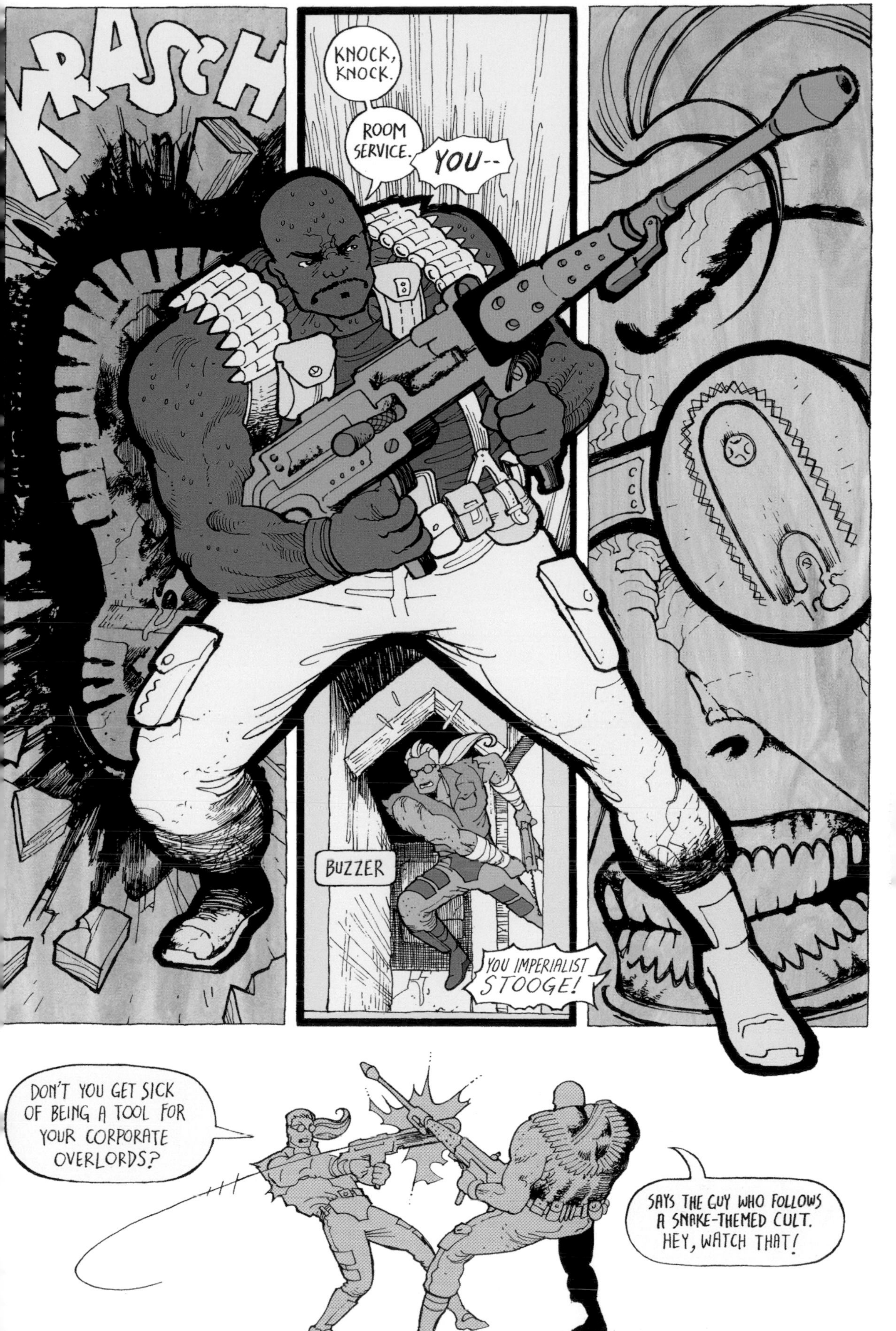
KRASCH
KNOCK, KNOCK.
ROOM SERVICE.
YOU--
BUZZER
YOU IMPERIALIST STOOGE!
DON'T YOU GET SICK OF BEING A TOOL FOR YOUR CORPORATE OVERLORDS?
SAYS THE GUY WHO FOLLOWS A SNAKE-THEMED CULT. HEY, WATCH THAT!

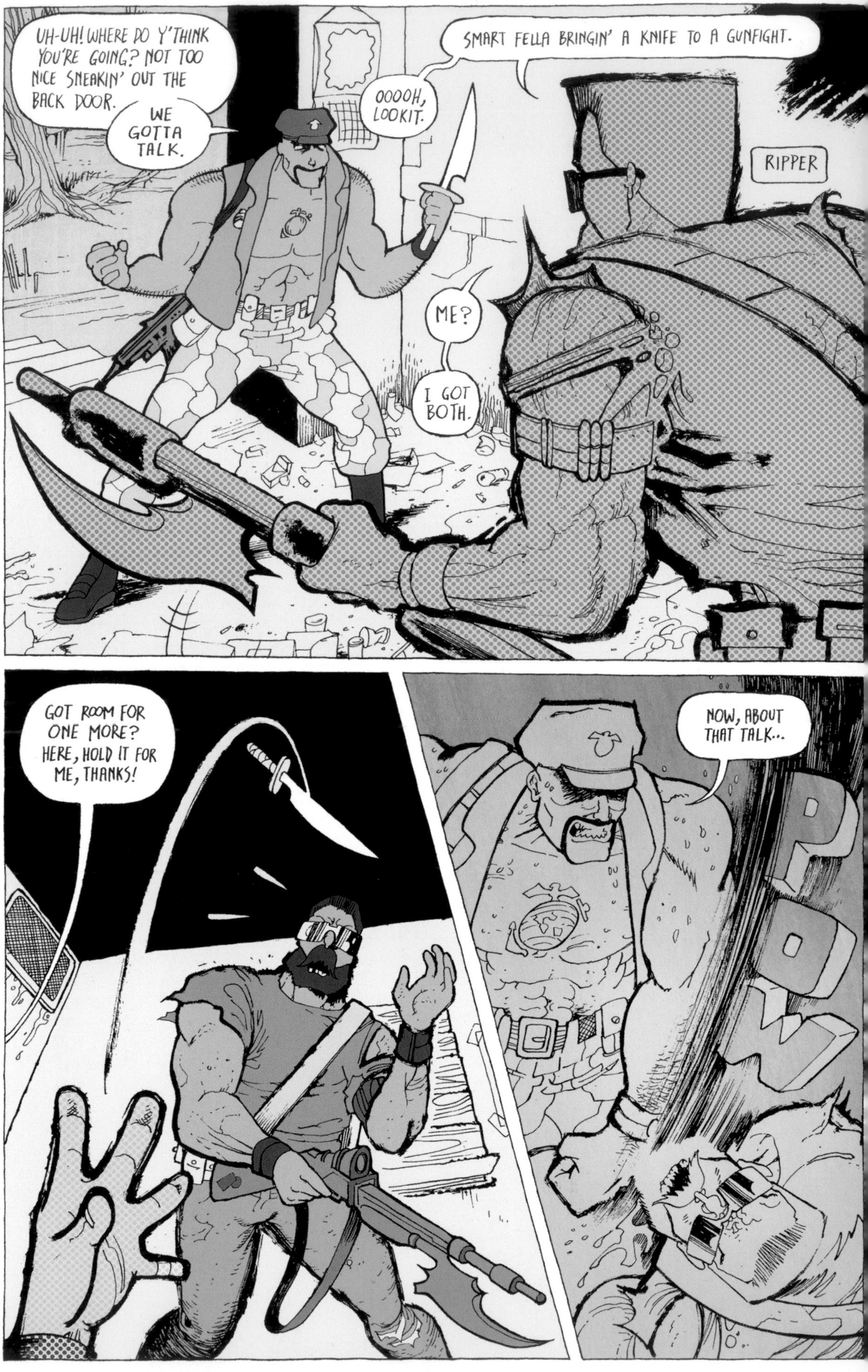
UH-UH! WHERE DO Y'THINK YOU'RE GOING? NOT TOO NICE SNEAKIN' OUT THE BACK DOOR.
WE GOTTA TALK.
OOOOH, LOOKIT.
SMART FELLA BRINGIN' A KNIFE TO A GUNFIGHT.
RIPPER
ME?
I GOT BOTH.
GOT ROOM FOR ONE MORE? HERE, HOLD IT FOR ME, THANKS!
NOW, ABOUT THAT TALK...
POW

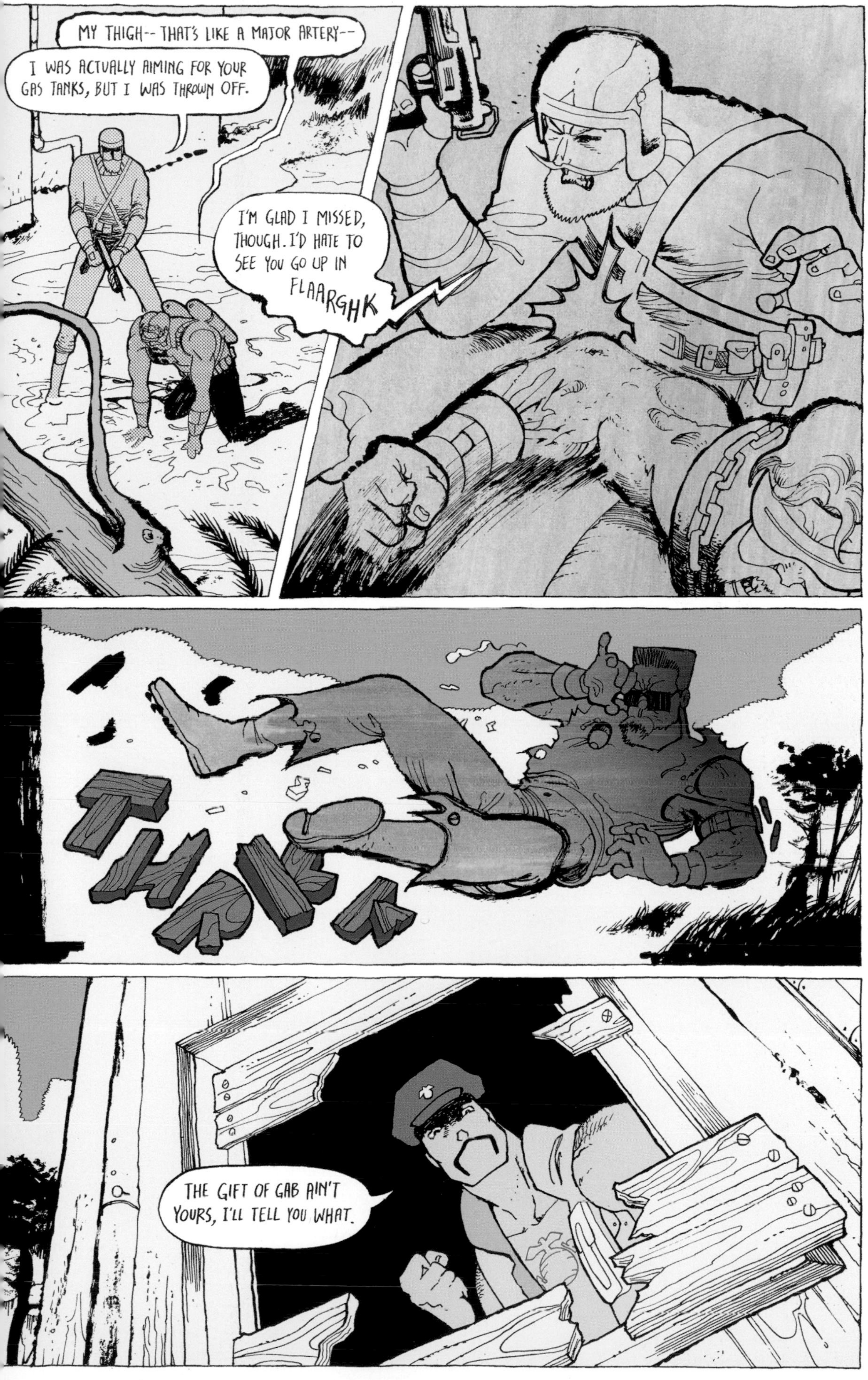
MY THIGH-- THAT'S LIKE A MAJOR ARTERY--
I WAS ACTUALLY AIMING FOR YOUR GAS TANKS, BUT I WAS THROWN OFF.
I'M GLAD I MISSED, THOUGH. I'D HATE TO SEE YOU GO UP IN FLAARGHK
THE GIFT OF GAB AIN'T YOURS, I'LL TELL YOU WHAT.

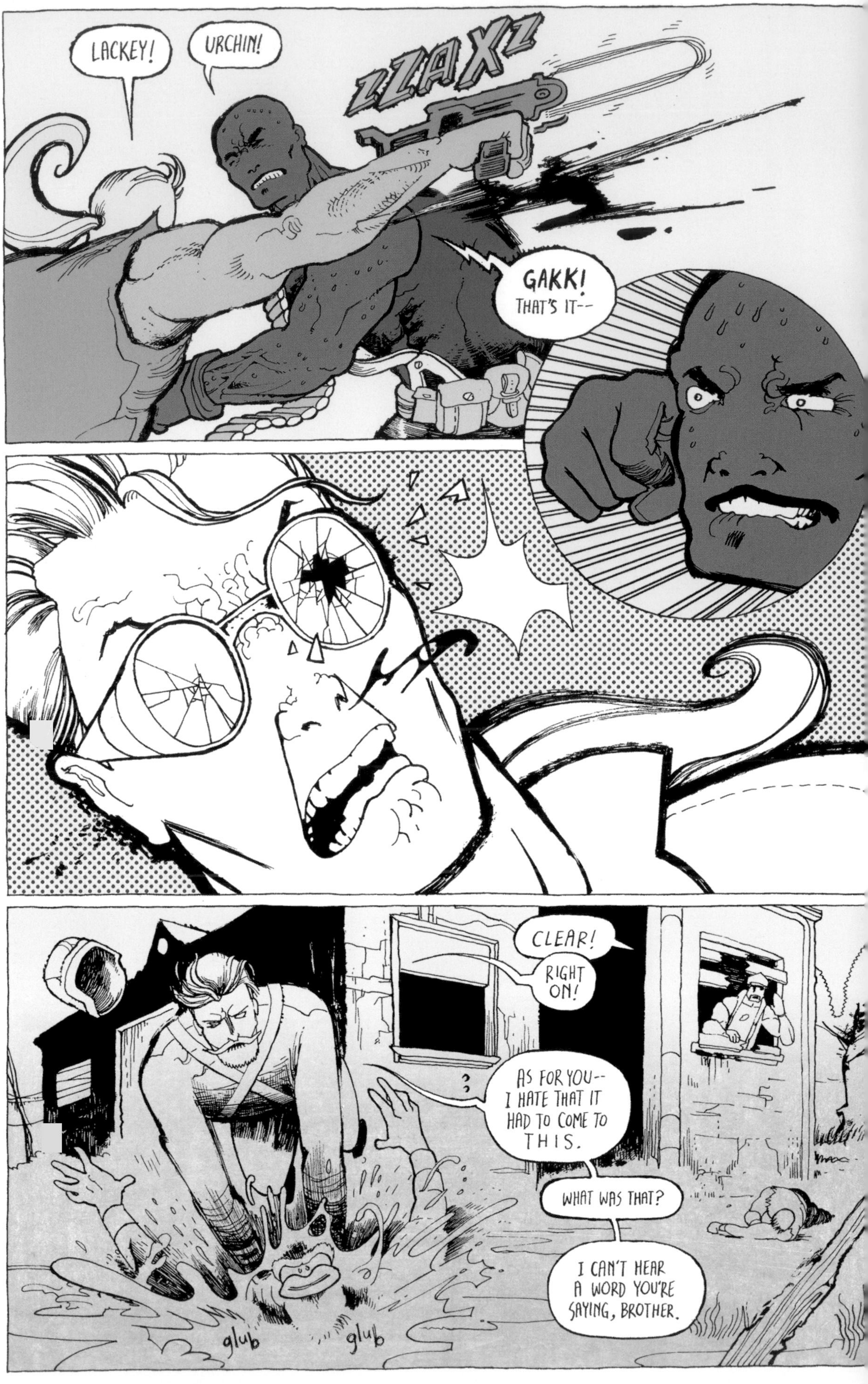
LACKEY!
URCHIN!
zZAXz
GAKK! THAT'S IT--
CLEAR!
RIGHT ON!
AS FOR YOU-- I HATE THAT IT HAD TO COME TO THIS.
WHAT WAS THAT?
I CAN'T HEAR A WORD YOU'RE SAYING, BROTHER.
glub
glub

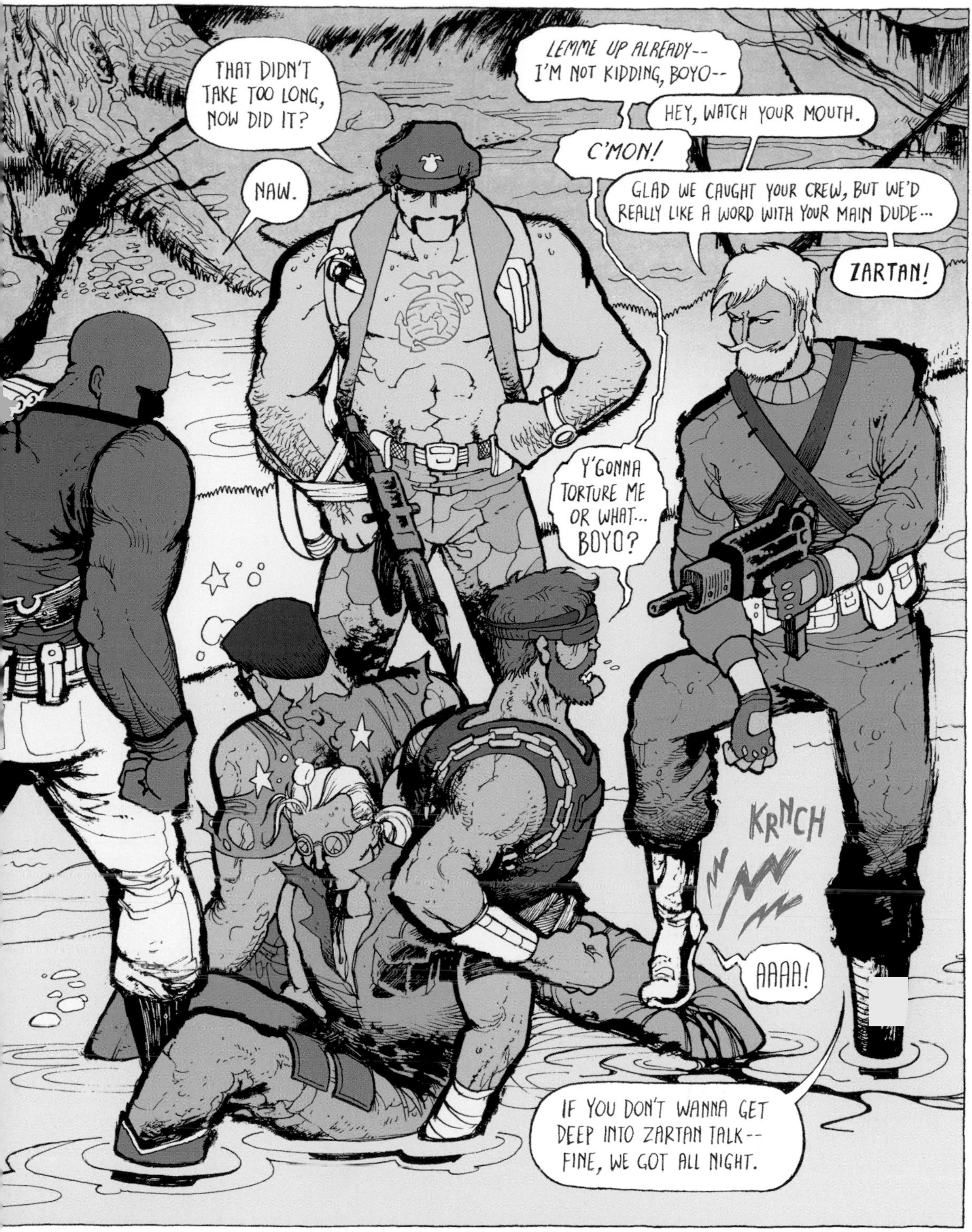
THAT DIDN'T TAKE TOO LONG, NOW DID IT?
NAW.
LEMME UP ALREADY-- I'M NOT KIDDING, BOYO--
C'MON!
HEY, WATCH YOUR MOUTH.
GLAD WE CAUGHT YOUR CREW, BUT WE'D REALLY LIKE A WORD WITH YOUR MAIN DUDE...
ZARTAN!
Y'GONNA TORTURE ME OR WHAT... BOYO?
KRNCH
AAAA!
IF YOU DON'T WANNA GET DEEP INTO ZARTAN TALK-- FINE, WE GOT ALL NIGHT.

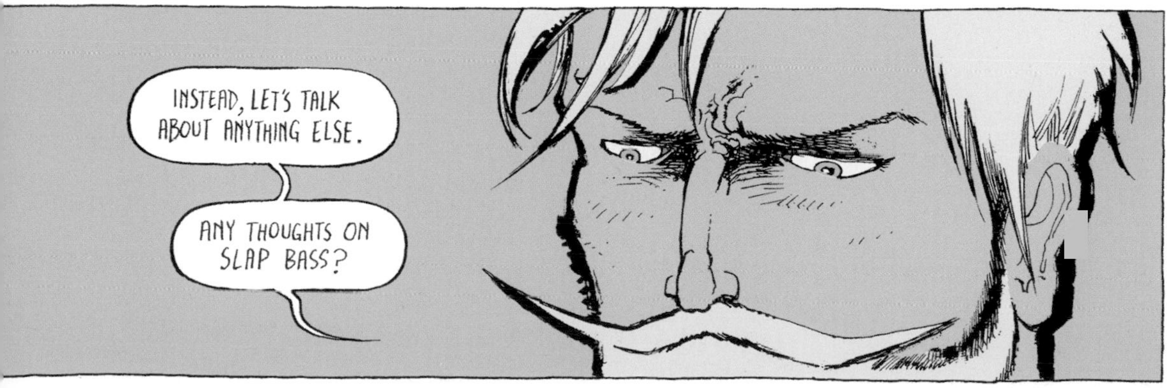
INSTEAD, LET'S TALK ABOUT ANYTHING ELSE.
ANY THOUGHTS ON SLAP BASS?

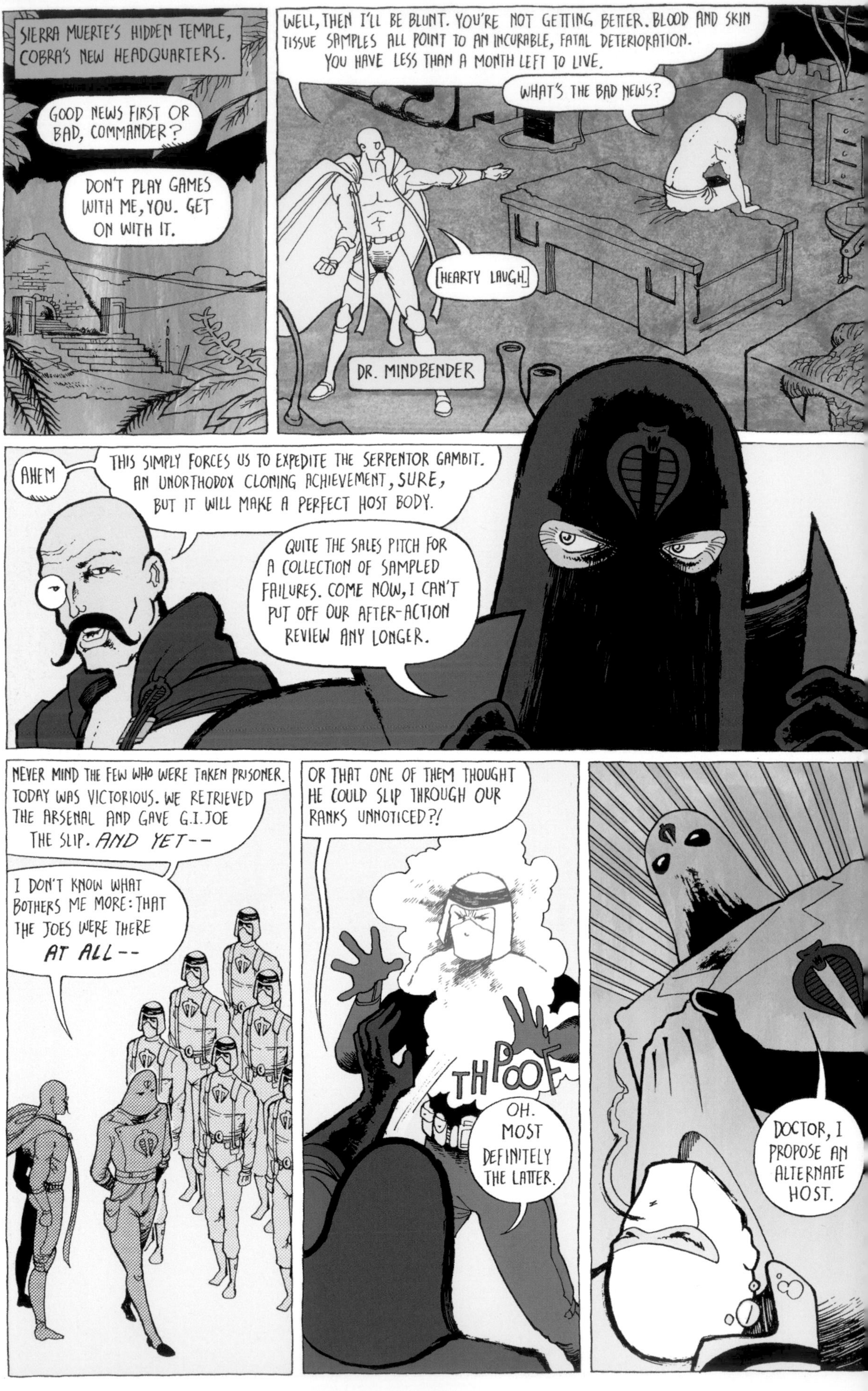
SIERRA MUERTE'S HIDDEN TEMPLE, COBRA'S NEW HEADQUARTERS.
GOOD NEWS FIRST OR BAD, COMMANDER?
DON'T PLAY GAMES WITH ME, YOU. GET ON WITH IT.
WELL, THEN I'LL BE BLUNT. YOU'RE NOT GETTING BETTER. BLOOD AND SKIN TISSUE SAMPLES ALL POINT TO AN INCURABLE, FATAL DETERIORATION. YOU HAVE LESS THAN A MONTH LEFT TO LIVE.
WHAT'S THE BAD NEWS?
[HEARTY LAUGH.]
DR. MINDBENDER
AHEM
THIS SIMPLY FORCES US TO EXPEDITE THE SERPENTOR GAMBIT. AN UNORTHODOX CLONING ACHIEVEMENT, SURE, BUT IT WILL MAKE A PERFECT HOST BODY.
QUITE THE SALES PITCH FOR A COLLECTION OF SAMPLED FAILURES. COME NOW, I CAN'T PUT OFF OUR AFTER-ACTION REVIEW ANY LONGER.
NEVER MIND THE FEW WHO WERE TAKEN PRISONER. TODAY WAS VICTORIOUS. WE RETRIEVED THE ARSENAL AND GAVE G.I. JOE THE SLIP. AND YET--
I DON'T KNOW WHAT BOTHERS ME MORE: THAT THE JOES WERE THERE AT ALL--
OR THAT ONE OF THEM THOUGHT HE COULD SLIP THROUGH OUR RANKS UNNOTICED?!
THPOOF
OH. MOST DEFINITELY THE LATTER.
DOCTOR, I PROPOSE AN ALTERNATE HOST.

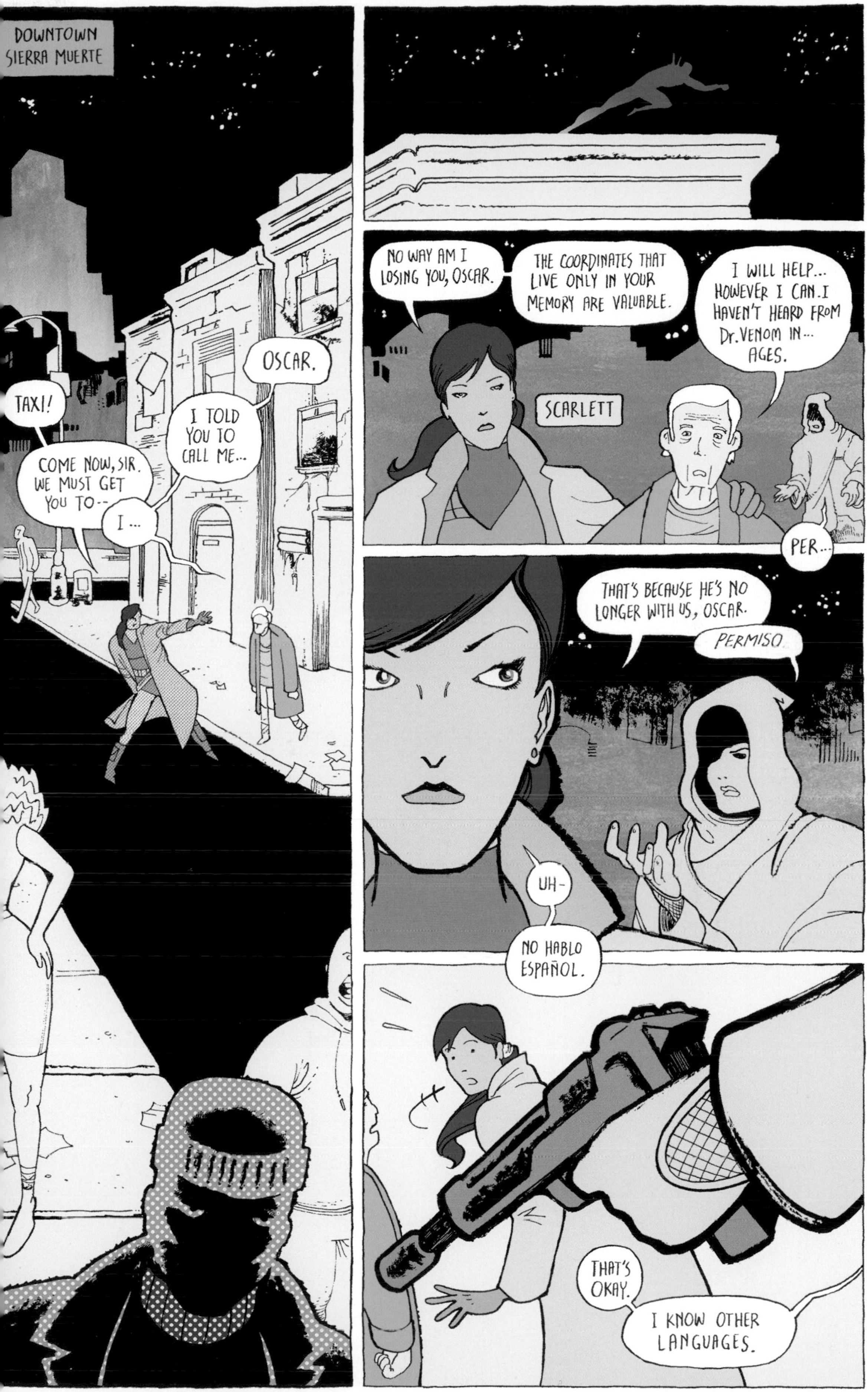
DOWNTOWN
SIERRA MUERTE
OSCAR.
TAXI!
I TOLD YOU TO CALL ME...
COME NOW, SIR. WE MUST GET YOU TO--
I...
NO WAY AM I LOSING YOU, OSCAR.
THE COORDINATES THAT LIVE ONLY IN YOUR MEMORY ARE VALUABLE.
I WILL HELP... HOWEVER I CAN. I HAVEN'T HEARD FROM Dr. VENOM IN... AGES.
SCARLETT
PER...
THAT'S BECAUSE HE'S NO LONGER WITH US, OSCAR.
PERMISO.
UH-
NO HABLO ESPAÑOL.
THAT'S OKAY.
I KNOW OTHER LANGUAGES.

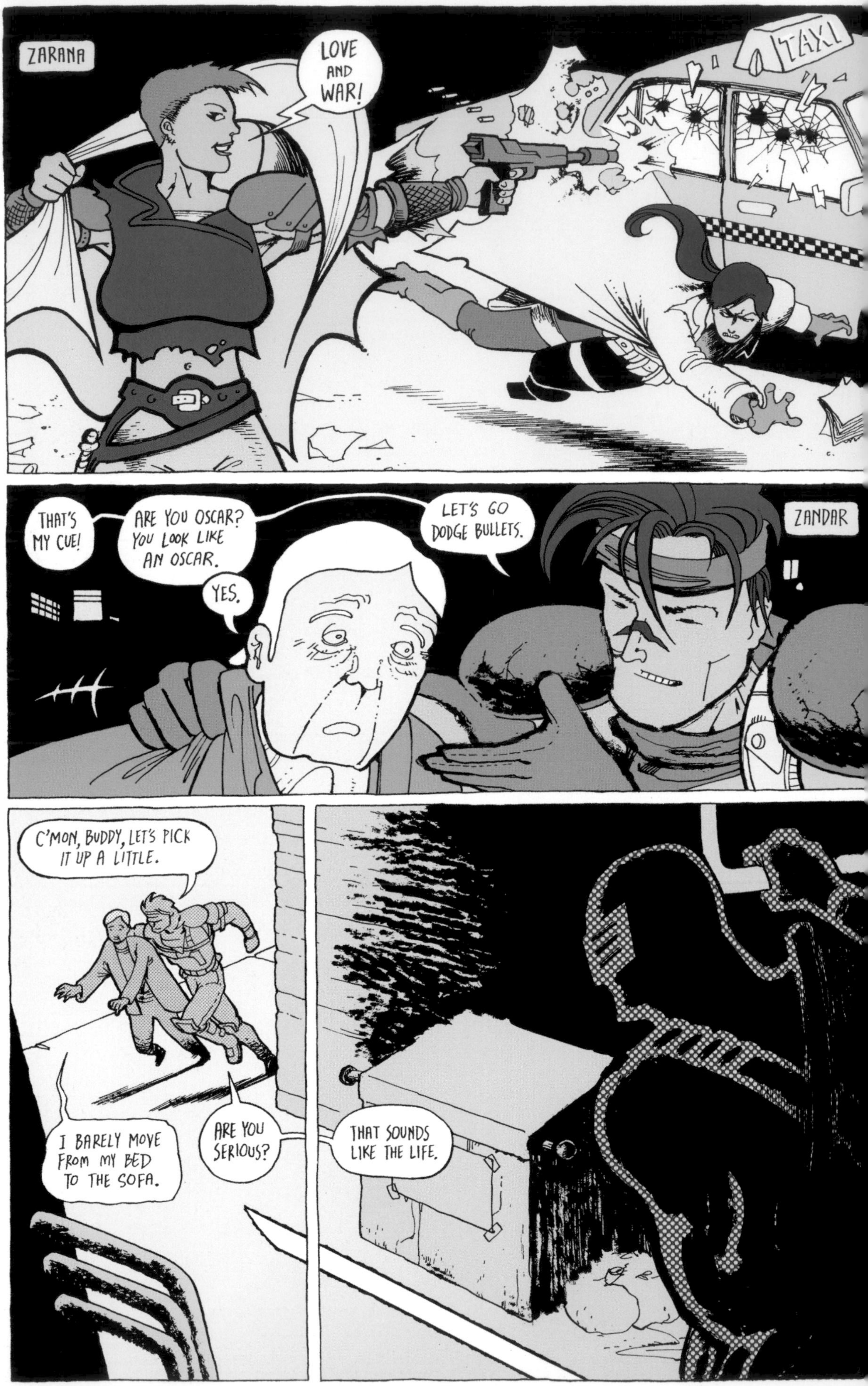
ZARANA
LOVE AND WAR!
THAT'S MY CUE!
ARE YOU OSCAR? YOU LOOK LIKE AN OSCAR.
YES.
LET'S GO DODGE BULLETS.
ZANDAR
C'MON, BUDDY, LET'S PICK IT UP A LITTLE.
I BARELY MOVE FROM MY BED TO THE SOFA.
ARE YOU SERIOUS?
THAT SOUNDS LIKE THE LIFE.

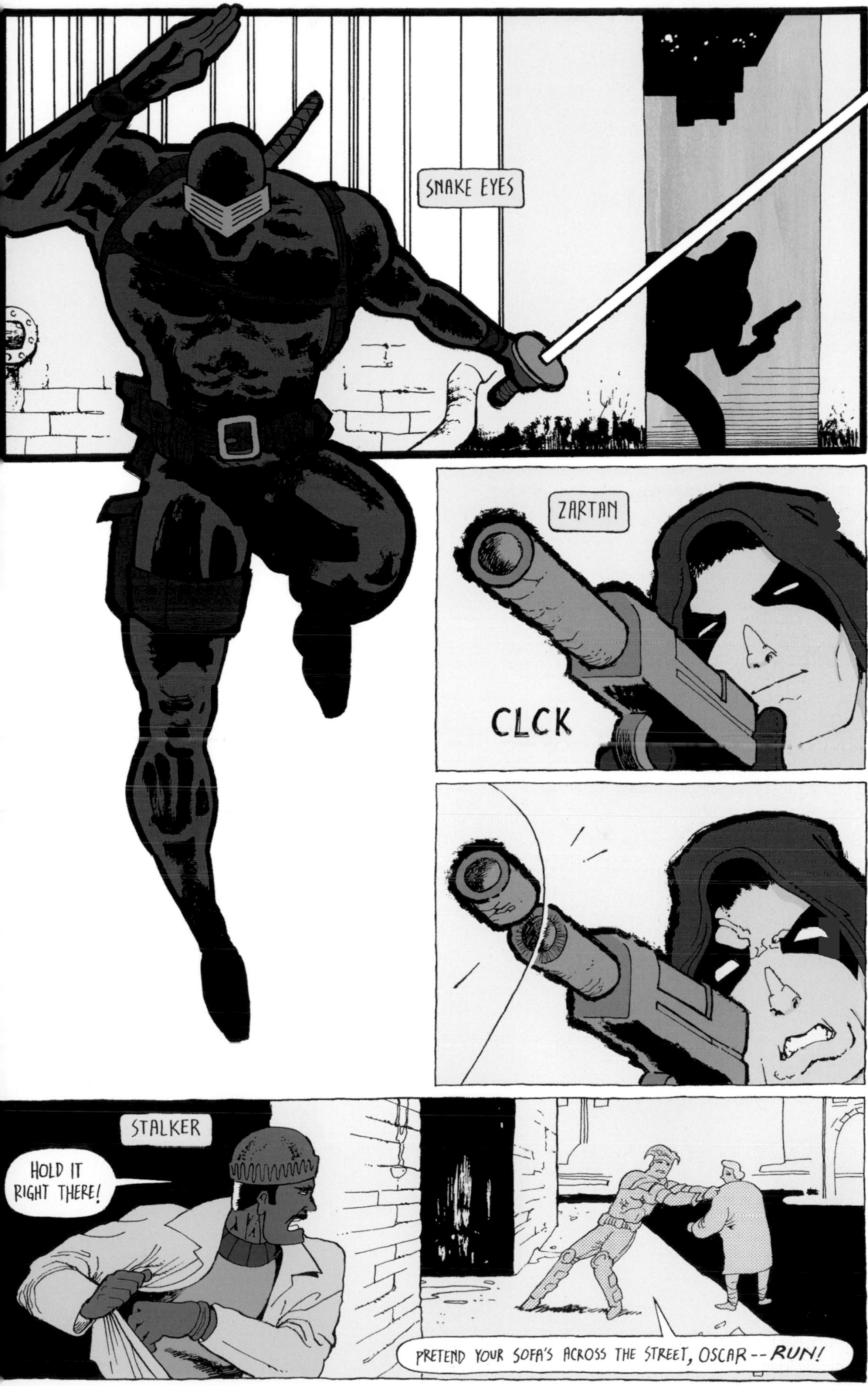
SNAKE EYES
ZARTAN
CLCK
STALKER
HOLD IT RIGHT THERE!
PRETEND YOUR SOFA'S ACROSS THE STREET, OSCAR--RUN!

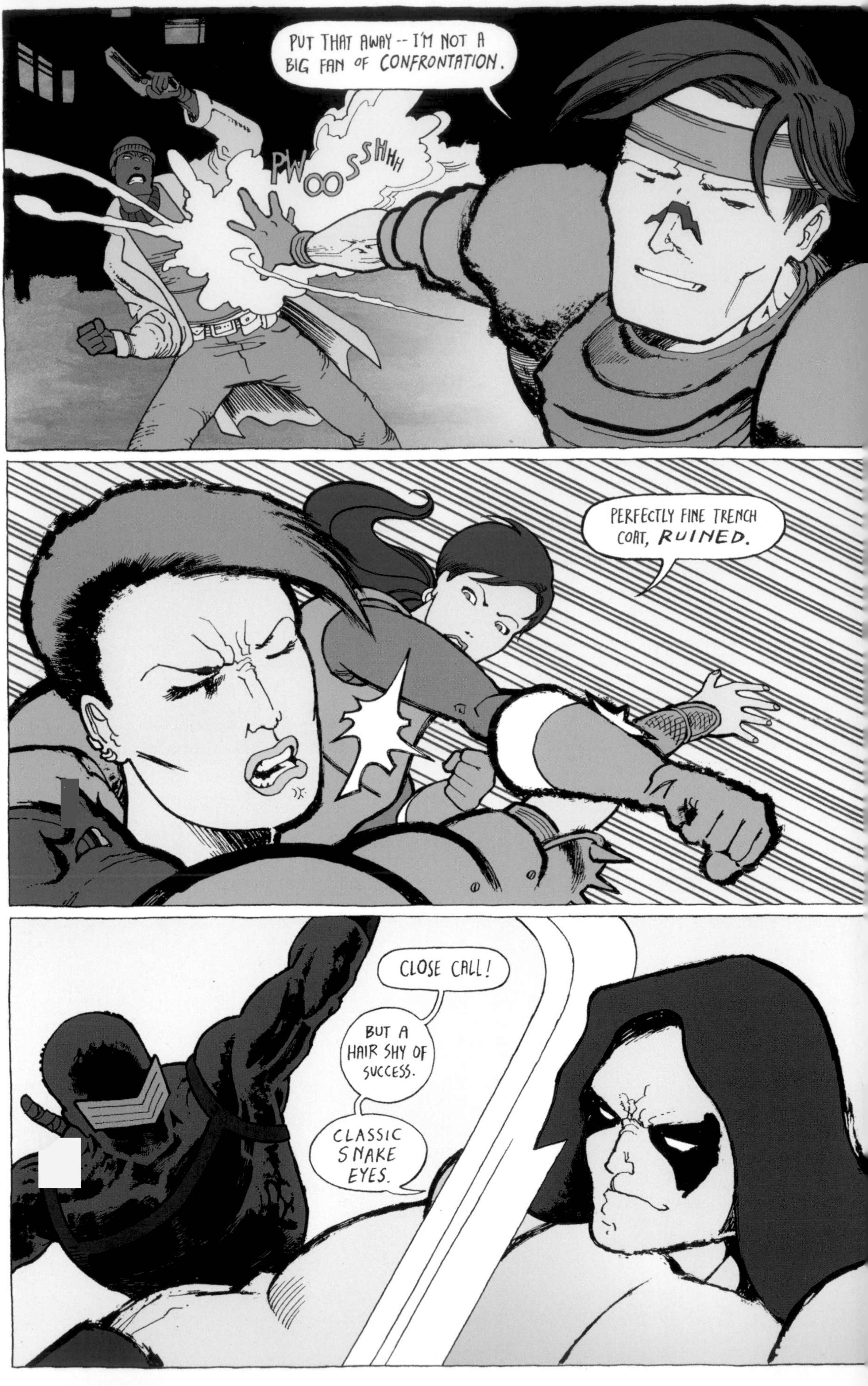
PUT THAT AWAY -- I'M NOT A BIG FAN OF CONFRONTATION.
PWOOSSHHH
PERFECTLY FINE TRENCH COAT, RUINED.
CLOSE CALL!
BUT A HAIR SHY OF SUCCESS.
CLASSIC SNAKE EYES.

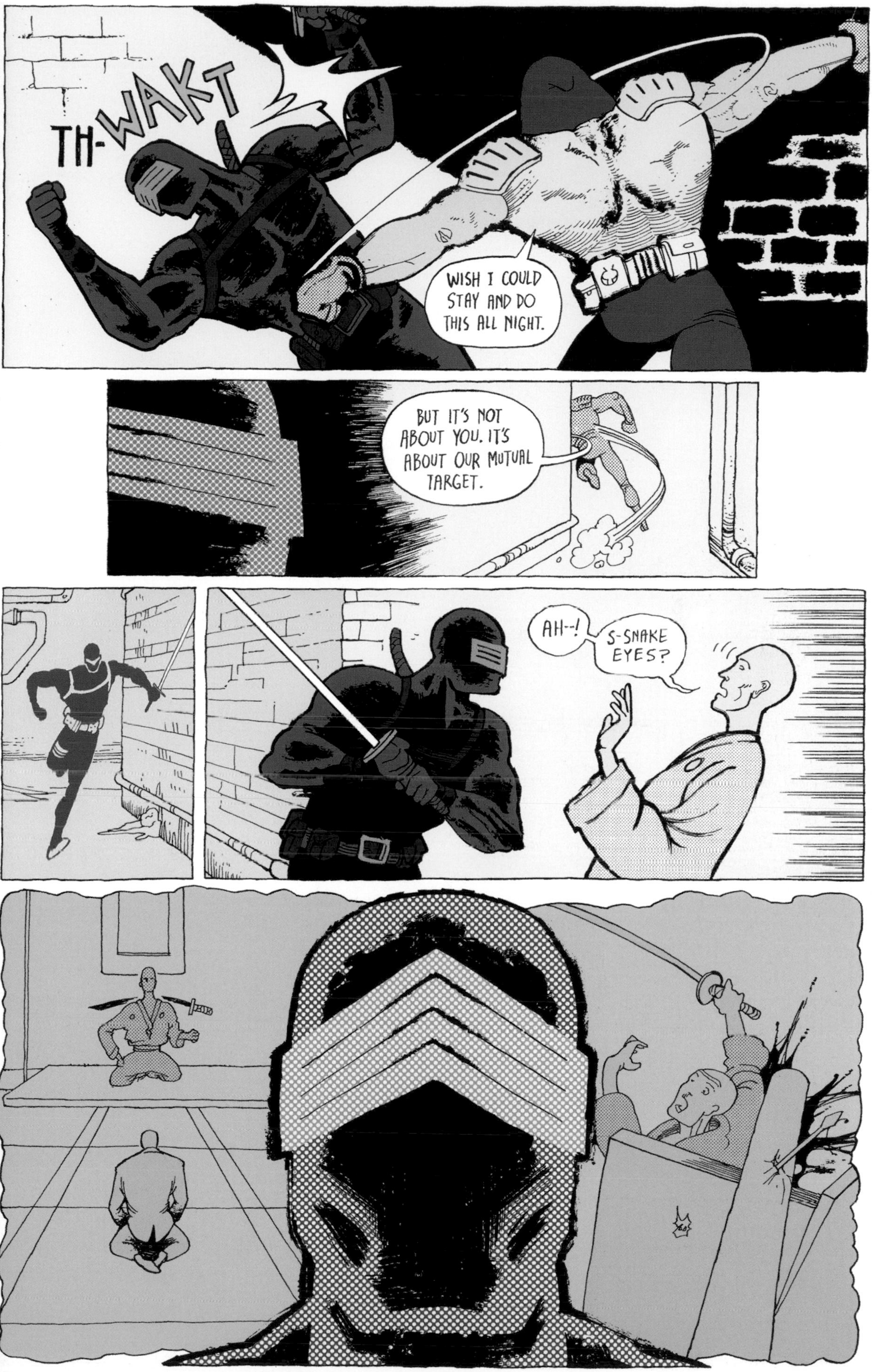
TH-WAKT
WISH I COULD STAY AND DO THIS ALL NIGHT.
BUT IT'S NOT ABOUT YOU. IT'S ABOUT OUR MUTUAL TARGET.
AH--!
S-SNAKE EYES?

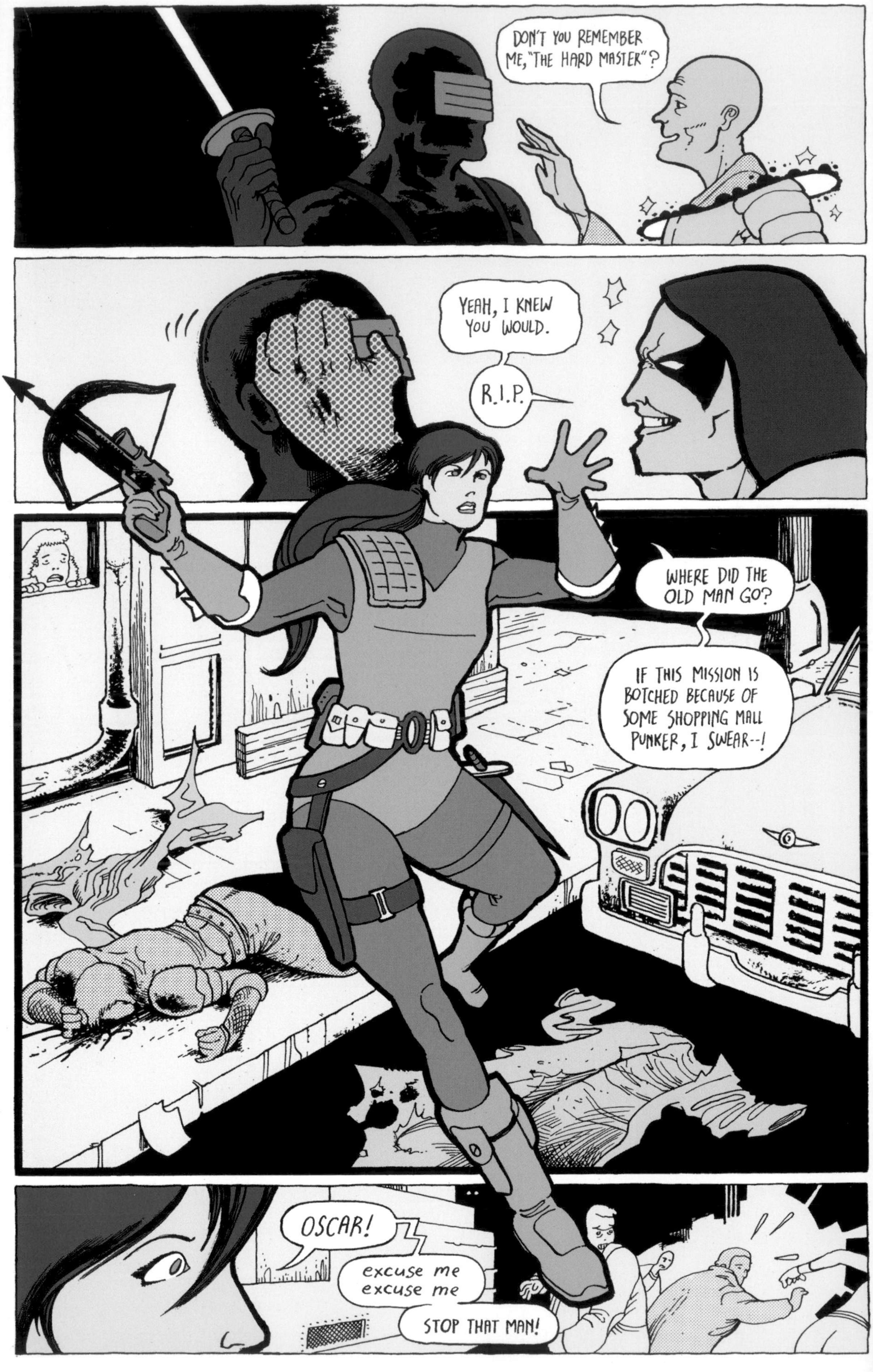
DON'T YOU REMEMBER ME, "THE HARD MASTER"?
YEAH, I KNEW YOU WOULD.
R.I.P.
WHERE DID THE OLD MAN GO?
IF THIS MISSION IS BOTCHED BECAUSE OF SOME SHOPPING MALL PUNKER, I SWEAR--!
OSCAR!
excuse me excuse me
STOP THAT MAN!

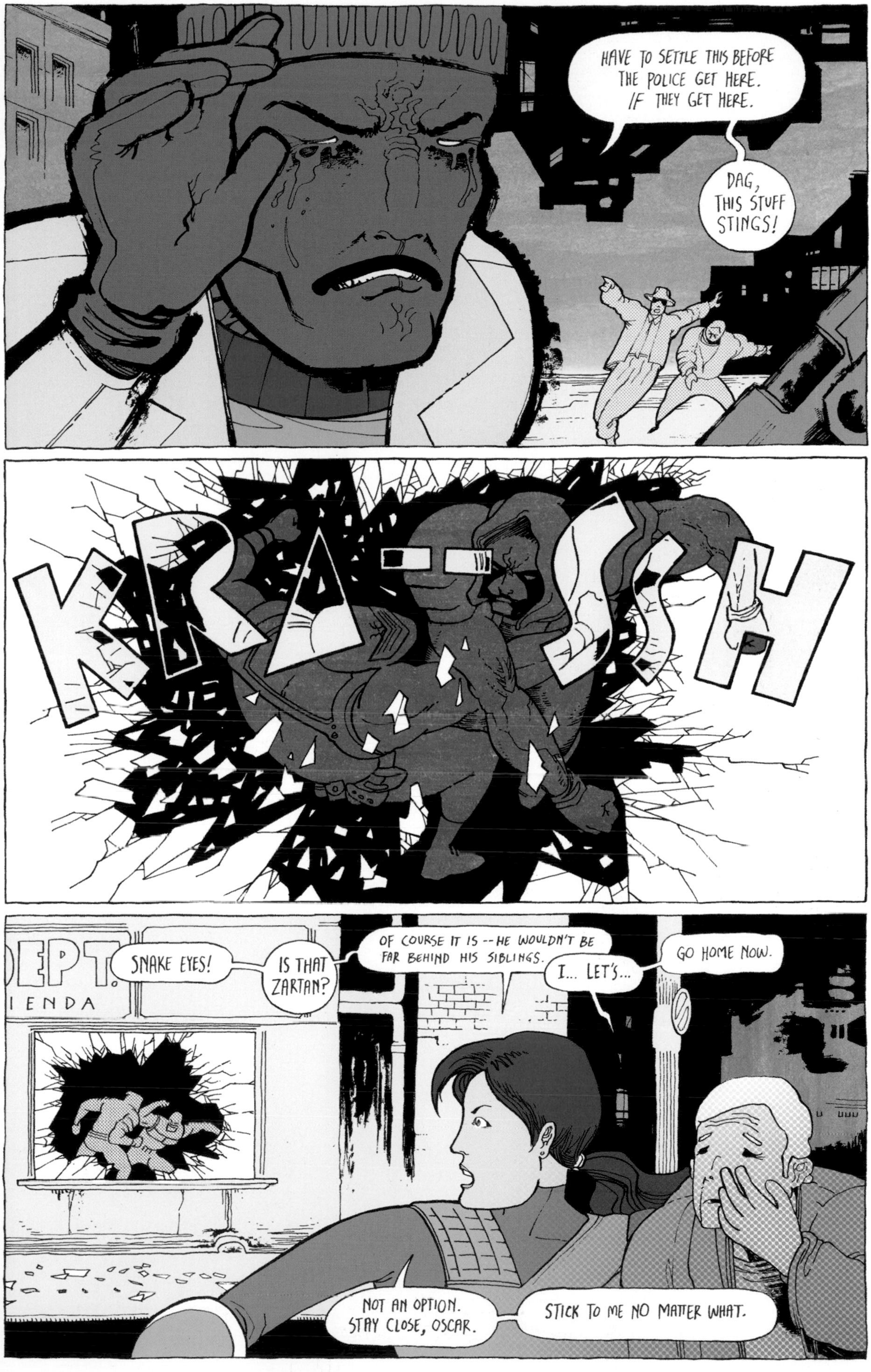
HAVE TO SETTLE THIS BEFORE THE POLICE GET HERE. IF THEY GET HERE.
DAG, THIS STUFF STINGS!
KRA-SSH
DEPT.
IENDA
SNAKE EYES!
IS THAT ZARTAN?
OF COURSE IT IS -- HE WOULDN'T BE FAR BEHIND HIS SIBLINGS.
I... LET'S...
GO HOME NOW.
NOT AN OPTION. STAY CLOSE, OSCAR.
STICK TO ME NO MATTER WHAT.

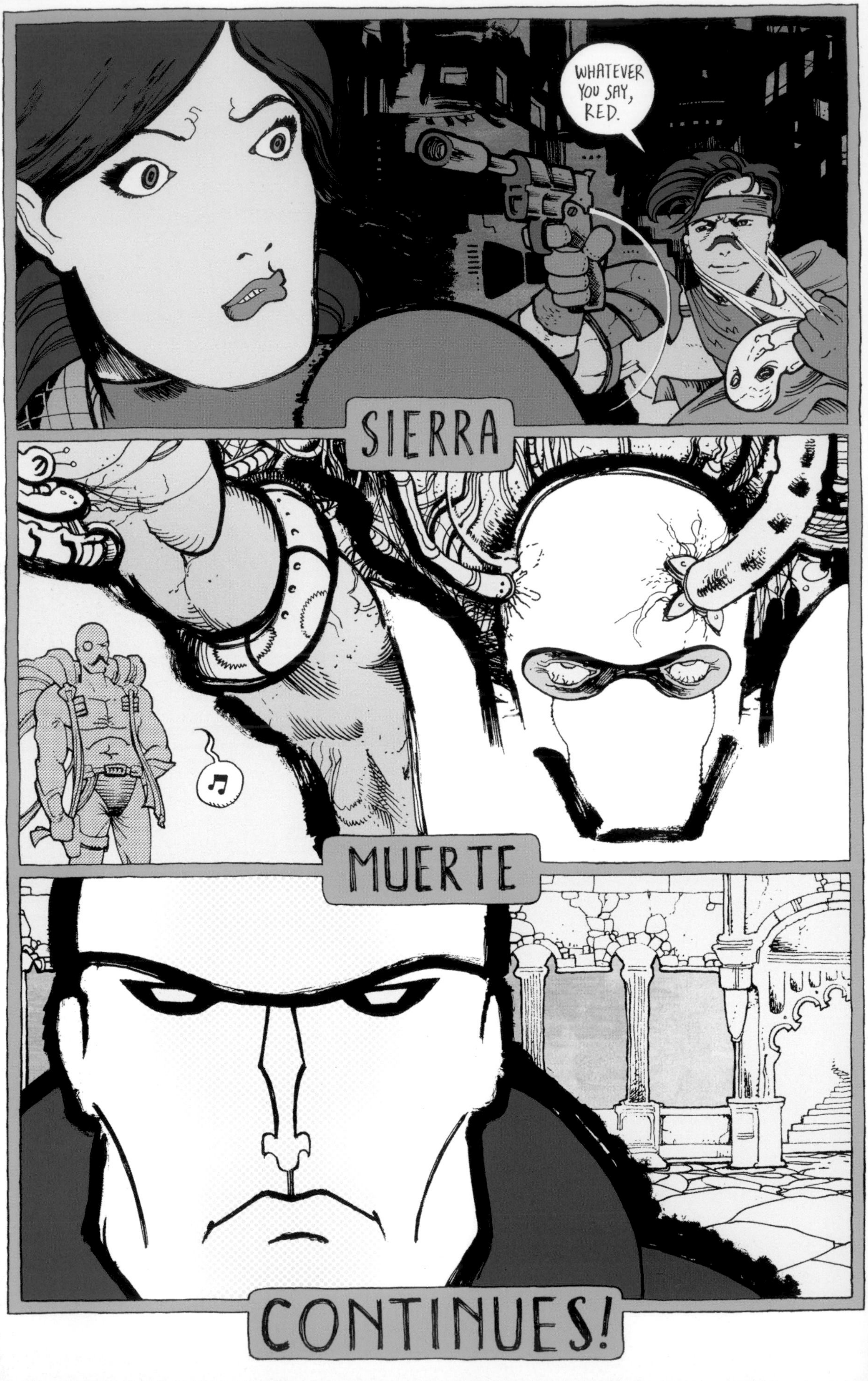
WHATEVER YOU SAY, RED.
SIERRA
MUERTE
CONTINUES!

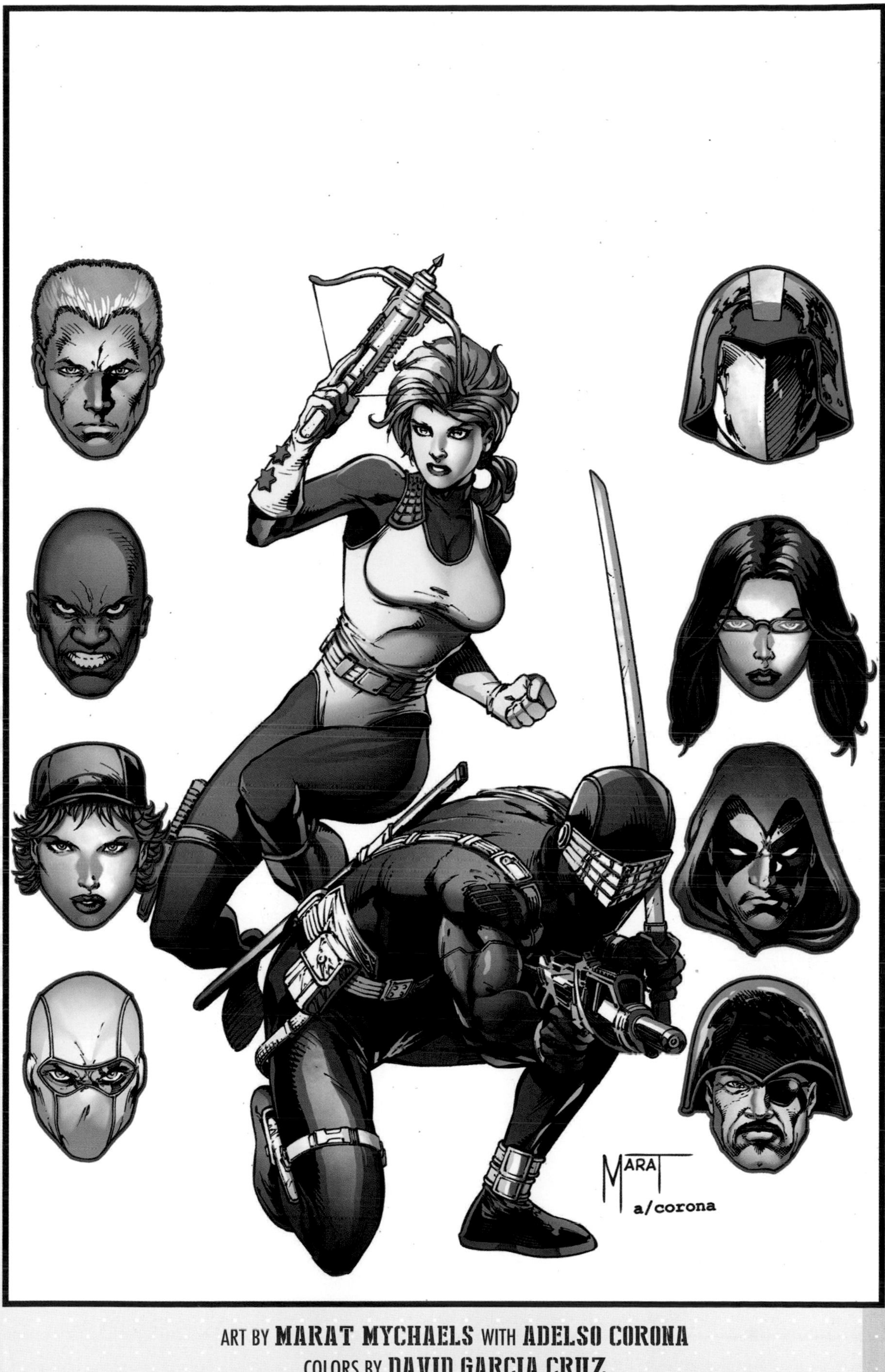
MARAT
a/corona

ART BY **MARAT MYCHAELS** WITH **ADELSO CORONA**
COLORS BY **DAVID GARCIA CRUZ**

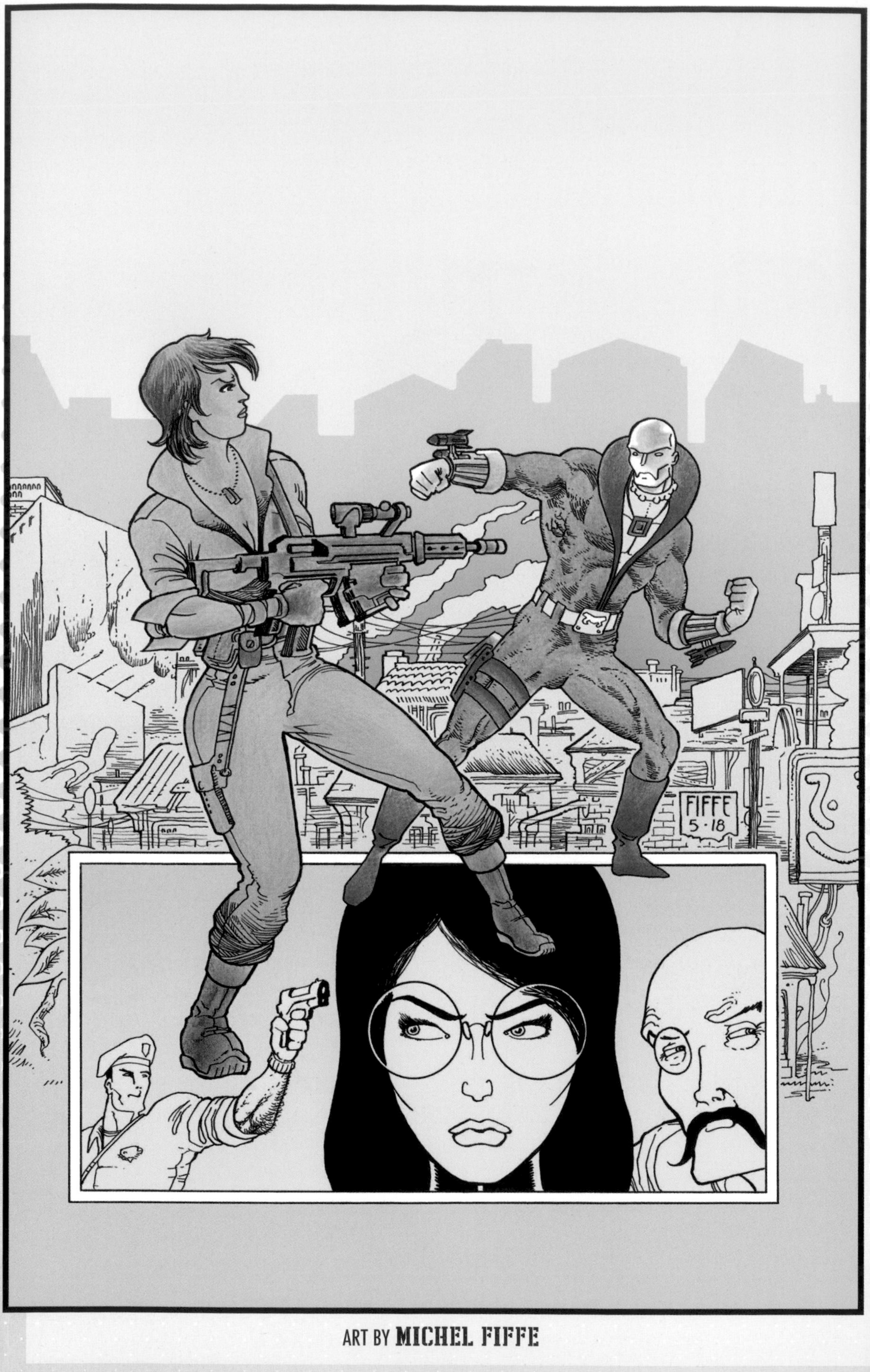
FIFFE
5-18

ART BY **MICHEL FIFFE**

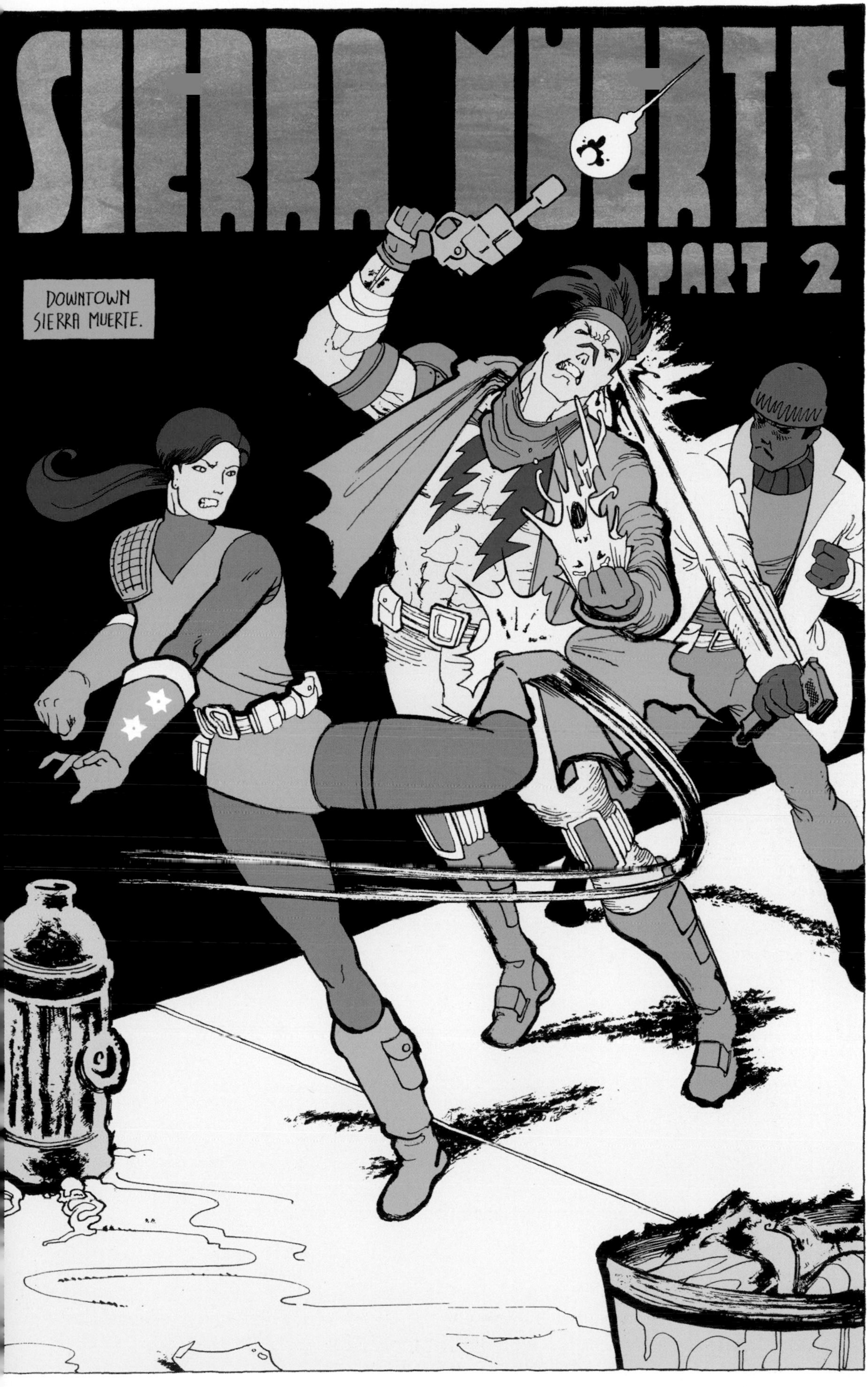
SIERRA MUERTE
PART 2
DOWNTOWN SIERRA MUERTE.

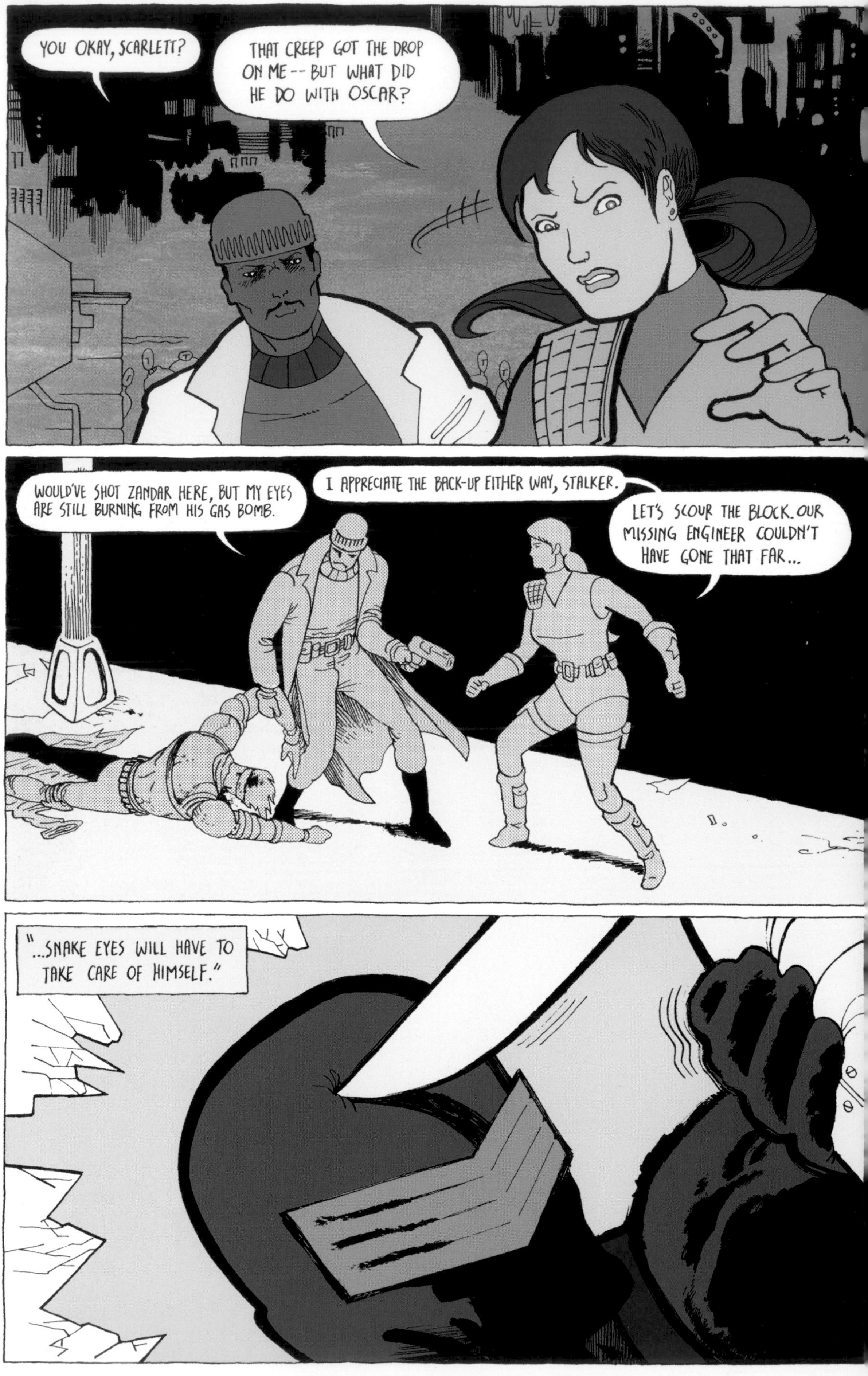
YOU OKAY, SCARLETT?
THAT CREEP GOT THE DROP ON ME -- BUT WHAT DID HE DO WITH OSCAR?
WOULD'VE SHOT ZANDAR HERE, BUT MY EYES ARE STILL BURNING FROM HIS GAS BOMB.
I APPRECIATE THE BACK-UP EITHER WAY, STALKER.
LET'S SCOUR THE BLOCK. OUR MISSING ENGINEER COULDN'T HAVE GONE THAT FAR...
"...SNAKE EYES WILL HAVE TO TAKE CARE OF HIMSELF."

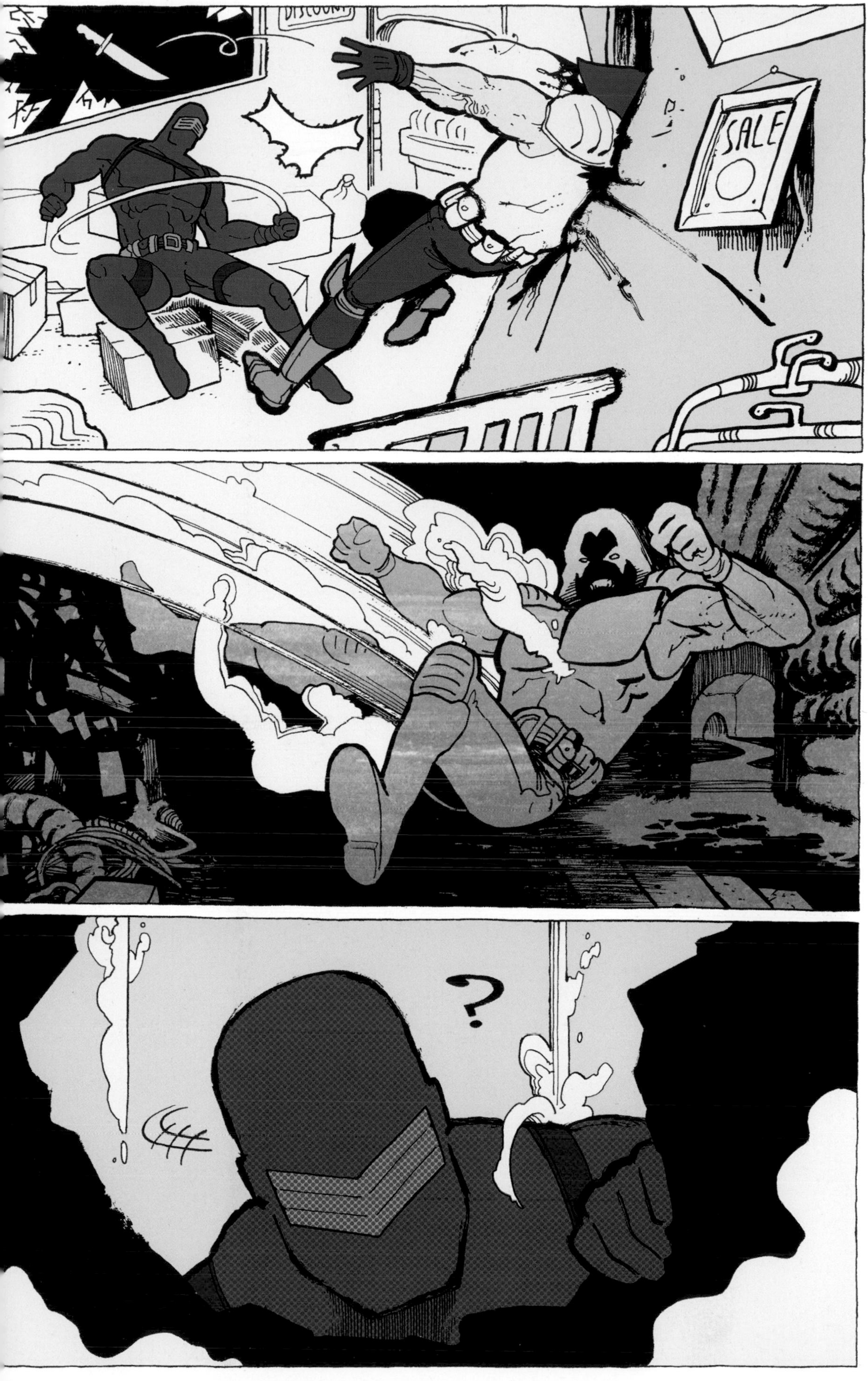
SALE
?

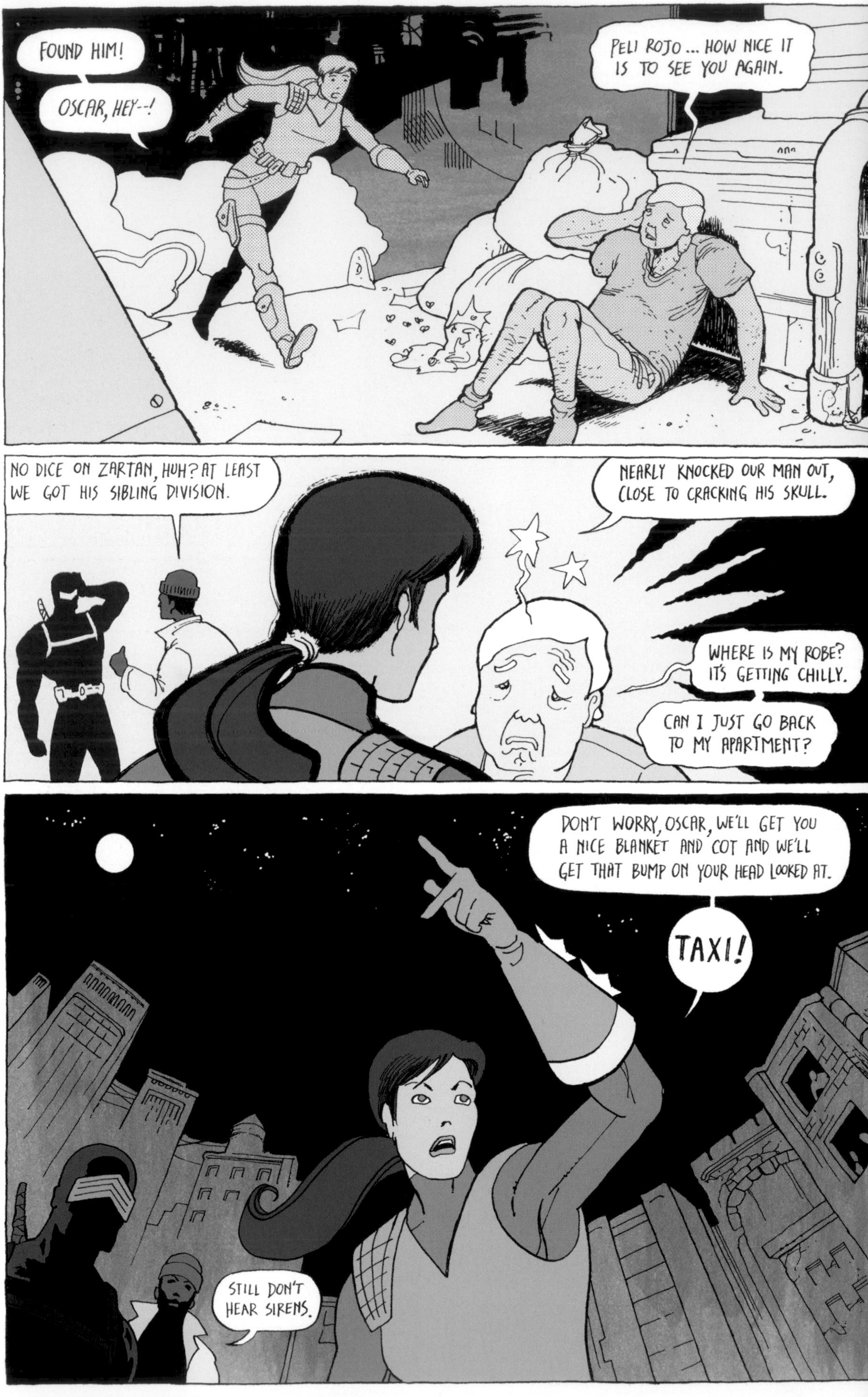
FOUND HIM!
OSCAR, HEY--!
PELI ROJO ... HOW NICE IT IS TO SEE YOU AGAIN.
NO DICE ON ZARTAN, HUH? AT LEAST WE GOT HIS SIBLING DIVISION.
NEARLY KNOCKED OUR MAN OUT, CLOSE TO CRACKING HIS SKULL.
WHERE IS MY ROBE? IT'S GETTING CHILLY.
CAN I JUST GO BACK TO MY APARTMENT?
DON'T WORRY, OSCAR, WE'LL GET YOU A NICE BLANKET AND COT AND WE'LL GET THAT BUMP ON YOUR HEAD LOOKED AT.
TAXI!
STILL DON'T HEAR SIRENS.

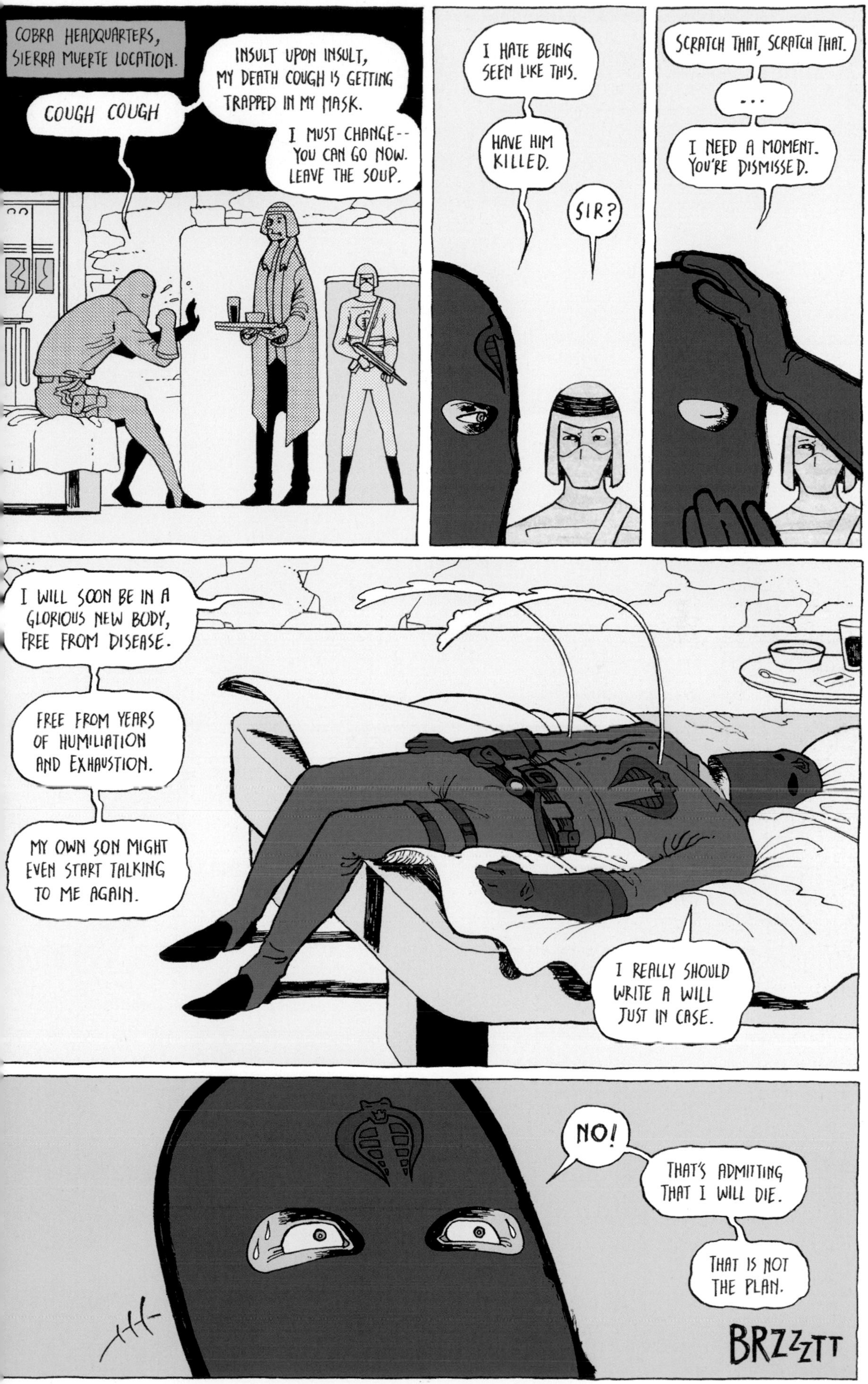
COBRA HEADQUARTERS, SIERRA MUERTE LOCATION.
COUGH COUGH
INSULT UPON INSULT, MY DEATH COUGH IS GETTING TRAPPED IN MY MASK.
I MUST CHANGE-- YOU CAN GO NOW. LEAVE THE SOUP.
I HATE BEING SEEN LIKE THIS.
HAVE HIM KILLED.
SIR?
SCRATCH THAT, SCRATCH THAT.
...
I NEED A MOMENT. YOU'RE DISMISSED.
I WILL SOON BE IN A GLORIOUS NEW BODY, FREE FROM DISEASE.
FREE FROM YEARS OF HUMILIATION AND EXHAUSTION.
MY OWN SON MIGHT EVEN START TALKING TO ME AGAIN.
I REALLY SHOULD WRITE A WILL JUST IN CASE.
NO!
THAT'S ADMITTING THAT I WILL DIE.
THAT IS NOT THE PLAN.
BRZZZTT

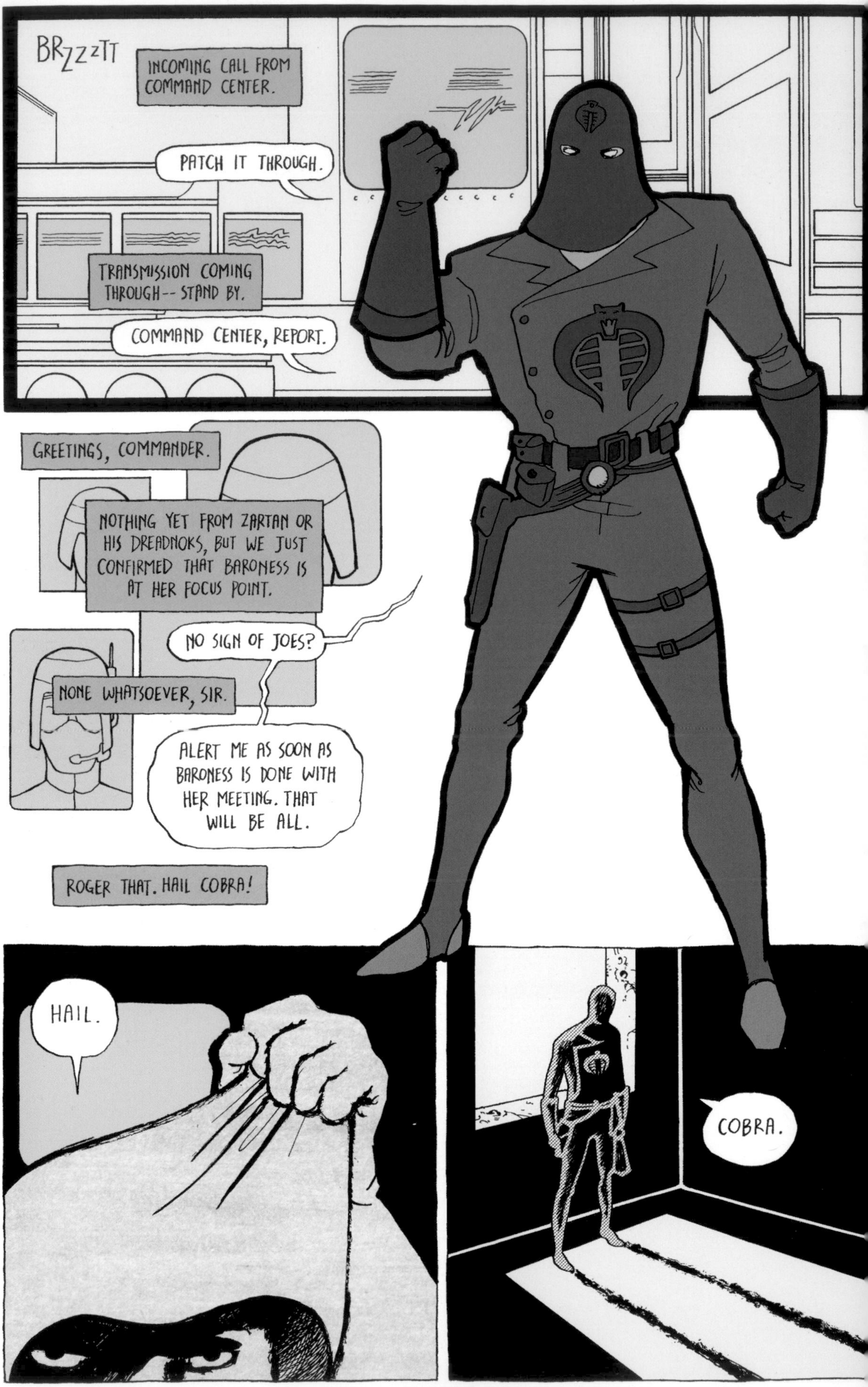
BRZZZTT
INCOMING CALL FROM COMMAND CENTER.
PATCH IT THROUGH.
TRANSMISSION COMING THROUGH-- STAND BY.
COMMAND CENTER, REPORT.
GREETINGS, COMMANDER.
NOTHING YET FROM ZARTAN OR HIS DREADNOKS, BUT WE JUST CONFIRMED THAT BARONESS IS AT HER FOCUS POINT.
NO SIGN OF JOES?
NONE WHATSOEVER, SIR.
ALERT ME AS SOON AS BARONESS IS DONE WITH HER MEETING. THAT WILL BE ALL.
ROGER THAT. HAIL COBRA!
HAIL.
COBRA.

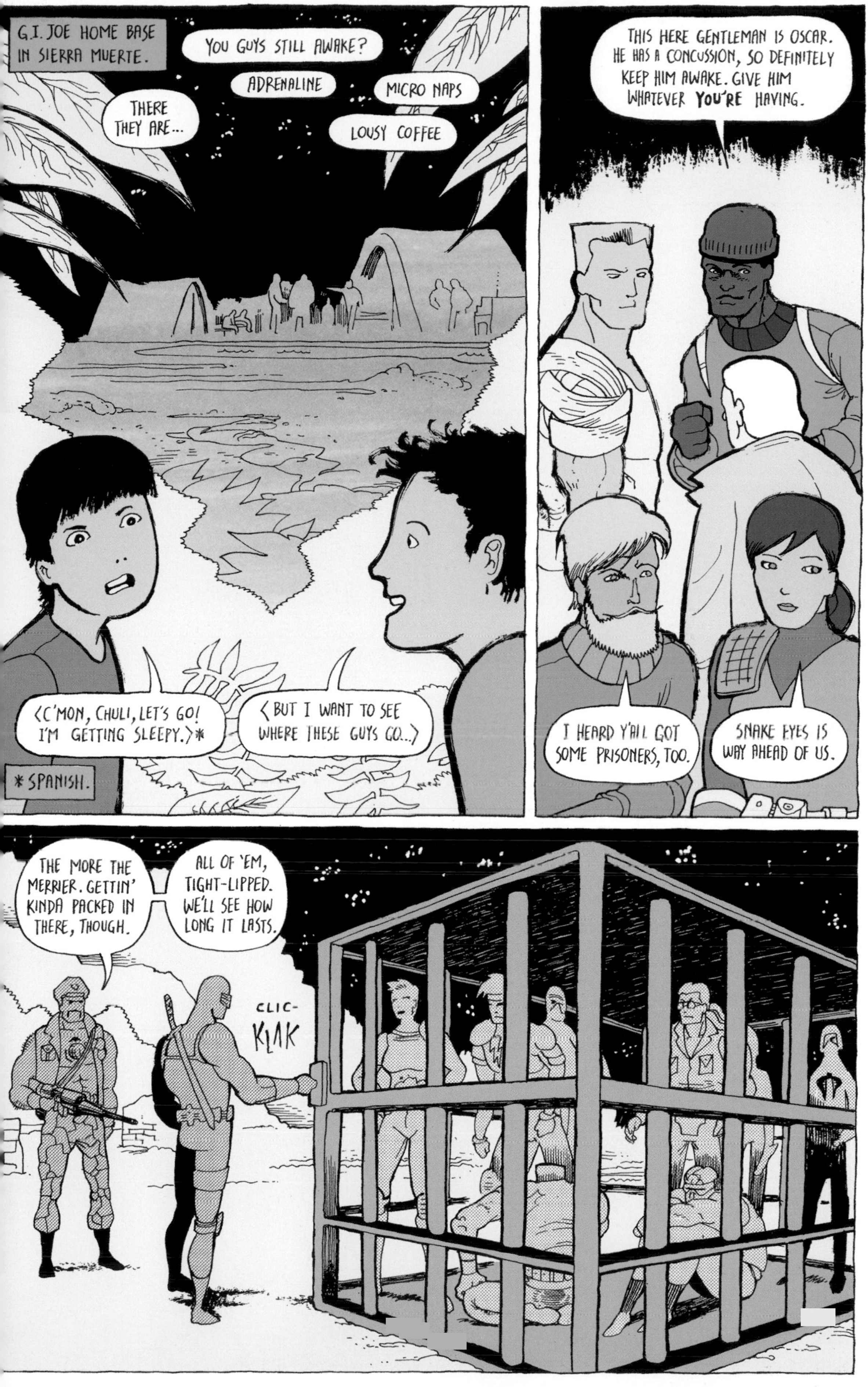
G.I. JOE HOME BASE IN SIERRA MUERTE.
YOU GUYS STILL AWAKE?
THERE THEY ARE...
ADRENALINE
MICRO NAPS
LOUSY COFFEE
<C'MON, CHULI, LET'S GO! I'M GETTING SLEEPY.>*
<BUT I WANT TO SEE WHERE THESE GUYS GO...>
* SPANISH.
THIS HERE GENTLEMAN IS OSCAR. HE HAS A CONCUSSION, SO DEFINITELY KEEP HIM AWAKE. GIVE HIM WHATEVER YOU'RE HAVING.
I HEARD Y'ALL GOT SOME PRISONERS, TOO.
SNAKE EYES IS WAY AHEAD OF US.
THE MORE THE MERRIER. GETTIN' KINDA PACKED IN THERE, THOUGH.
ALL OF 'EM, TIGHT-LIPPED. WE'LL SEE HOW LONG IT LASTS.
CLIC-
KLAK

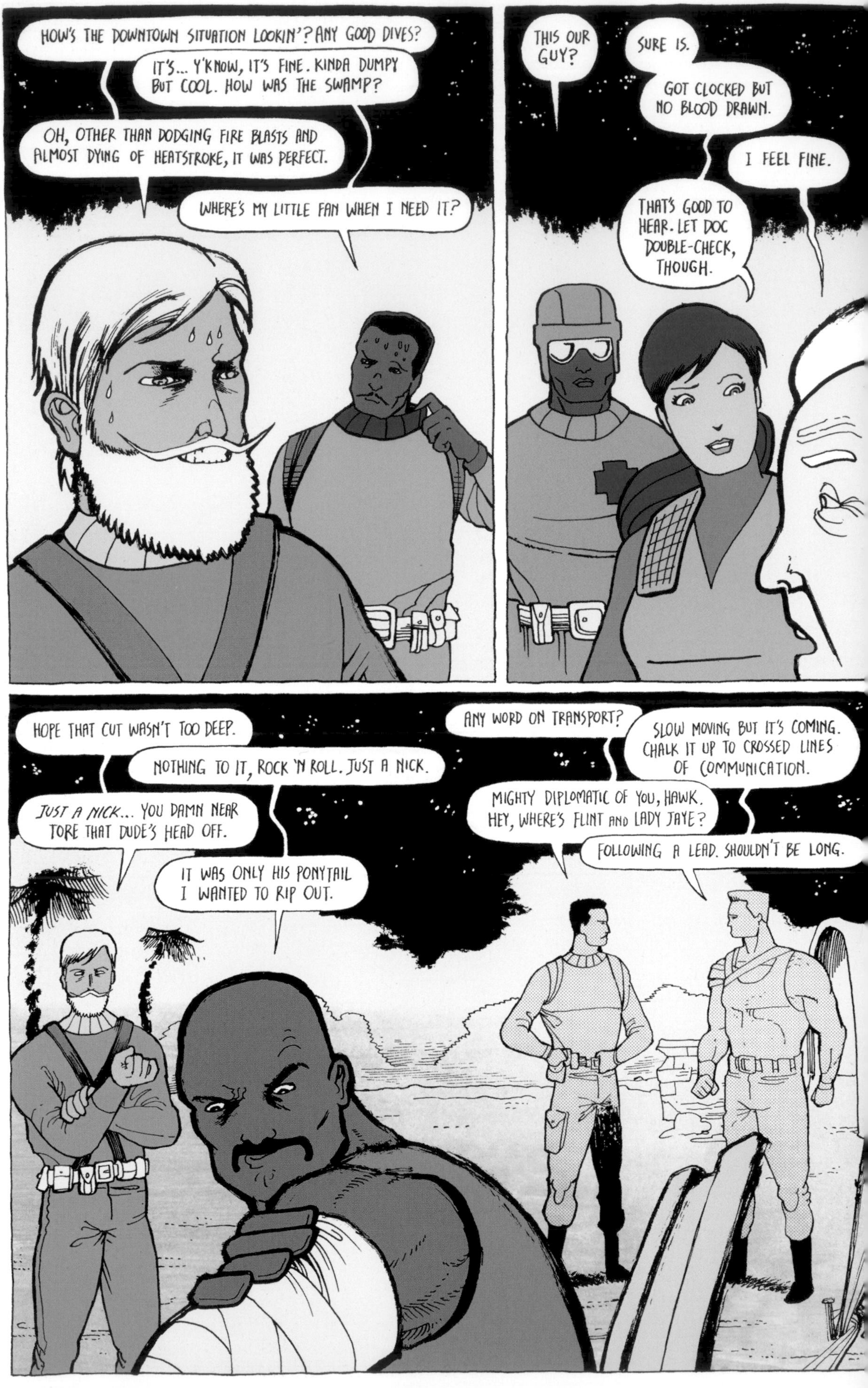
HOW'S THE DOWNTOWN SITUATION LOOKIN'? ANY GOOD DIVES?
IT'S... Y'KNOW, IT'S FINE. KINDA DUMPY BUT COOL. HOW WAS THE SWAMP?
OH, OTHER THAN DODGING FIRE BLASTS AND ALMOST DYING OF HEATSTROKE, IT WAS PERFECT.
WHERE'S MY LITTLE FAN WHEN I NEED IT?
THIS OUR GUY?
SURE IS.
GOT CLOCKED BUT NO BLOOD DRAWN.
I FEEL FINE.
THAT'S GOOD TO HEAR. LET DOC DOUBLE-CHECK, THOUGH.
HOPE THAT CUT WASN'T TOO DEEP.
NOTHING TO IT, ROCK 'N ROLL. JUST A NICK.
JUST A NICK... YOU DAMN NEAR TORE THAT DUDE'S HEAD OFF.
IT WAS ONLY HIS PONYTAIL I WANTED TO RIP OUT.
ANY WORD ON TRANSPORT?
SLOW MOVING BUT IT'S COMING. CHALK IT UP TO CROSSED LINES OF COMMUNICATION.
MIGHTY DIPLOMATIC OF YOU, HAWK. HEY, WHERE'S FLINT AND LADY JAYE?
FOLLOWING A LEAD. SHOULDN'T BE LONG.

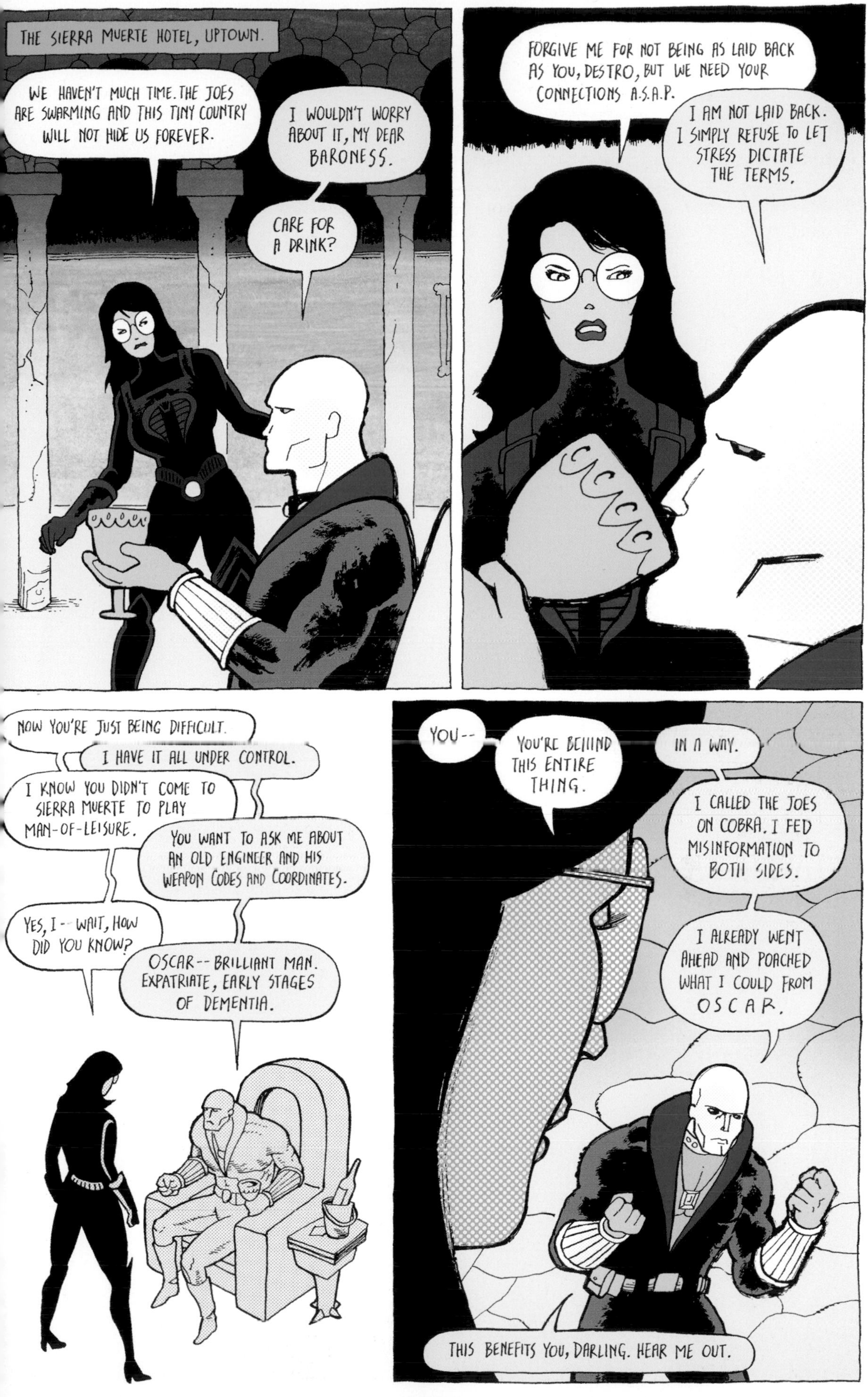
THE SIERRA MUERTE HOTEL, UPTOWN.
WE HAVEN'T MUCH TIME. THE JOES ARE SWARMING AND THIS TINY COUNTRY WILL NOT HIDE US FOREVER.
I WOULDN'T WORRY ABOUT IT, MY DEAR BARONESS.
CARE FOR A DRINK?
FORGIVE ME FOR NOT BEING AS LAID BACK AS YOU, DESTRO, BUT WE NEED YOUR CONNECTIONS A.S.A.P.
I AM NOT LAID BACK. I SIMPLY REFUSE TO LET STRESS DICTATE THE TERMS.
NOW YOU'RE JUST BEING DIFFICULT.
I HAVE IT ALL UNDER CONTROL.
I KNOW YOU DIDN'T COME TO SIERRA MUERTE TO PLAY MAN-OF-LEISURE.
YOU WANT TO ASK ME ABOUT AN OLD ENGINEER AND HIS WEAPON CODES AND COORDINATES.
YES, I-- WAIT, HOW DID YOU KNOW?
OSCAR-- BRILLIANT MAN. EXPATRIATE, EARLY STAGES OF DEMENTIA.
YOU--
YOU'RE BEHIND THIS ENTIRE THING.
IN A WAY.
I CALLED THE JOES ON COBRA. I FED MISINFORMATION TO BOTH SIDES.
I ALREADY WENT AHEAD AND POACHED WHAT I COULD FROM OSCAR.
THIS BENEFITS YOU, DARLING. HEAR ME OUT.

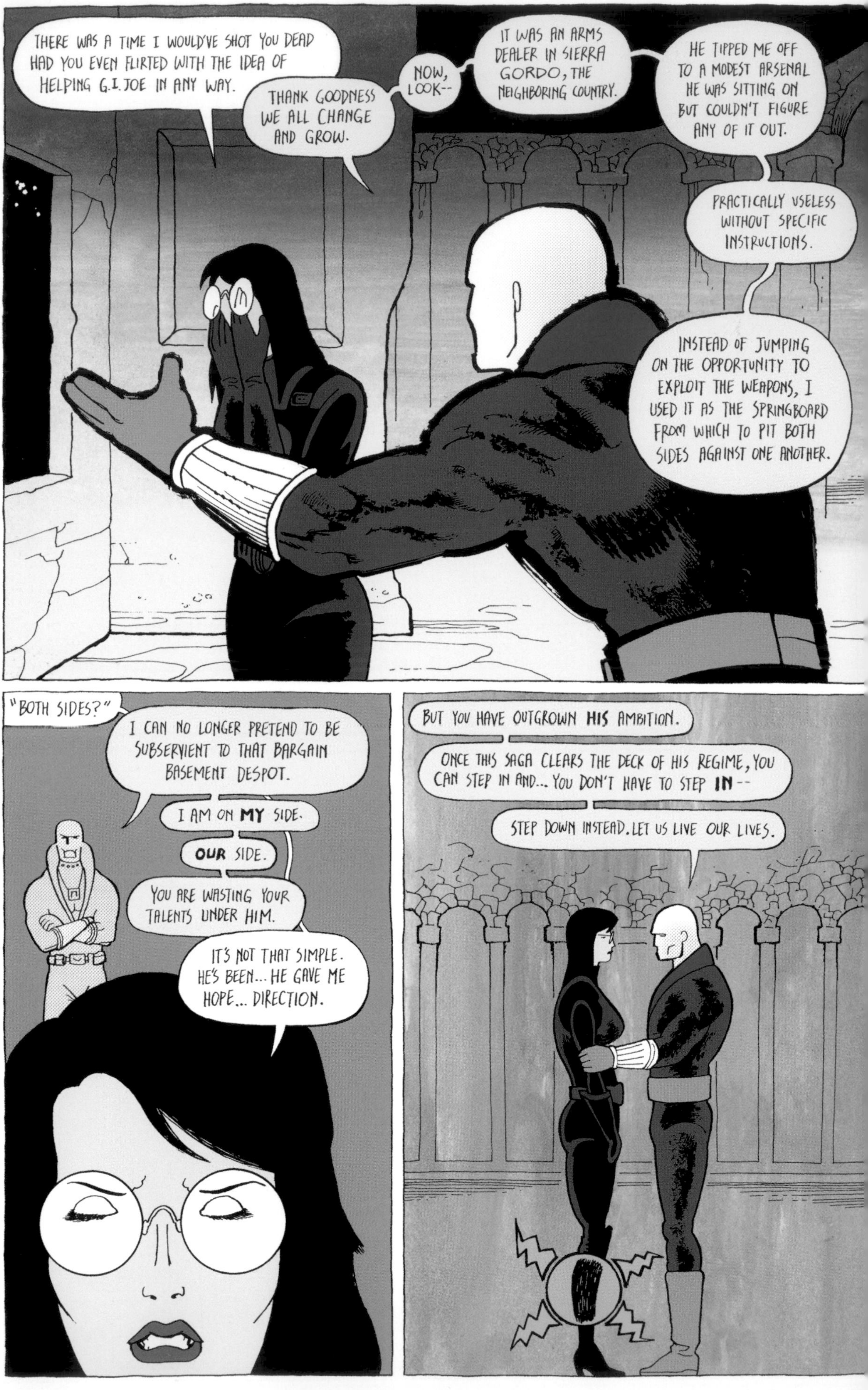
THERE WAS A TIME I WOULD'VE SHOT YOU DEAD HAD YOU EVEN FLIRTED WITH THE IDEA OF HELPING G.I. JOE IN ANY WAY.
THANK GOODNESS WE ALL CHANGE AND GROW.
NOW, LOOK--
IT WAS AN ARMS DEALER IN SIERRA GORDO, THE NEIGHBORING COUNTRY.
HE TIPPED ME OFF TO A MODEST ARSENAL HE WAS SITTING ON BUT COULDN'T FIGURE ANY OF IT OUT.
PRACTICALLY USELESS WITHOUT SPECIFIC INSTRUCTIONS.
INSTEAD OF JUMPING ON THE OPPORTUNITY TO EXPLOIT THE WEAPONS, I USED IT AS THE SPRINGBOARD FROM WHICH TO PIT BOTH SIDES AGAINST ONE ANOTHER.
"BOTH SIDES?"
I CAN NO LONGER PRETEND TO BE SUBSERVIENT TO THAT BARGAIN BASEMENT DESPOT.
I AM ON **MY** SIDE.
OUR SIDE.
YOU ARE WASTING YOUR TALENTS UNDER HIM.
IT'S NOT THAT SIMPLE. HE'S BEEN... HE GAVE ME HOPE... DIRECTION.
BUT YOU HAVE OUTGROWN **HIS** AMBITION.
ONCE THIS SAGA CLEARS THE DECK OF HIS REGIME, YOU CAN STEP IN AND... YOU DON'T HAVE TO STEP **IN**--
STEP DOWN INSTEAD. LET US LIVE OUR LIVES.

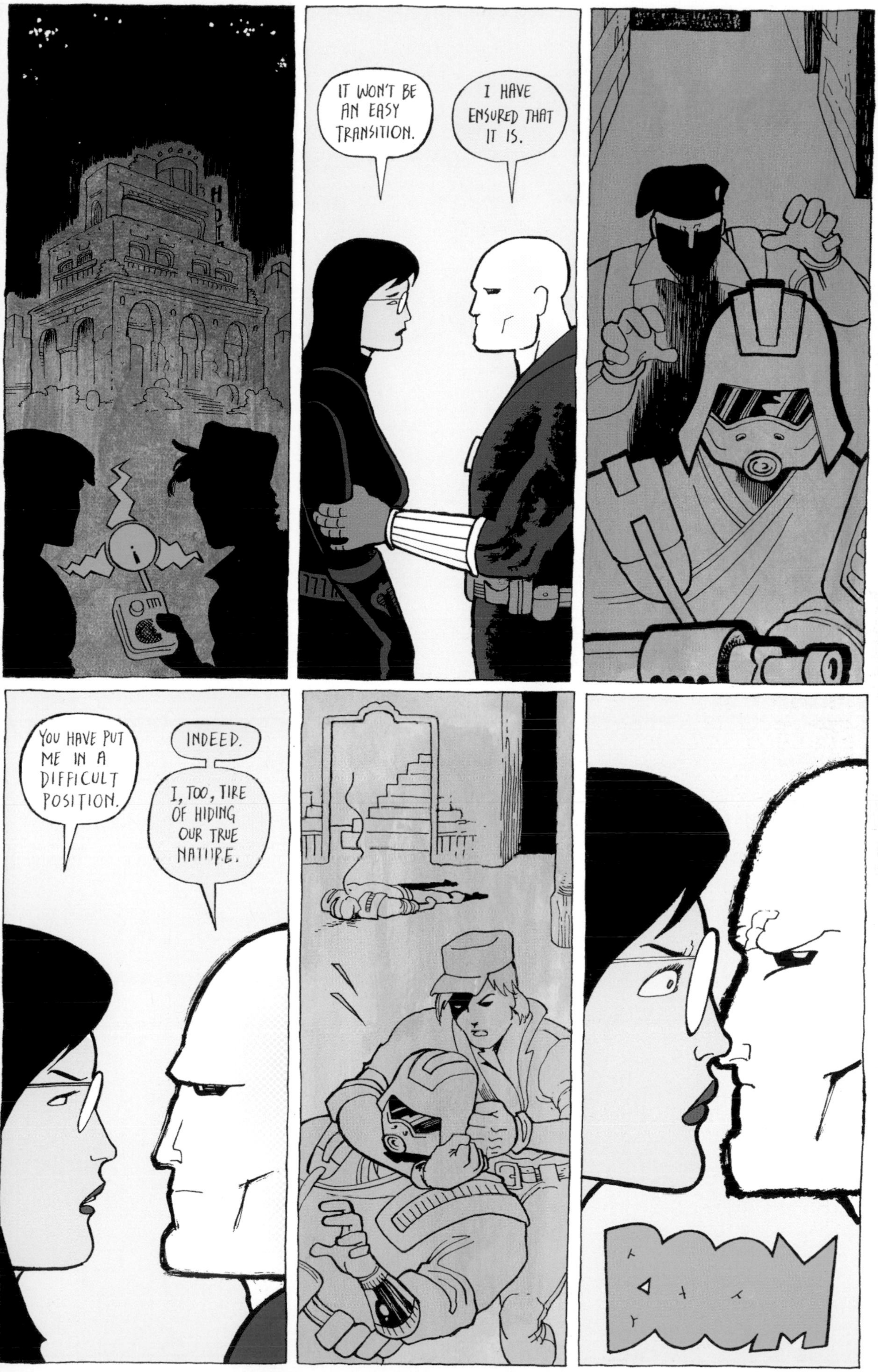

IT WON'T BE AN EASY TRANSITION.
I HAVE ENSURED THAT IT IS.
YOU HAVE PUT ME IN A DIFFICULT POSITION.
INDEED.
I, TOO, TIRE OF HIDING OUR TRUE NATURE.
BOOM

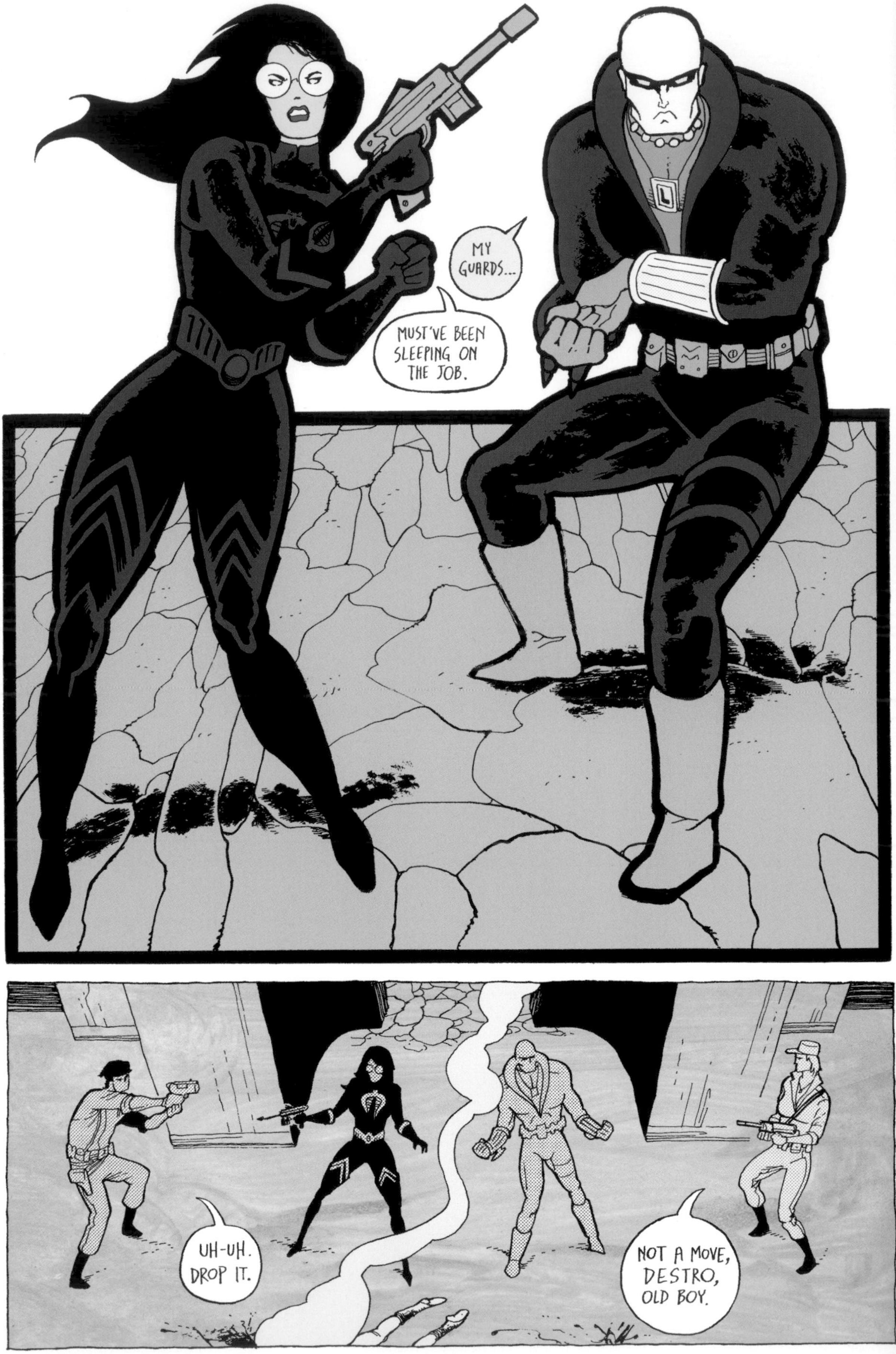
MY GUARDS...
MUST'VE BEEN SLEEPING ON THE JOB.
UH-UH. DROP IT.
NOT A MOVE, DESTRO, OLD BOY.

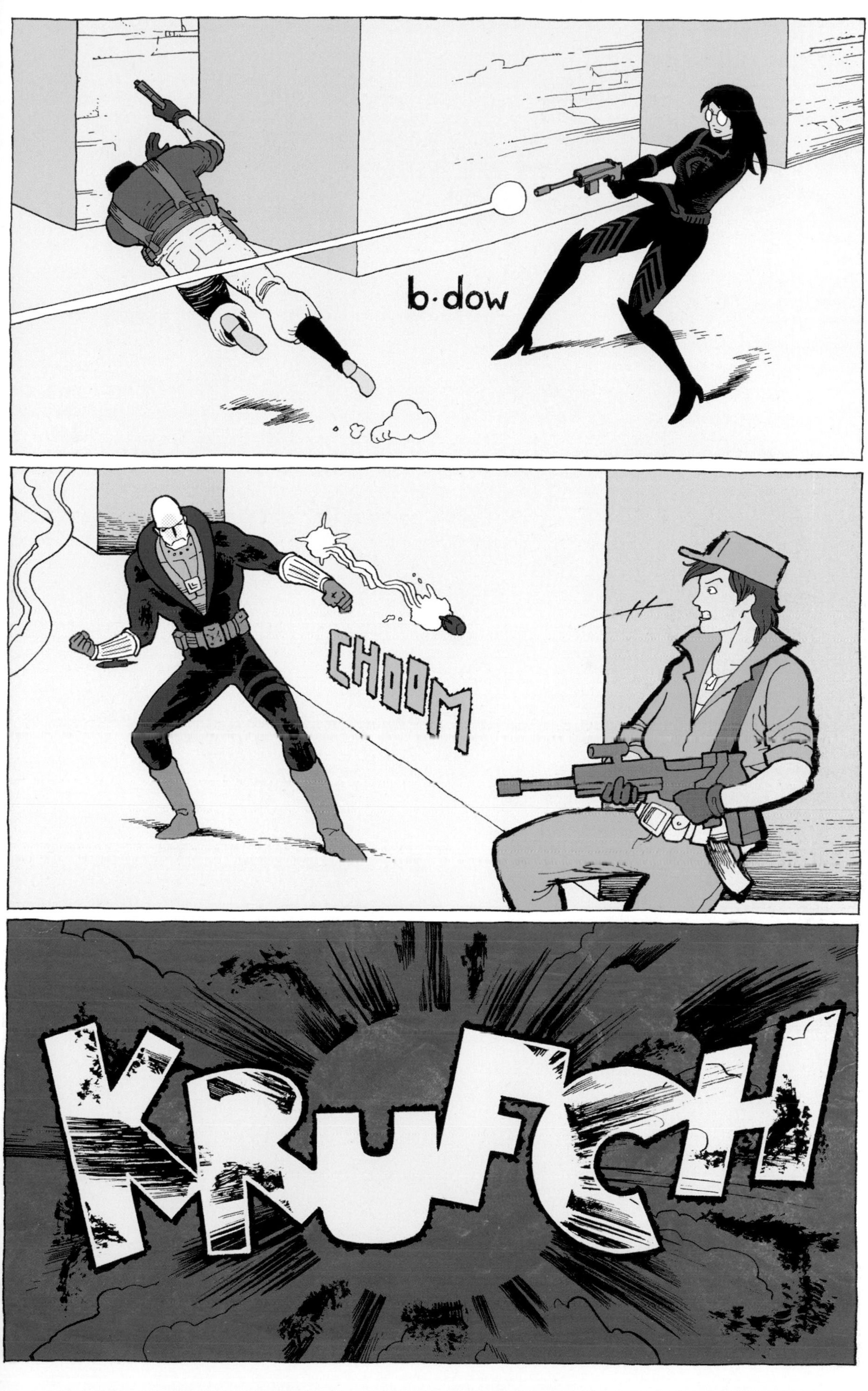
b·dow
CHOOM
KRUFCH!

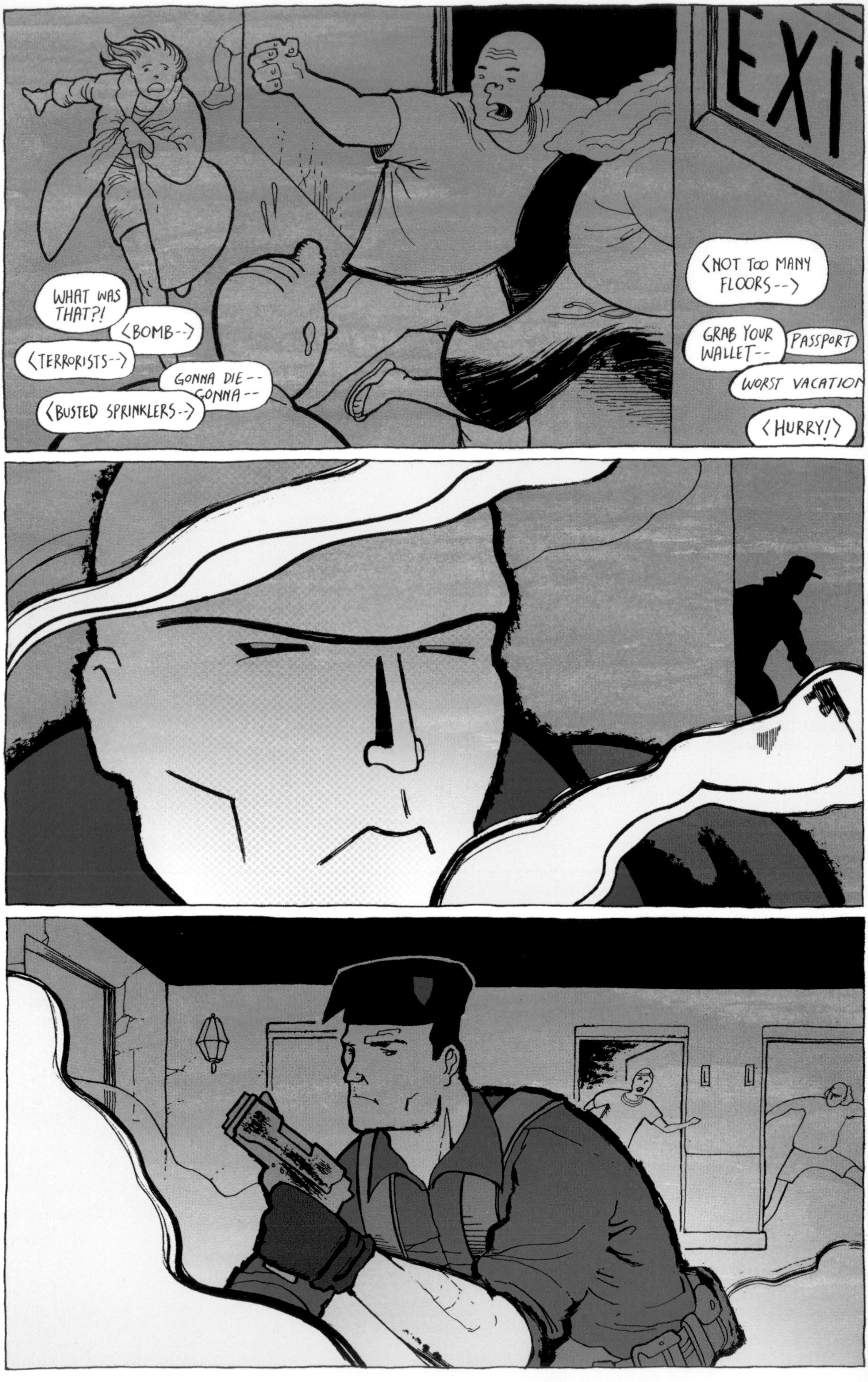
WHAT WAS THAT?!
<BOMB-->
<TERRORISTS-->
GONNA DIE-- GONNA--
<BUSTED SPRINKLERS-->
<NOT TOO MANY FLOORS-->
GRAB YOUR WALLET--
PASSPORT
WORST VACATIO
<HURRY!>

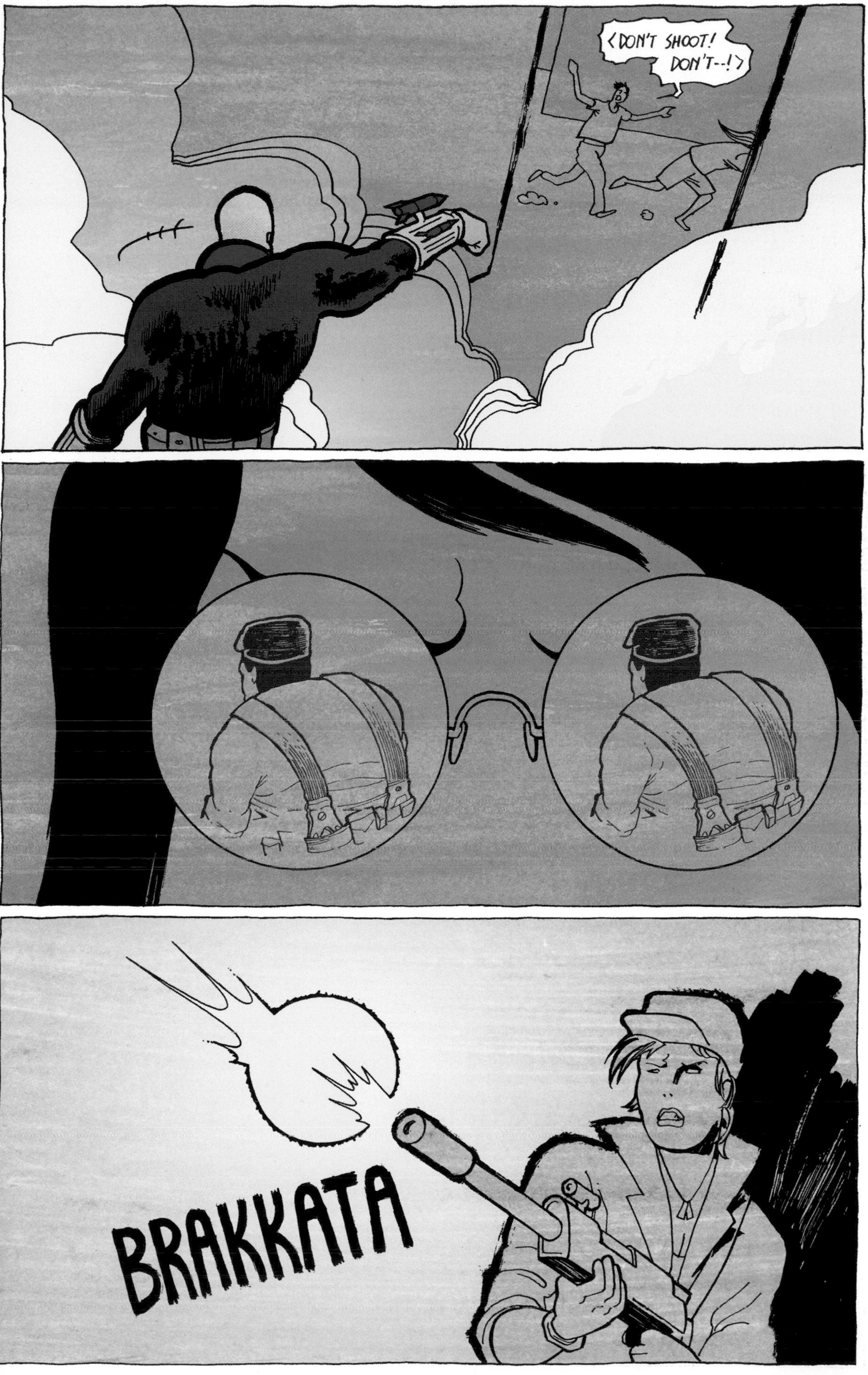
<DON'T SHOOT! DON'T--!>
BRAKKATA

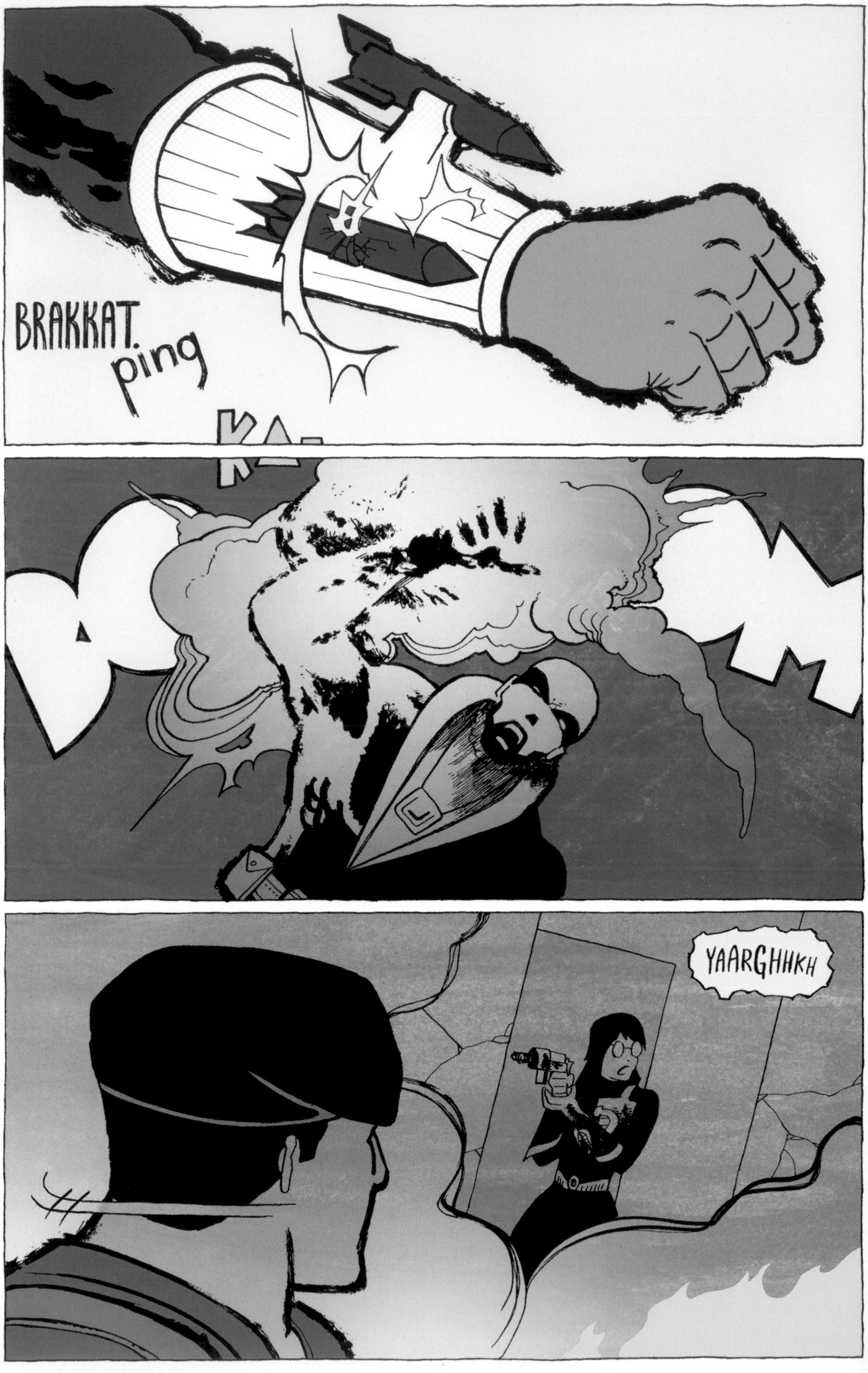
BRAKKAT.
ping
KA-BOOM
YAARGHHKH

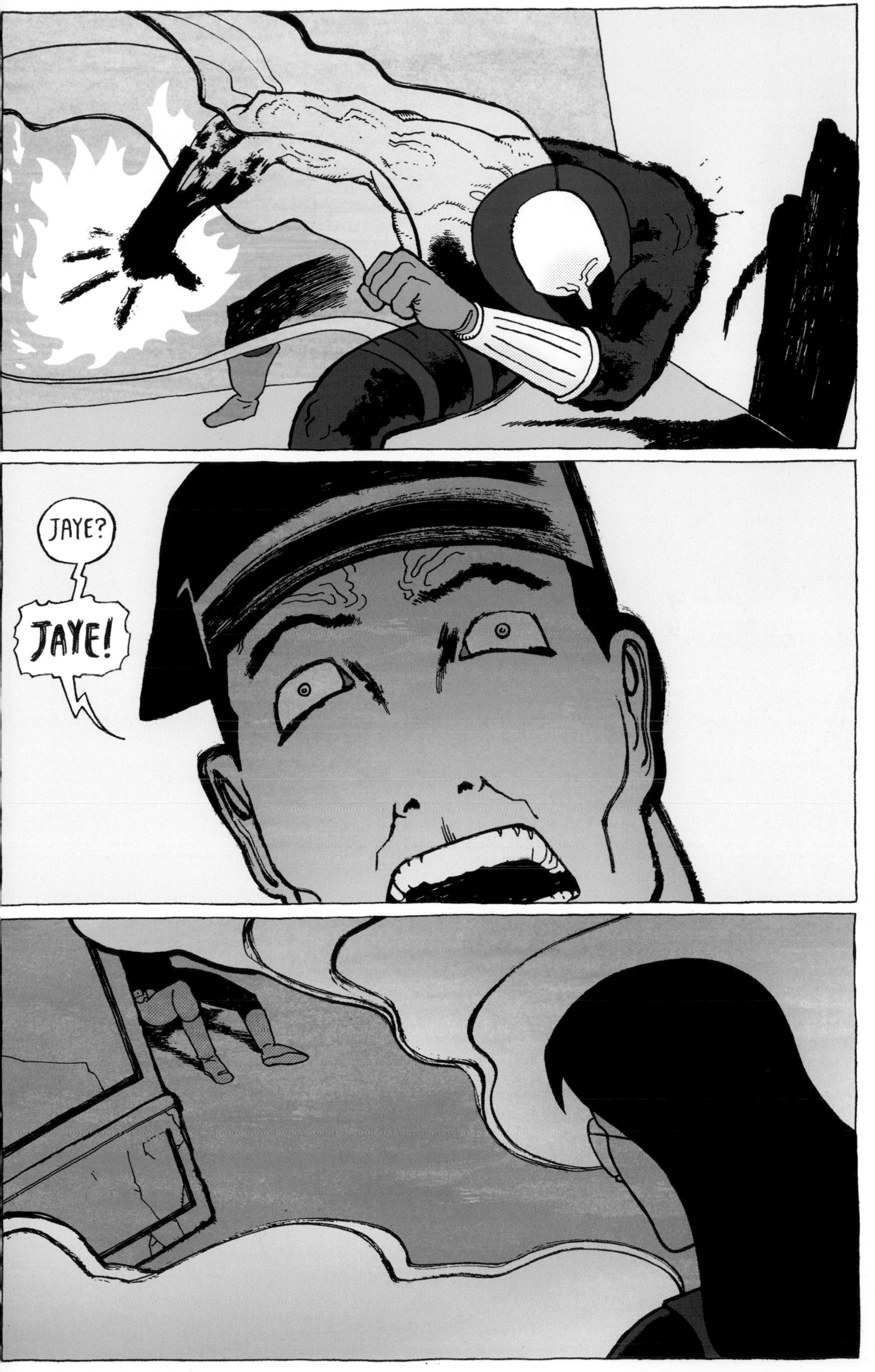
JAYE?
JAYE!

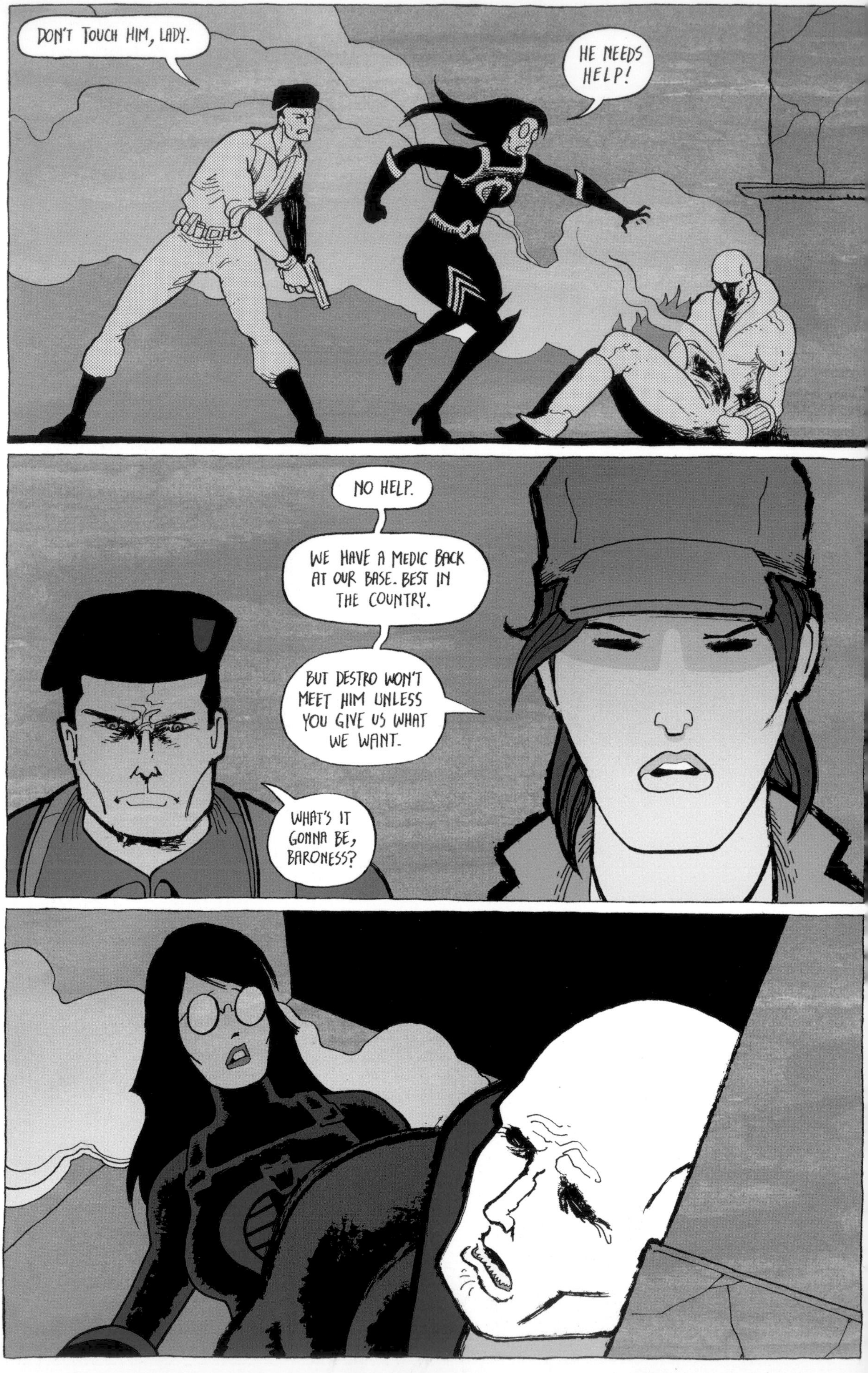
DON'T TOUCH HIM, LADY.
HE NEEDS HELP!
NO HELP.
WE HAVE A MEDIC BACK AT OUR BASE. BEST IN THE COUNTRY.
BUT DESTRO WON'T MEET HIM UNLESS YOU GIVE US WHAT WE WANT.
WHAT'S IT GONNA BE, BARONESS?

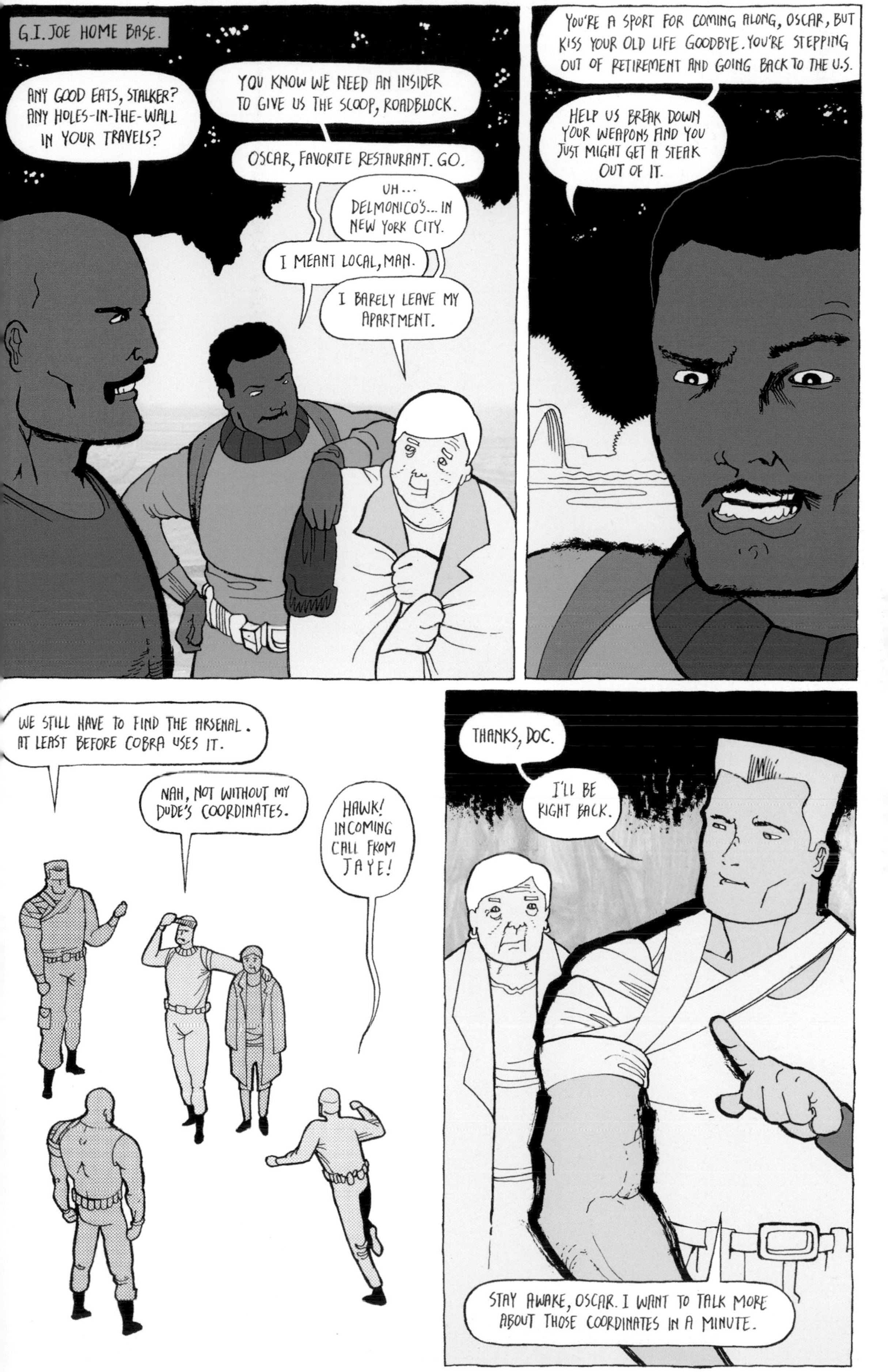
G.I. JOE HOME BASE.
ANY GOOD EATS, STALKER? ANY HOLES-IN-THE-WALL IN YOUR TRAVELS?
YOU KNOW WE NEED AN INSIDER TO GIVE US THE SCOOP, ROADBLOCK.
OSCAR, FAVORITE RESTAURANT. GO.
UH... DELMONICO'S... IN NEW YORK CITY.
I MEANT LOCAL, MAN.
I BARELY LEAVE MY APARTMENT.
YOU'RE A SPORT FOR COMING ALONG, OSCAR, BUT KISS YOUR OLD LIFE GOODBYE. YOU'RE STEPPING OUT OF RETIREMENT AND GOING BACK TO THE U.S.
HELP US BREAK DOWN YOUR WEAPONS AND YOU JUST MIGHT GET A STEAK OUT OF IT.
WE STILL HAVE TO FIND THE ARSENAL. AT LEAST BEFORE COBRA USES IT.
NAH, NOT WITHOUT MY DUDE'S COORDINATES.
HAWK! INCOMING CALL FROM JAYE!
THANKS, DOC.
I'LL BE RIGHT BACK.
STAY AWAKE, OSCAR. I WANT TO TALK MORE ABOUT THOSE COORDINATES IN A MINUTE.

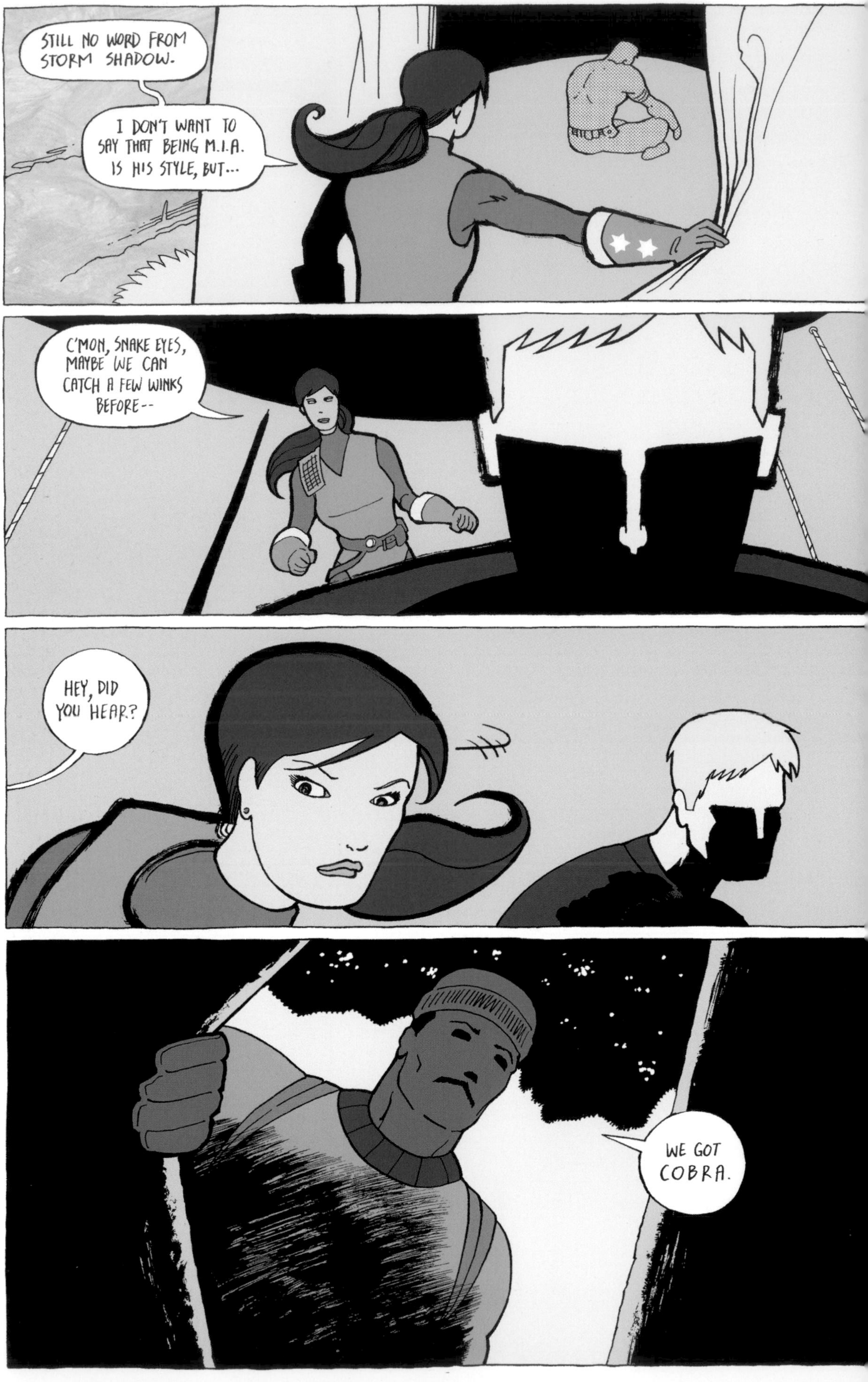
STILL NO WORD FROM STORM SHADOW.
I DON'T WANT TO SAY THAT BEING M.I.A. IS HIS STYLE, BUT...
C'MON, SNAKE EYES, MAYBE WE CAN CATCH A FEW WINKS BEFORE--
HEY, DID YOU HEAR?
WE GOT COBRA.

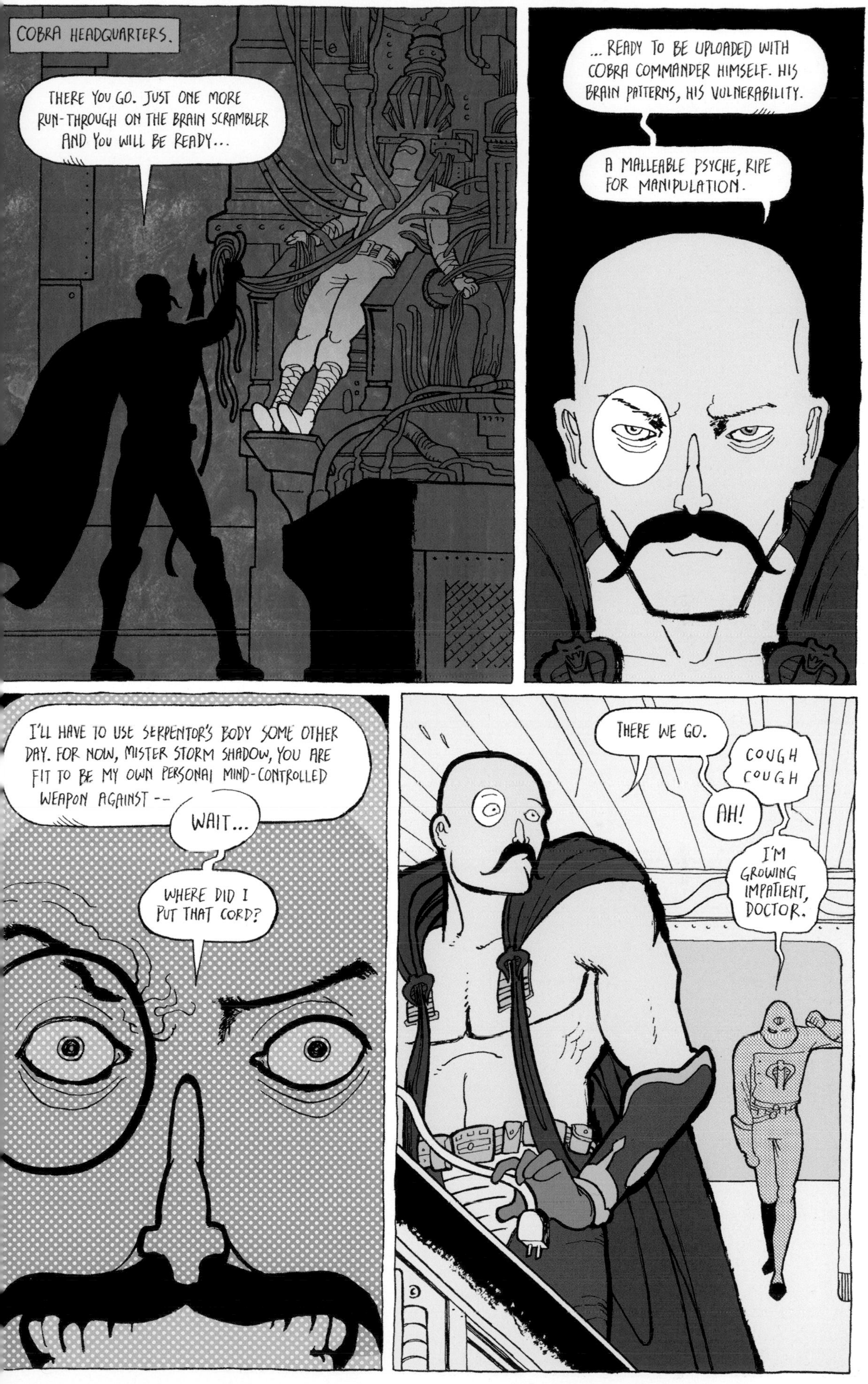
COBRA HEADQUARTERS.
THERE YOU GO. JUST ONE MORE RUN-THROUGH ON THE BRAIN SCRAMBLER AND YOU WILL BE READY...
... READY TO BE UPLOADED WITH COBRA COMMANDER HIMSELF. HIS BRAIN PATTERNS, HIS VULNERABILITY.
A MALLEABLE PSYCHE, RIPE FOR MANIPULATION.
I'LL HAVE TO USE SERPENTOR'S BODY SOME OTHER DAY. FOR NOW, MISTER STORM SHADOW, YOU ARE FIT TO BE MY OWN PERSONAL MIND-CONTROLLED WEAPON AGAINST --
WAIT...
WHERE DID I PUT THAT CORD?
THERE WE GO.
AH!
COUGH COUGH
I'M GROWING IMPATIENT, DOCTOR.

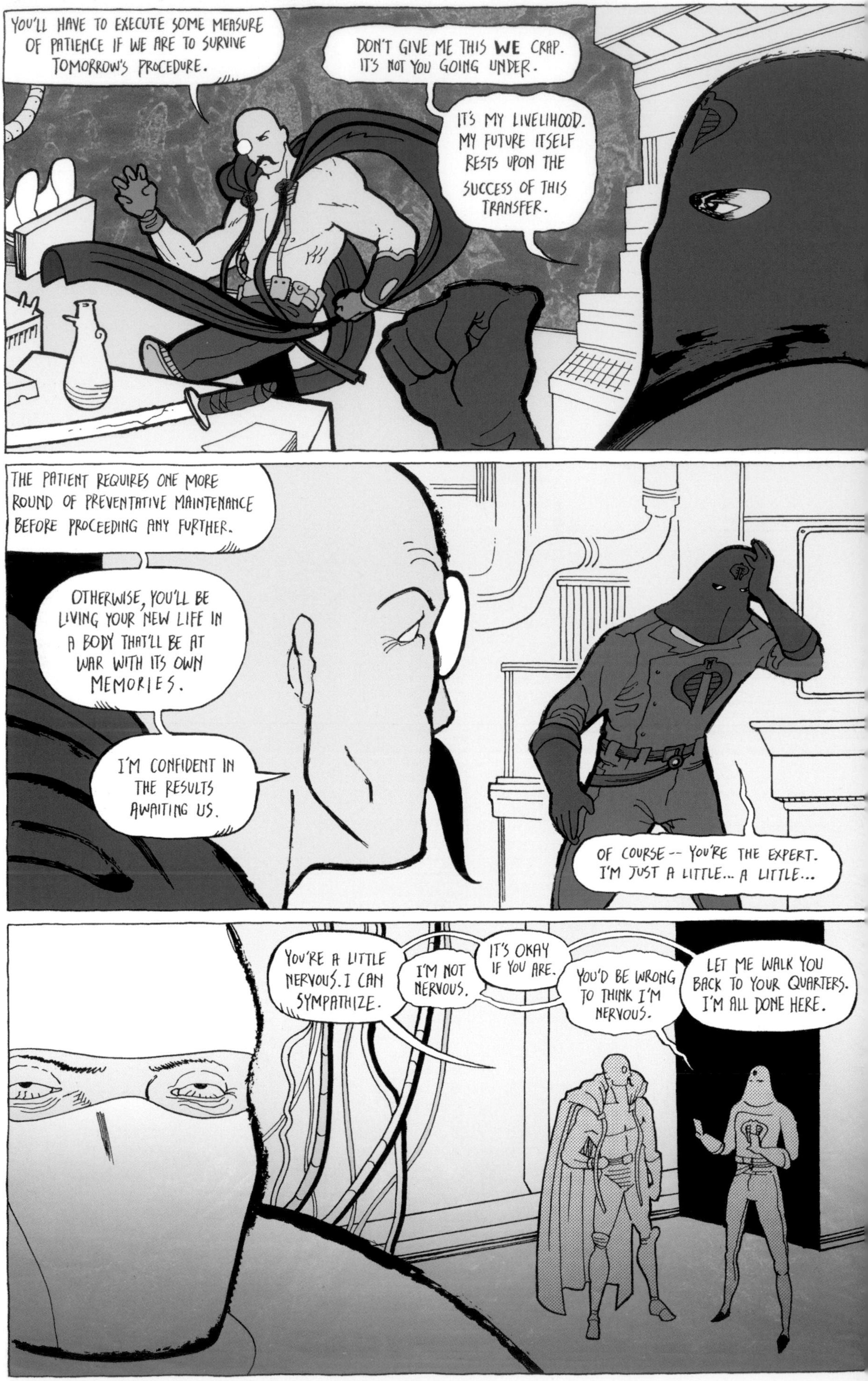
YOU'LL HAVE TO EXECUTE SOME MEASURE OF PATIENCE IF WE ARE TO SURVIVE TOMORROW'S PROCEDURE.
DON'T GIVE ME THIS **WE** CRAP. IT'S NOT YOU GOING UNDER.
IT'S MY LIVELIHOOD. MY FUTURE ITSELF RESTS UPON THE SUCCESS OF THIS TRANSFER.
THE PATIENT REQUIRES ONE MORE ROUND OF PREVENTATIVE MAINTENANCE BEFORE PROCEEDING ANY FURTHER.
OTHERWISE, YOU'LL BE LIVING YOUR NEW LIFE IN A BODY THAT'LL BE AT WAR WITH ITS OWN MEMORIES.
I'M CONFIDENT IN THE RESULTS AWAITING US.
OF COURSE -- YOU'RE THE EXPERT. I'M JUST A LITTLE... A LITTLE...
YOU'RE A LITTLE NERVOUS. I CAN SYMPATHIZE.
I'M NOT NERVOUS.
IT'S OKAY IF YOU ARE.
YOU'D BE WRONG TO THINK I'M NERVOUS.
LET ME WALK YOU BACK TO YOUR QUARTERS. I'M ALL DONE HERE.

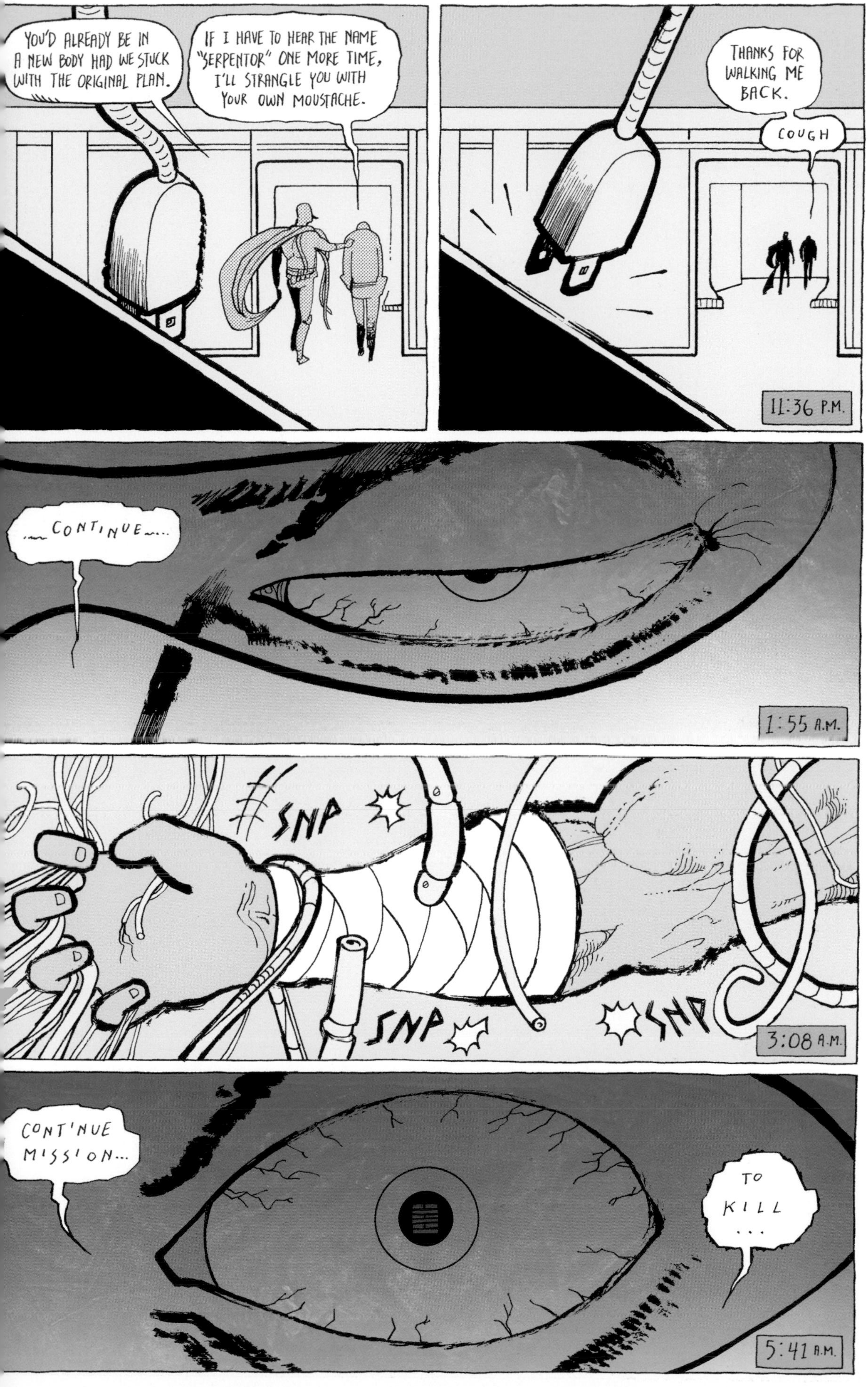
YOU'D ALREADY BE IN A NEW BODY HAD WE STUCK WITH THE ORIGINAL PLAN.
IF I HAVE TO HEAR THE NAME "SERPENTOR" ONE MORE TIME, I'LL STRANGLE YOU WITH YOUR OWN MOUSTACHE.
THANKS FOR WALKING ME BACK.
COUGH
11:36 P.M.
...CONTINUE...
1:55 A.M.
SNP
SNP
SNP
3:08 A.M.
CONT'NUE MISSION...
TO KILL ...
5:41 A.M.

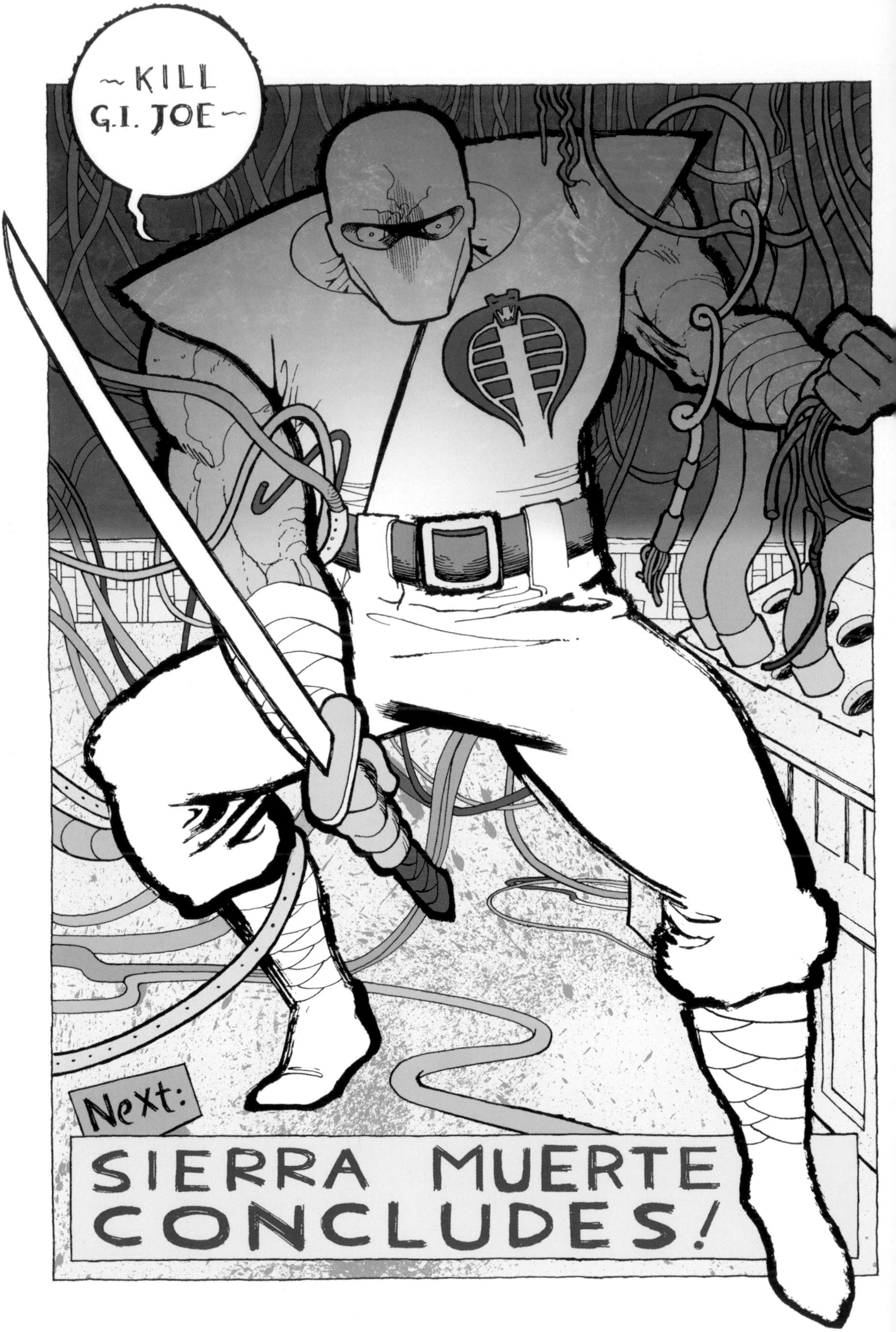
~KILL G.I. JOE~
Next:
SIERRA MUERTE CONCLUDES!

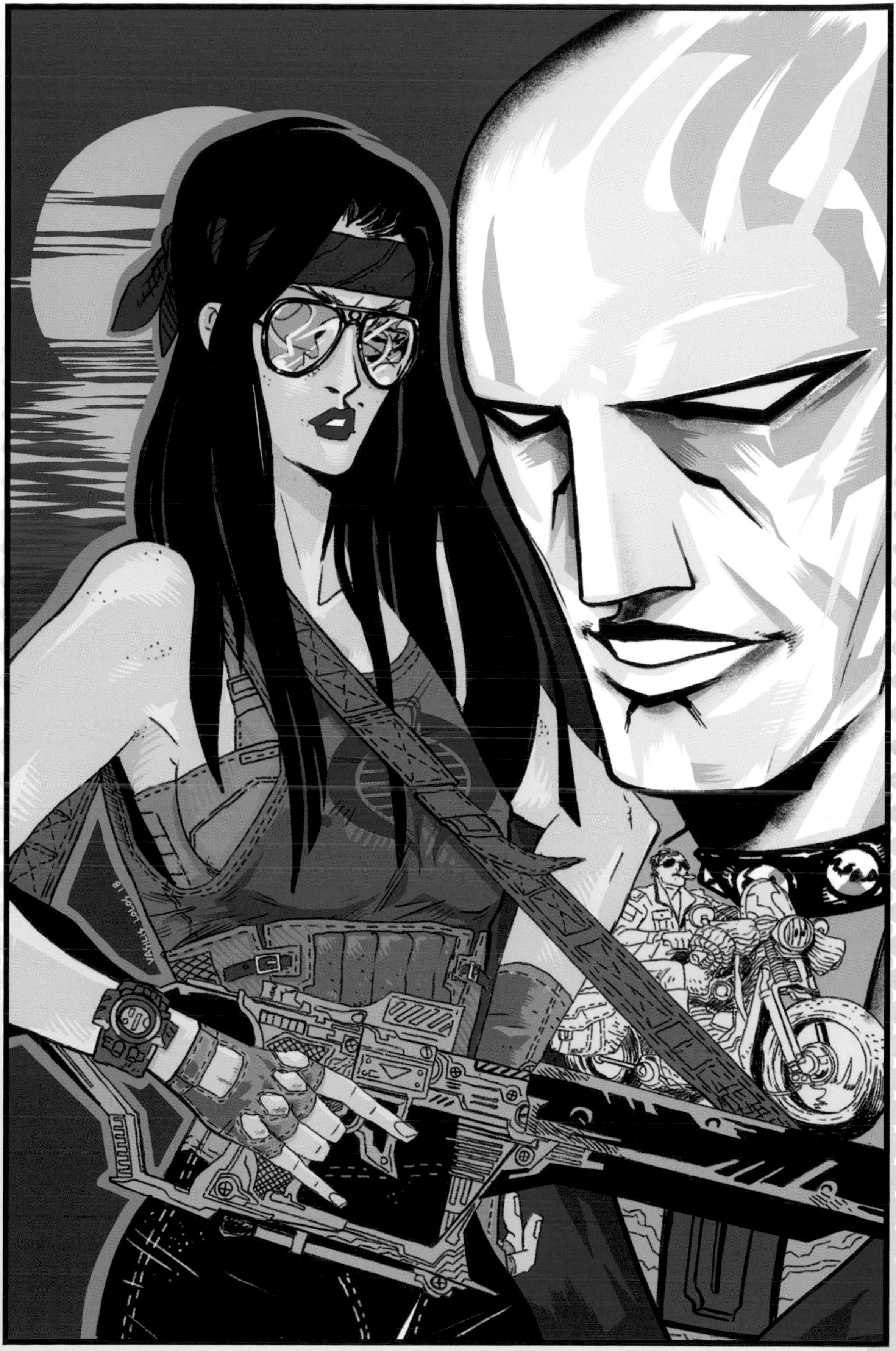

ART BY **VASILIS LOLOS**

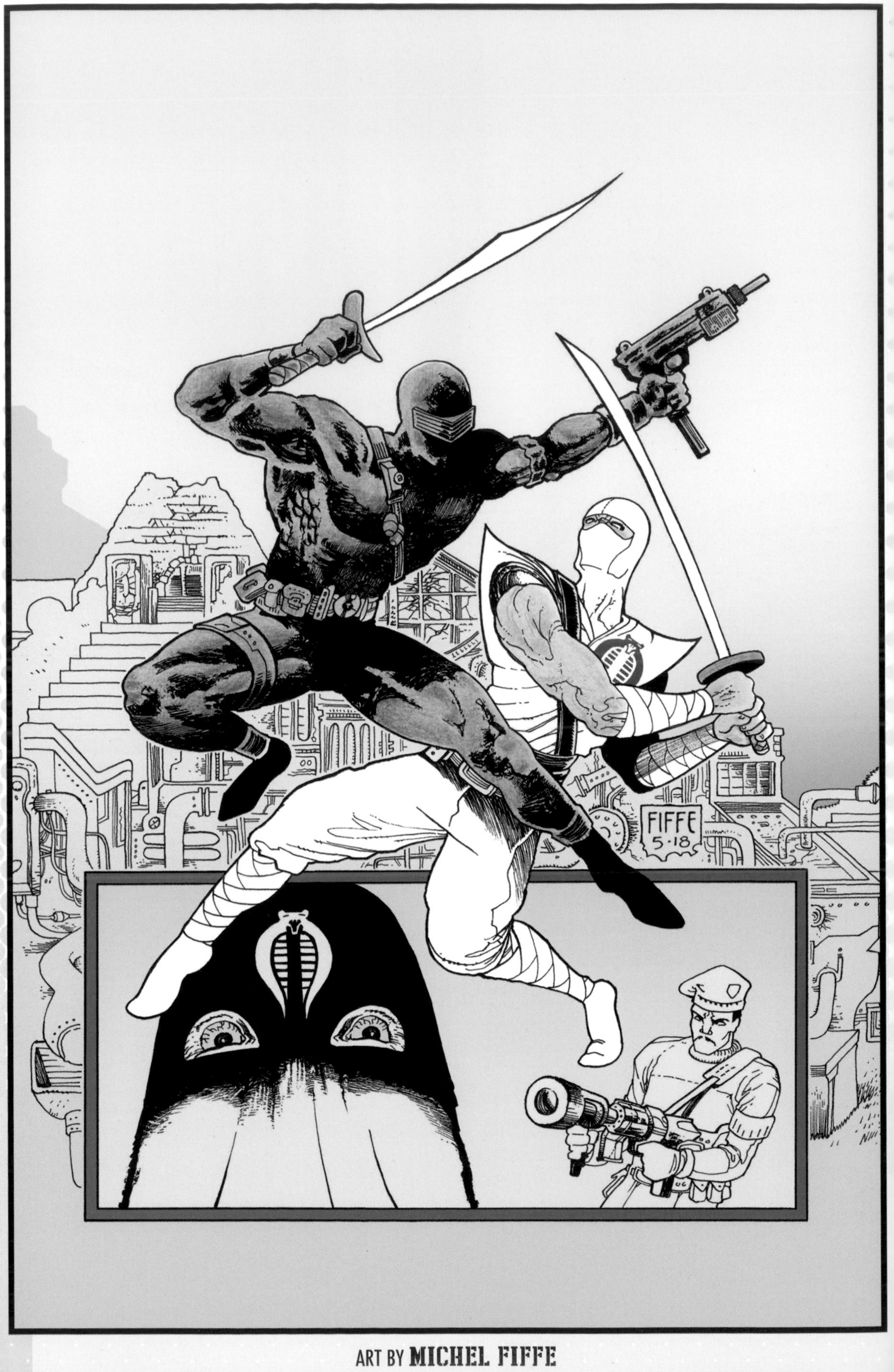
FIFFE
5·18

ART BY **MICHEL FIFFE**

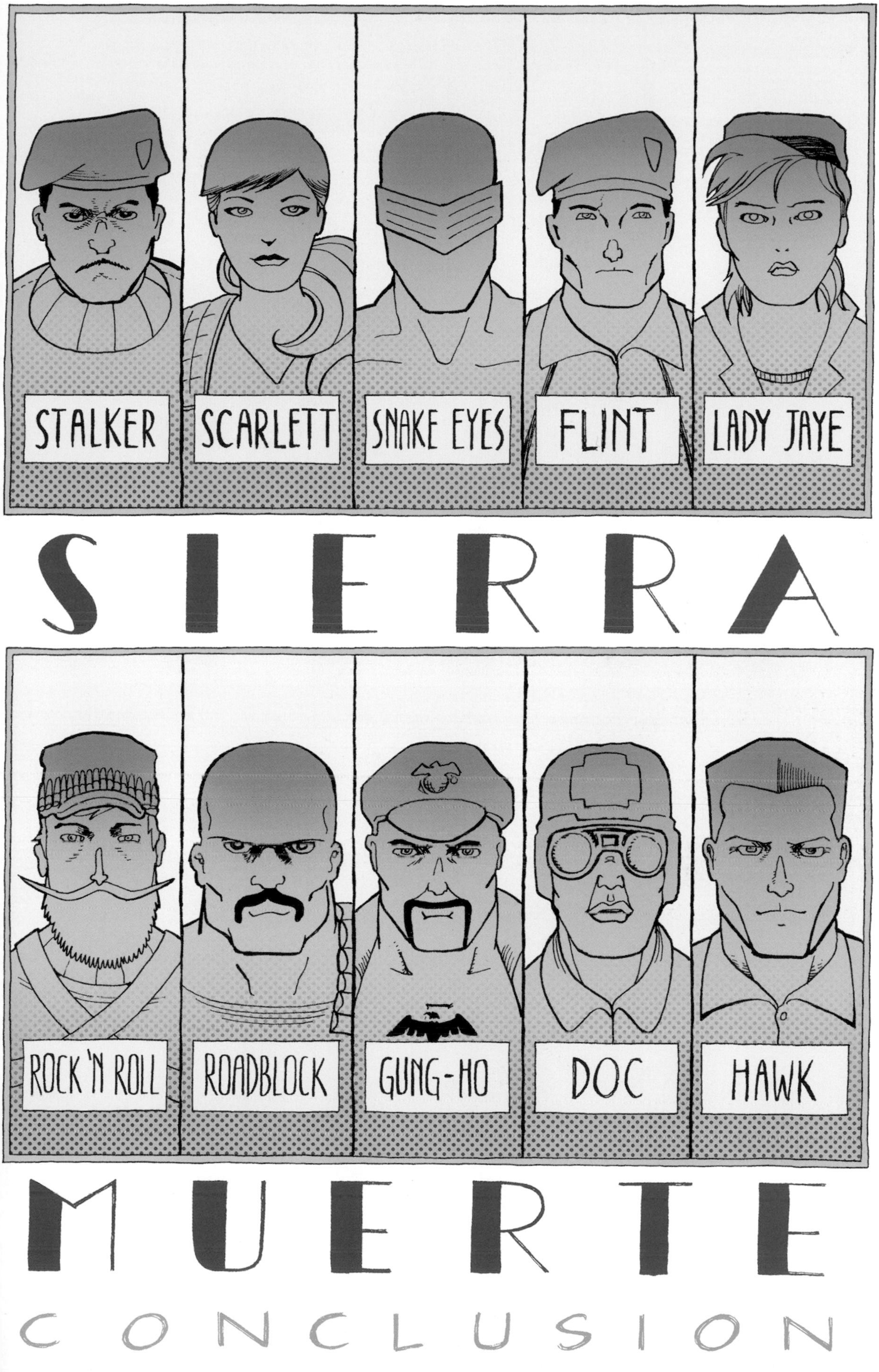
STALKER
SCARLETT
SNAKE EYES
FLINT
LADY JAYE
SIERRA
ROCK 'N ROLL
ROADBLOCK
GUNG-HO
DOC
HAWK
MUERTE
CONCLUSION

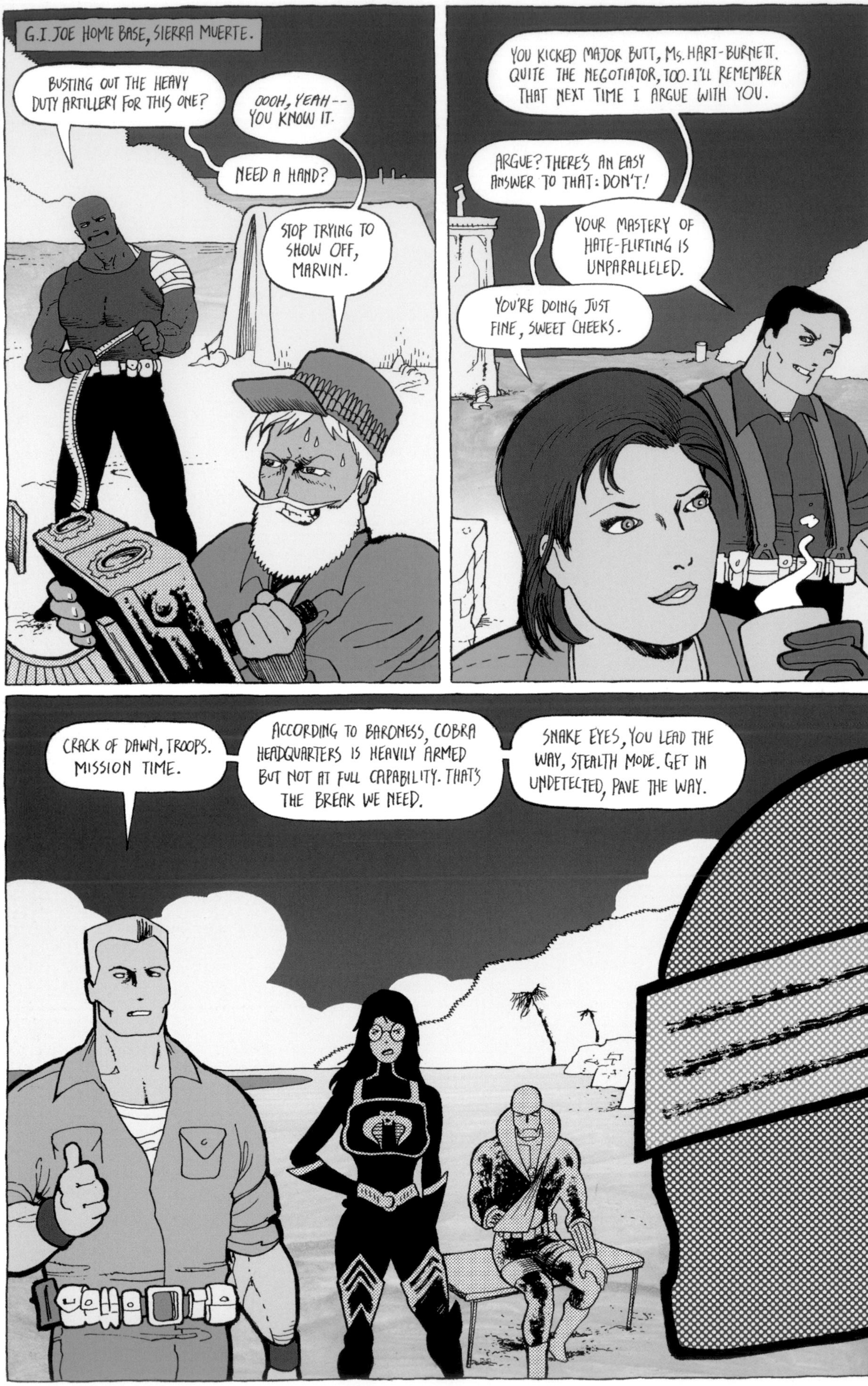
G.I. JOE HOME BASE, SIERRA MUERTE.
BUSTING OUT THE HEAVY DUTY ARTILLERY FOR THIS ONE?
OOOH, YEAH-- YOU KNOW IT.
NEED A HAND?
STOP TRYING TO SHOW OFF, MARVIN.
YOU KICKED MAJOR BUTT, Ms. HART-BURNETT. QUITE THE NEGOTIATOR, TOO. I'LL REMEMBER THAT NEXT TIME I ARGUE WITH YOU.
ARGUE? THERE'S AN EASY ANSWER TO THAT: DON'T!
YOUR MASTERY OF HATE-FLIRTING IS UNPARALLELED.
YOU'RE DOING JUST FINE, SWEET CHEEKS.
CRACK OF DAWN, TROOPS. MISSION TIME.
ACCORDING TO BARONESS, COBRA HEADQUARTERS IS HEAVILY ARMED BUT NOT AT FULL CAPABILITY. THAT'S THE BREAK WE NEED.
SNAKE EYES, YOU LEAD THE WAY, STEALTH MODE. GET IN UNDETECTED, PAVE THE WAY.

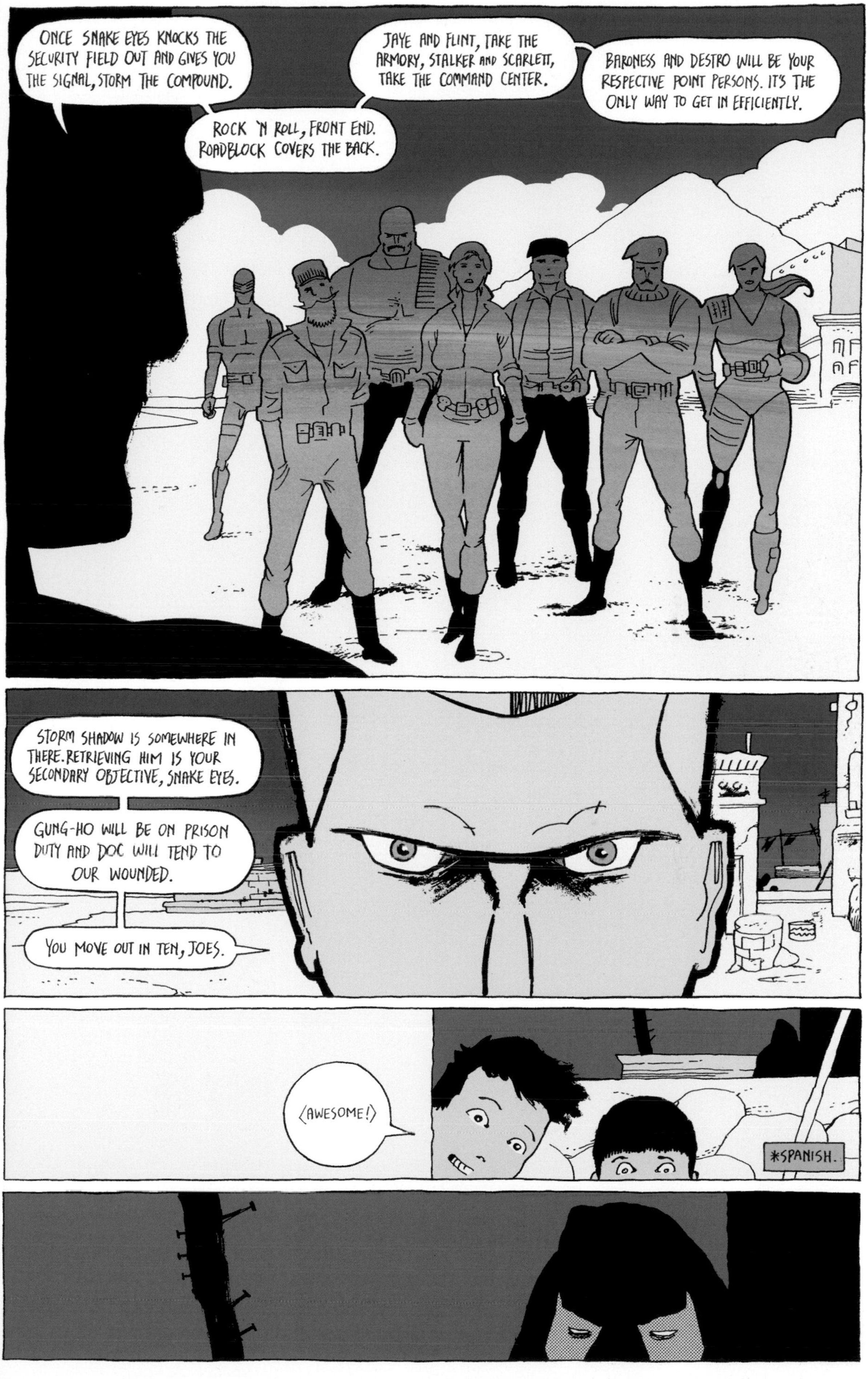
ONCE SNAKE EYES KNOCKS THE SECURITY FIELD OUT AND GIVES YOU THE SIGNAL, STORM THE COMPOUND.
ROCK 'N ROLL, FRONT END. ROADBLOCK COVERS THE BACK.
JAYE AND FLINT, TAKE THE ARMORY, STALKER AND SCARLETT, TAKE THE COMMAND CENTER.
BARONESS AND DESTRO WILL BE YOUR RESPECTIVE POINT PERSONS. IT'S THE ONLY WAY TO GET IN EFFICIENTLY.
STORM SHADOW IS SOMEWHERE IN THERE. RETRIEVING HIM IS YOUR SECONDARY OBJECTIVE, SNAKE EYES.
GUNG-HO WILL BE ON PRISON DUTY AND DOC WILL TEND TO OUR WOUNDED.
YOU MOVE OUT IN TEN, JOES.
⟨AWESOME!⟩
*SPANISH.

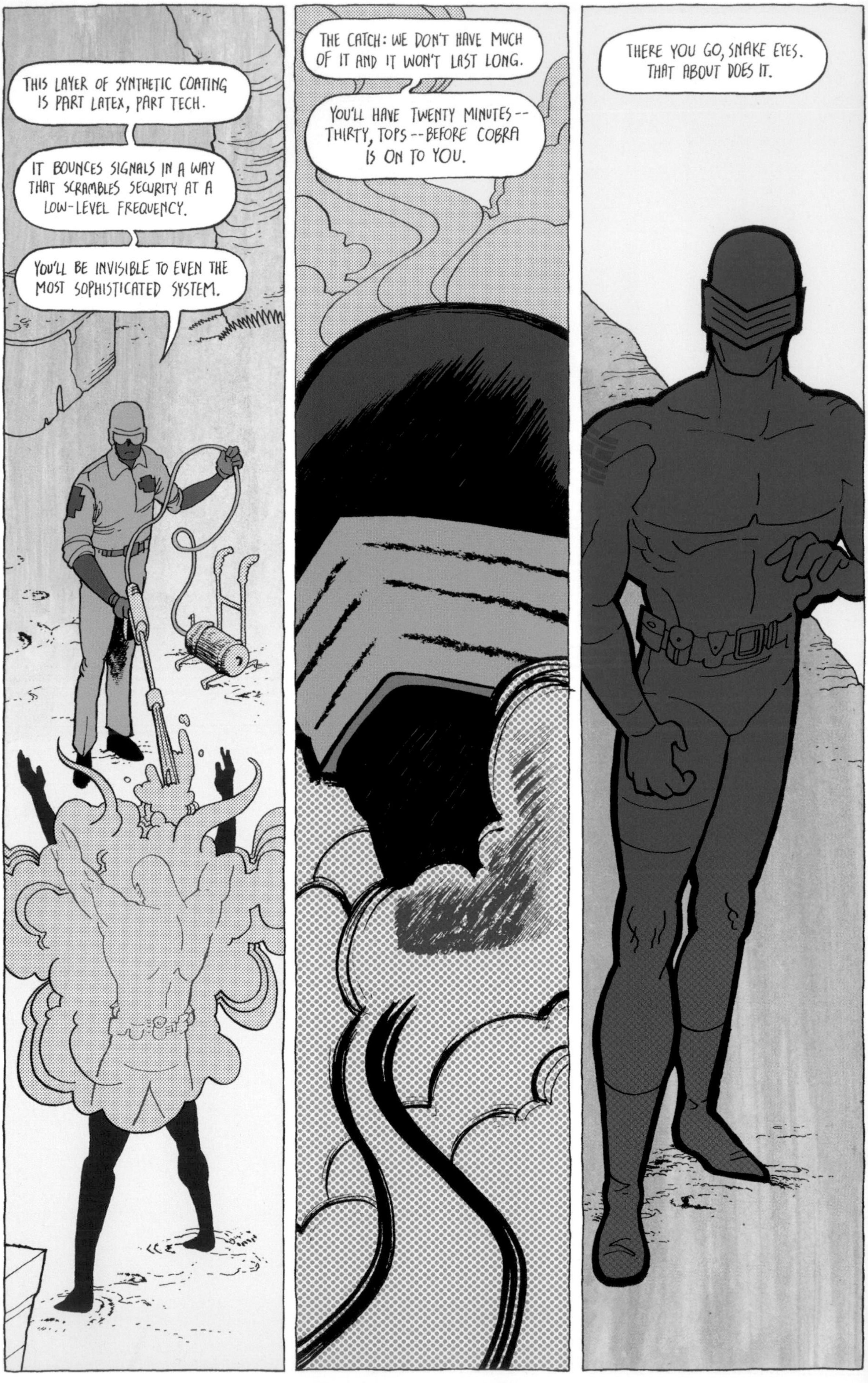
THIS LAYER OF SYNTHETIC COATING IS PART LATEX, PART TECH.
IT BOUNCES SIGNALS IN A WAY THAT SCRAMBLES SECURITY AT A LOW-LEVEL FREQUENCY.
YOU'LL BE INVISIBLE TO EVEN THE MOST SOPHISTICATED SYSTEM.
THE CATCH: WE DON'T HAVE MUCH OF IT AND IT WON'T LAST LONG.
YOU'LL HAVE TWENTY MINUTES--THIRTY, TOPS--BEFORE COBRA IS ON TO YOU.
THERE YOU GO, SNAKE EYES. THAT ABOUT DOES IT.

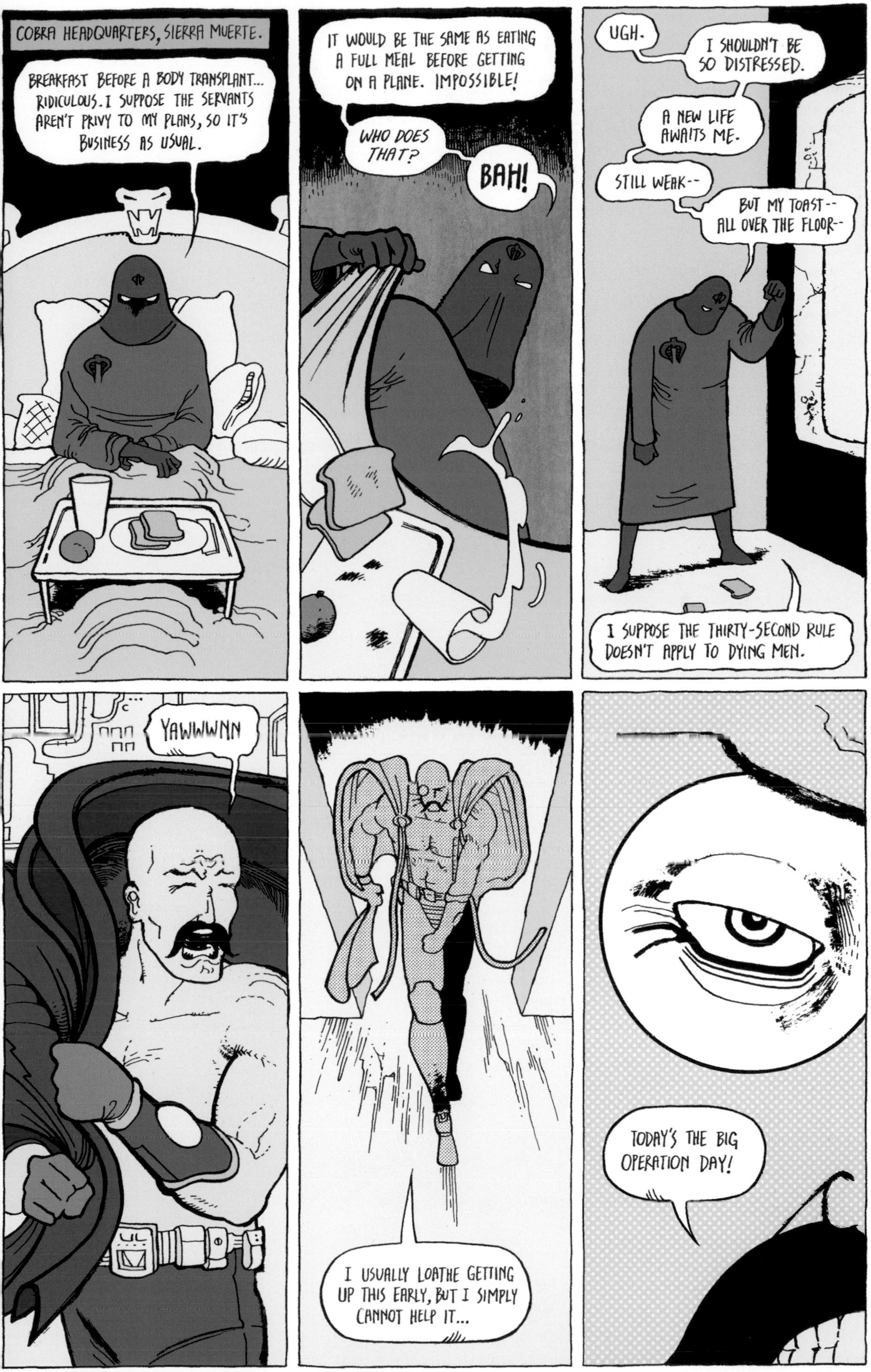
COBRA HEADQUARTERS, SIERRA MUERTE.
BREAKFAST BEFORE A BODY TRANSPLANT... RIDICULOUS. I SUPPOSE THE SERVANTS AREN'T PRIVY TO MY PLANS, SO IT'S BUSINESS AS USUAL.
IT WOULD BE THE SAME AS EATING A FULL MEAL BEFORE GETTING ON A PLANE. IMPOSSIBLE!
WHO DOES THAT?
BAH!
UGH.
I SHOULDN'T BE SO DISTRESSED.
A NEW LIFE AWAITS ME.
STILL WEAK--
BUT MY TOAST-- ALL OVER THE FLOOR--
I SUPPOSE THE THIRTY-SECOND RULE DOESN'T APPLY TO DYING MEN.
YAWWWNN
I USUALLY LOATHE GETTING UP THIS EARLY, BUT I SIMPLY CANNOT HELP IT...
TODAY'S THE BIG OPERATION DAY!

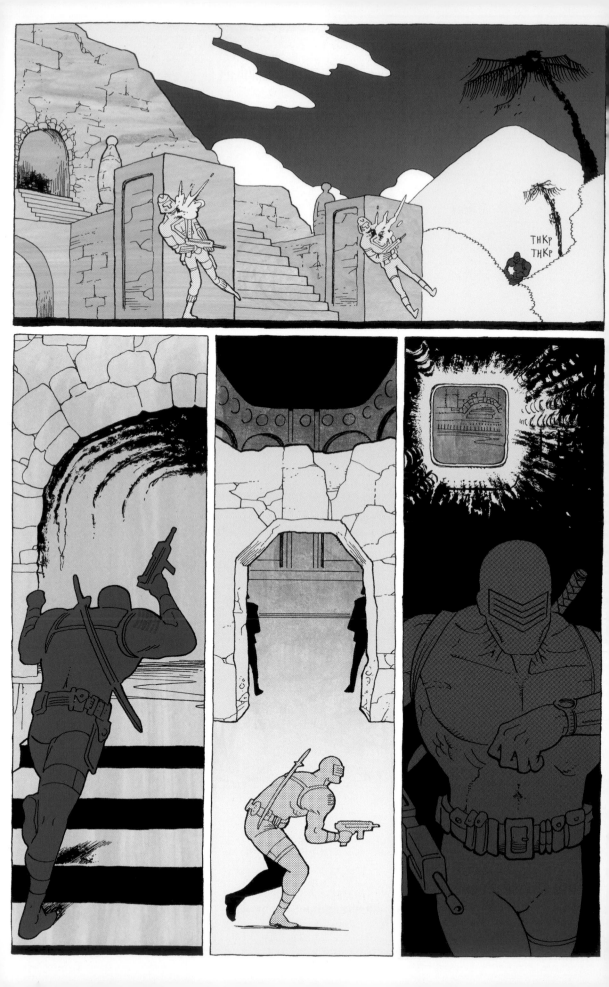

THKP
THKP

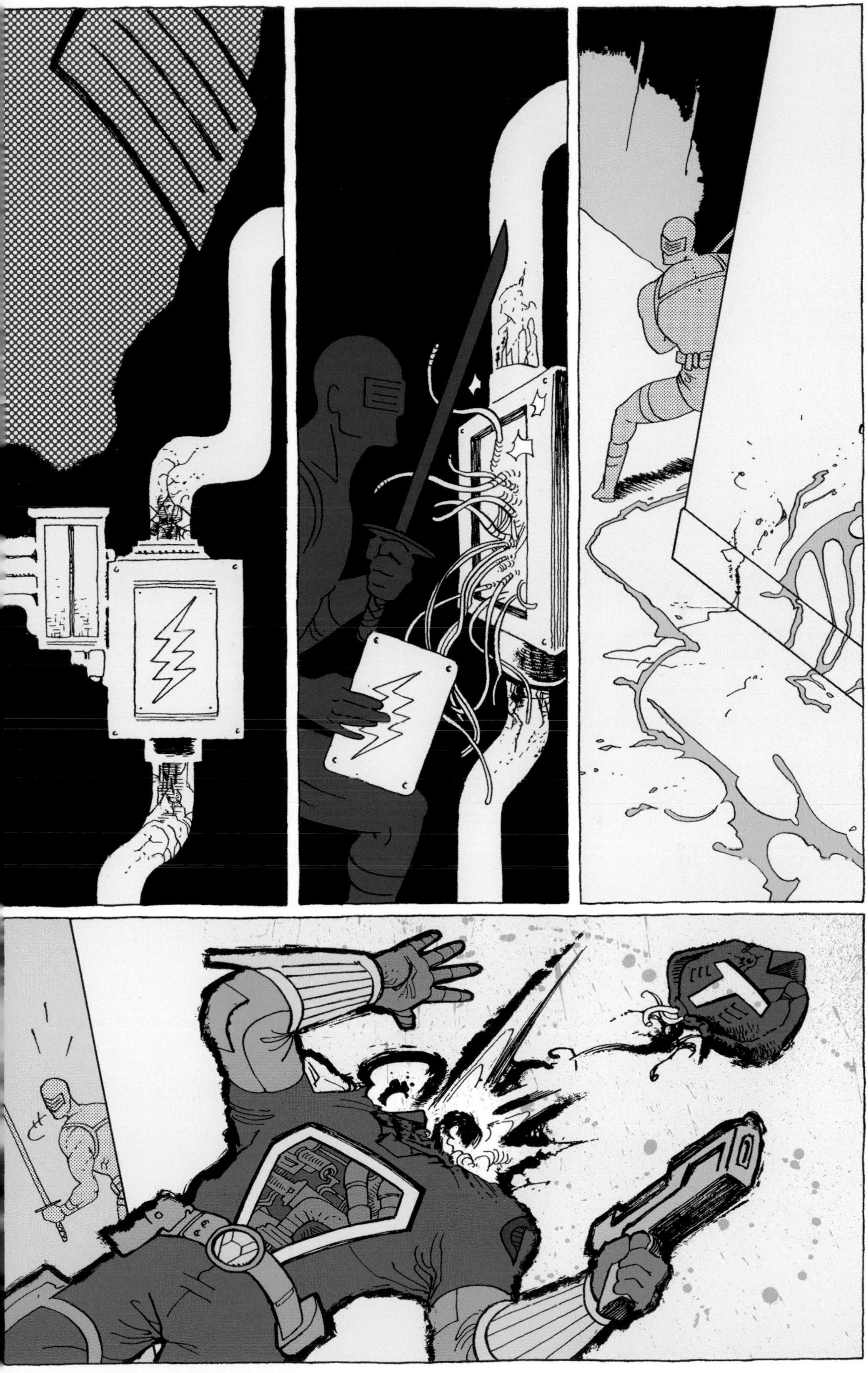

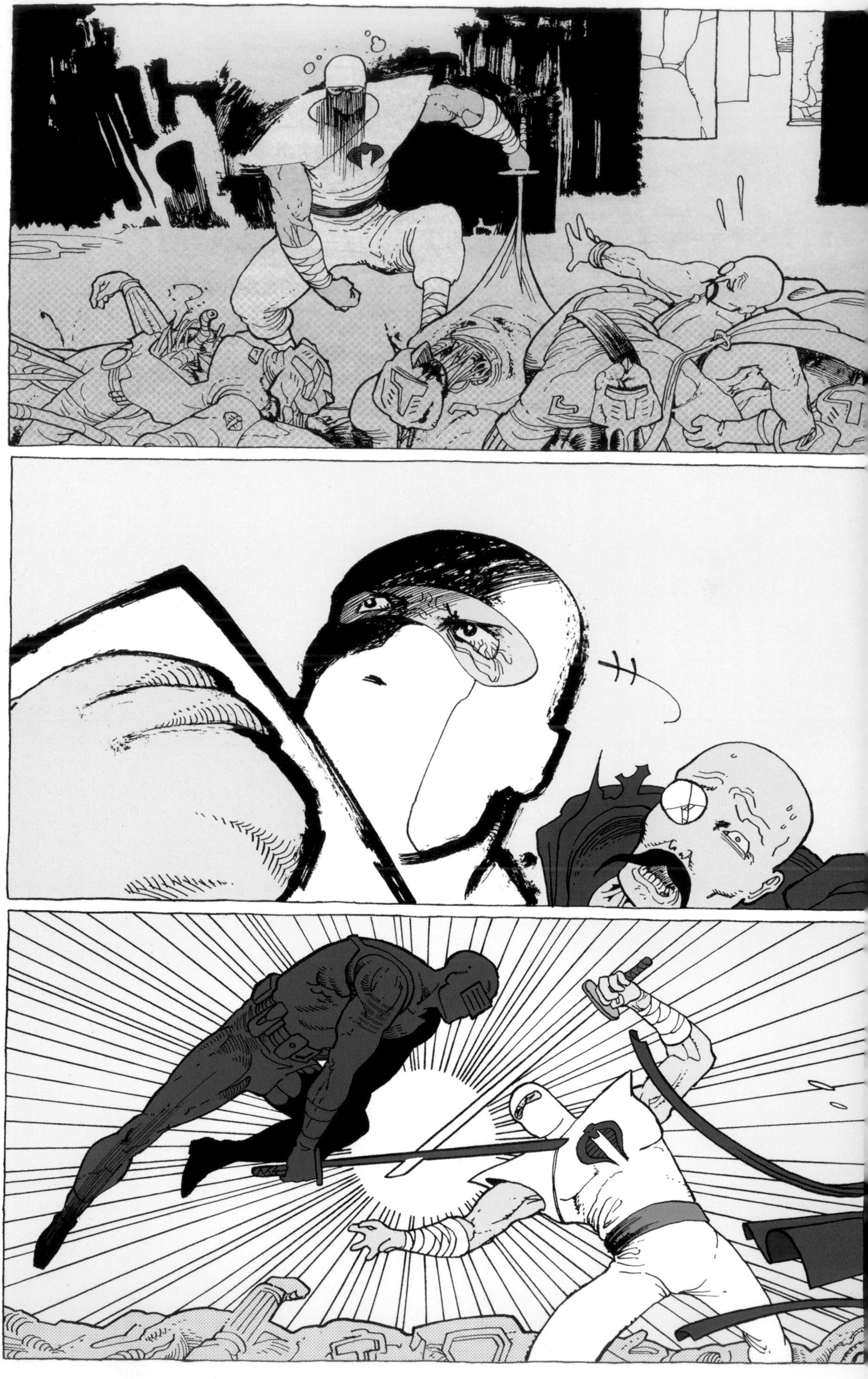

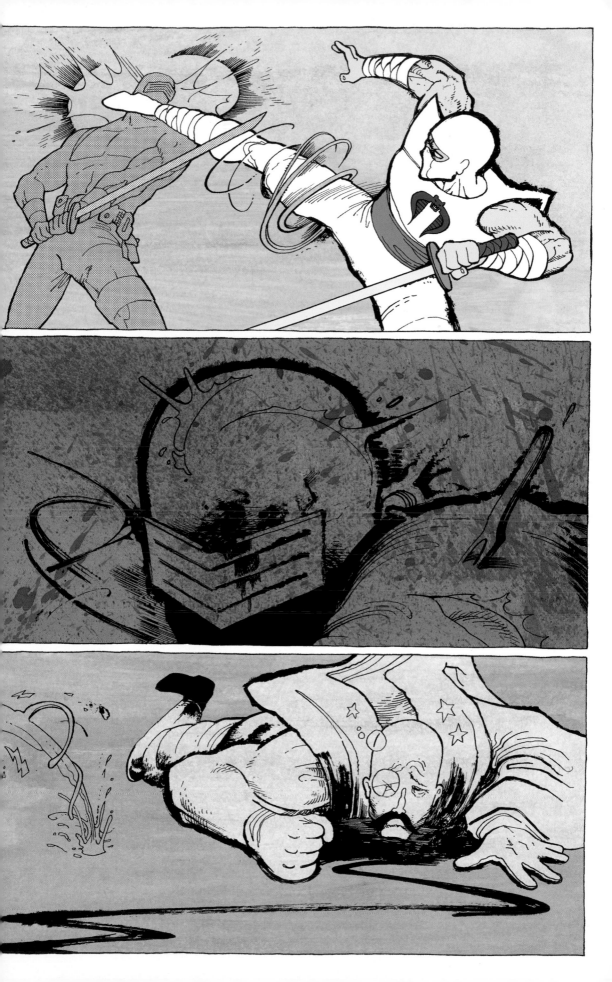

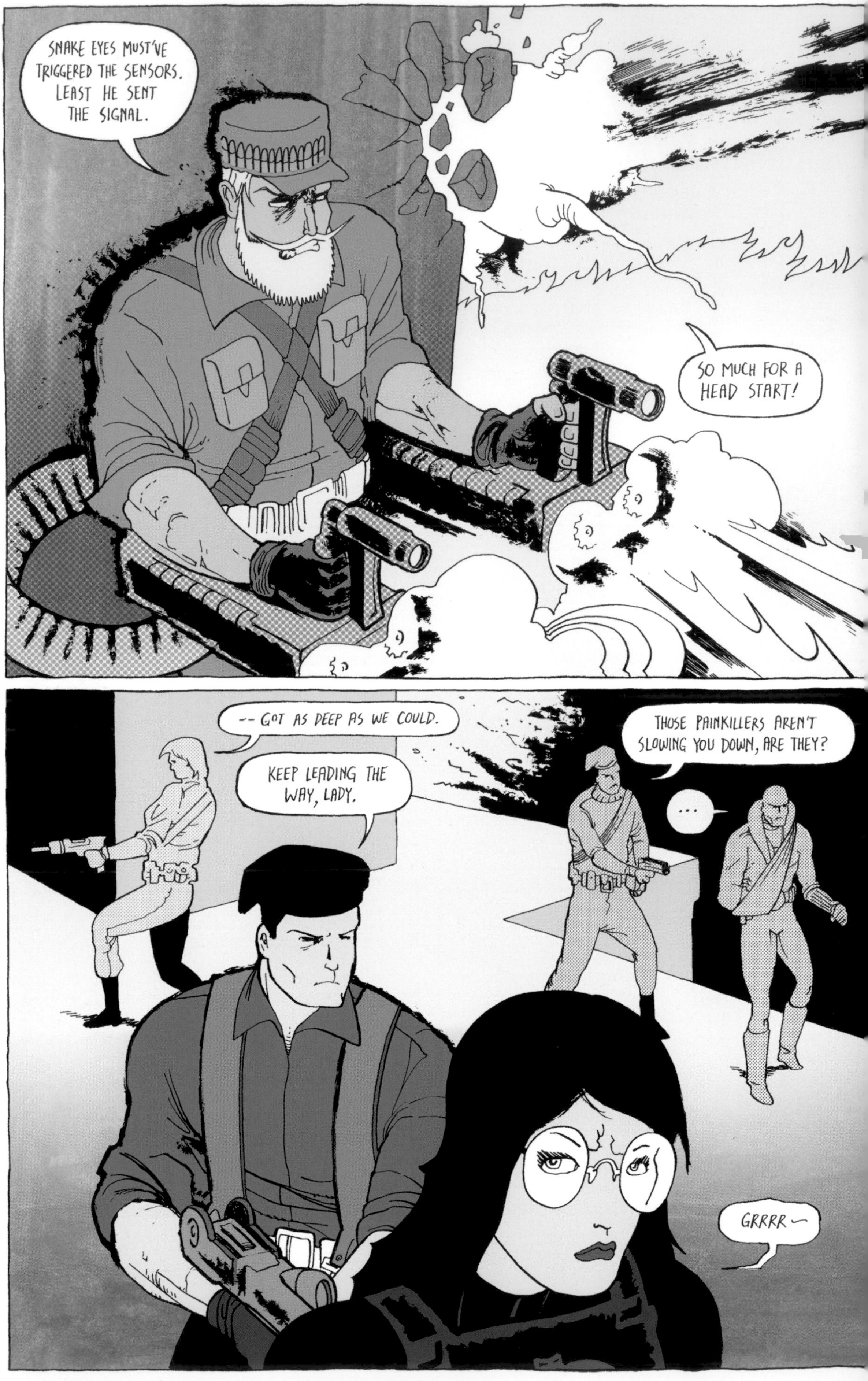
SNAKE EYES MUST'VE TRIGGERED THE SENSORS. LEAST HE SENT THE SIGNAL.
SO MUCH FOR A HEAD START!
-- GOT AS DEEP AS WE COULD.
KEEP LEADING THE WAY, LADY.
THOSE PAINKILLERS AREN'T SLOWING YOU DOWN, ARE THEY?
...
GRRRR--

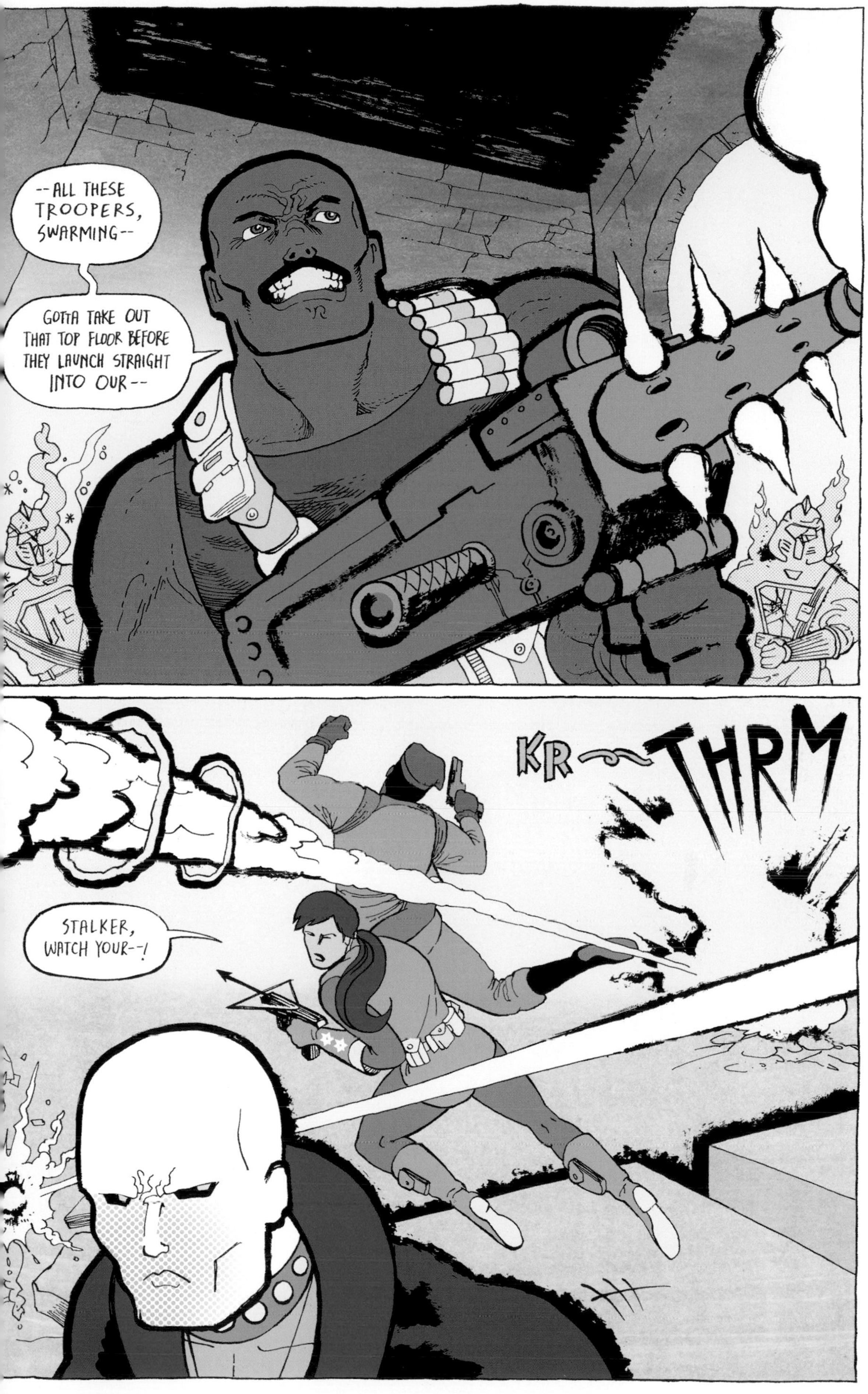
--ALL THESE TROOPERS, SWARMING--
GOTTA TAKE OUT THAT TOP FLOOR BEFORE THEY LAUNCH STRAIGHT INTO OUR--
KR--THRM
STALKER, WATCH YOUR--!

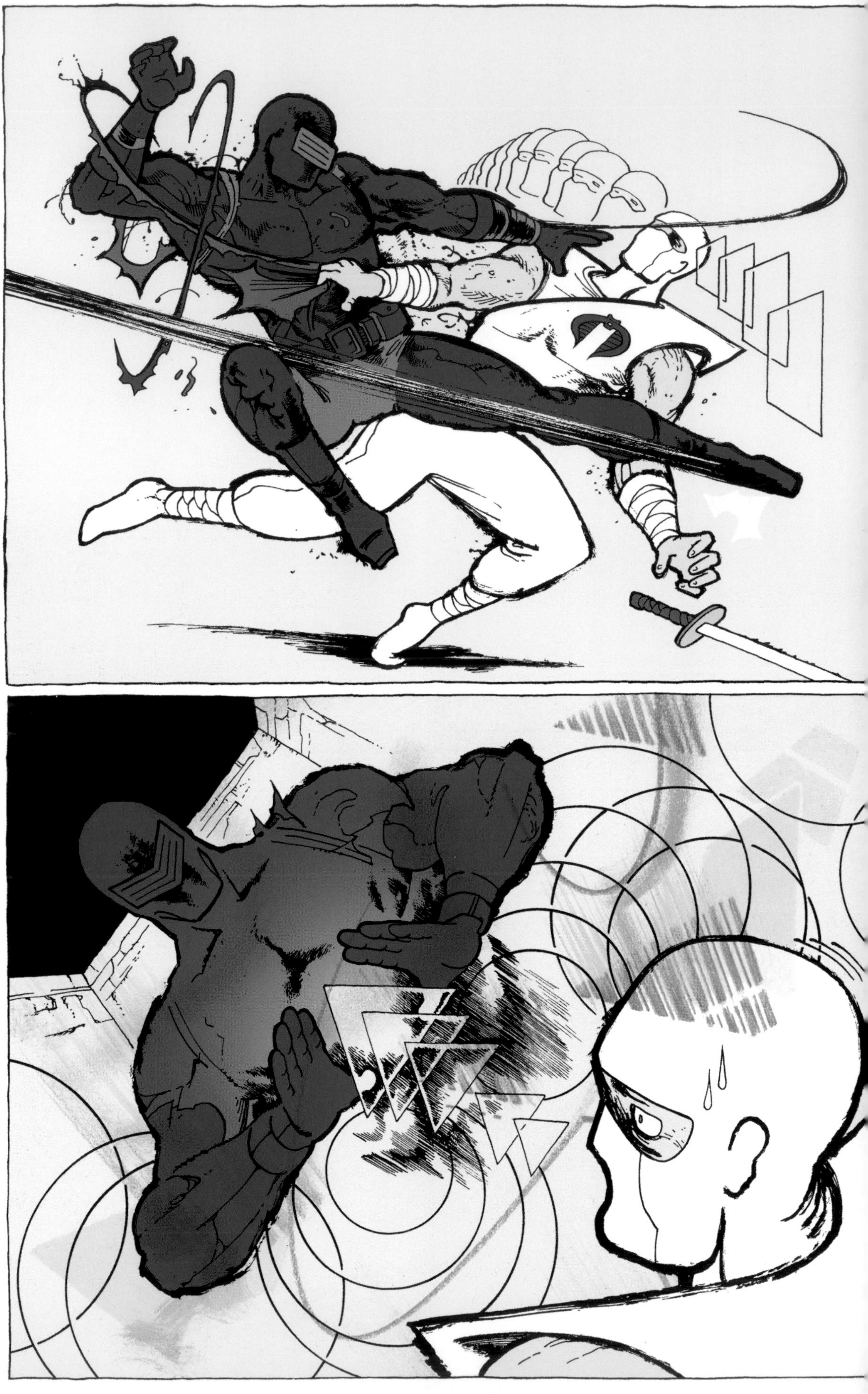

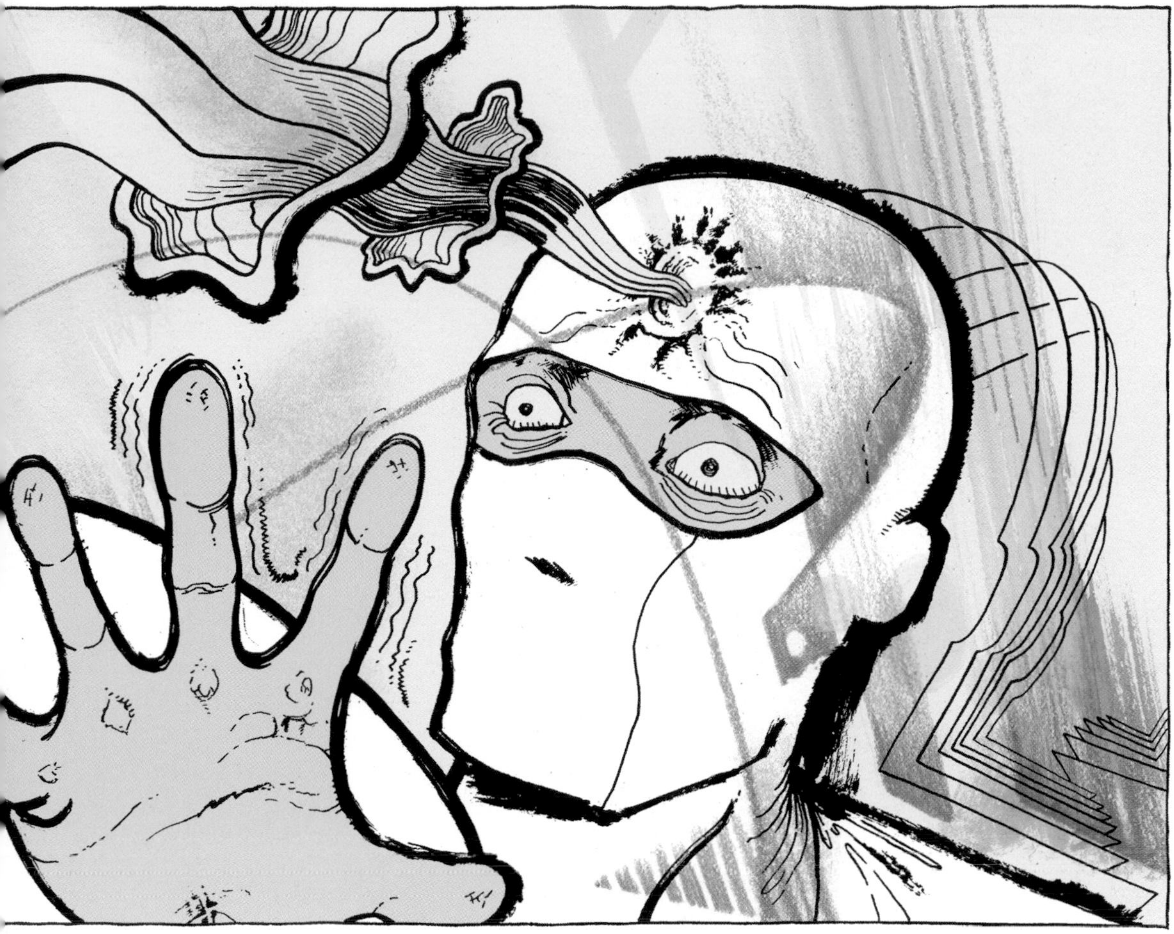

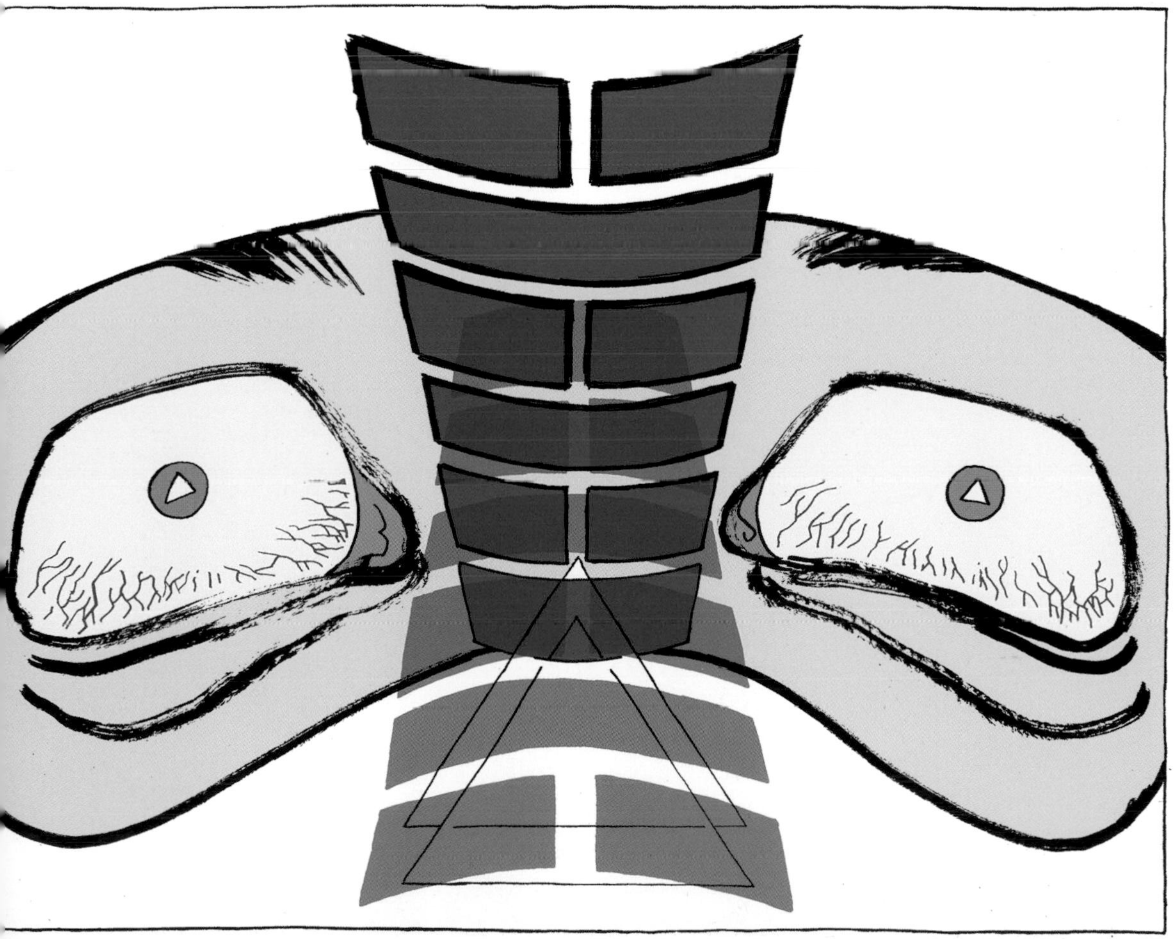

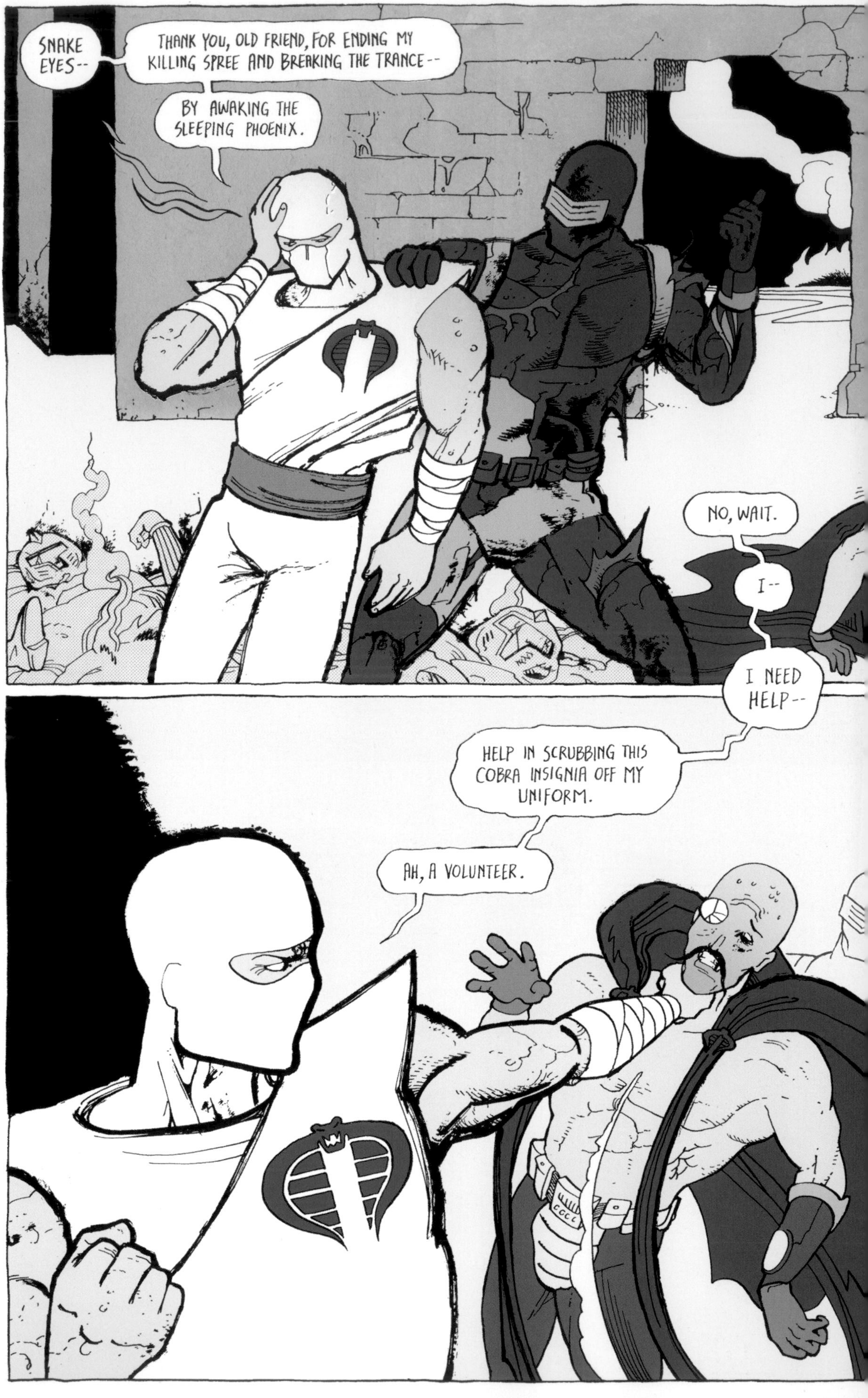
SNAKE EYES--
THANK YOU, OLD FRIEND, FOR ENDING MY KILLING SPREE AND BREAKING THE TRANCE--
BY AWAKING THE SLEEPING PHOENIX.
NO, WAIT.
I--
I NEED HELP--
HELP IN SCRUBBING THIS COBRA INSIGNIA OFF MY UNIFORM.
AH, A VOLUNTEER.

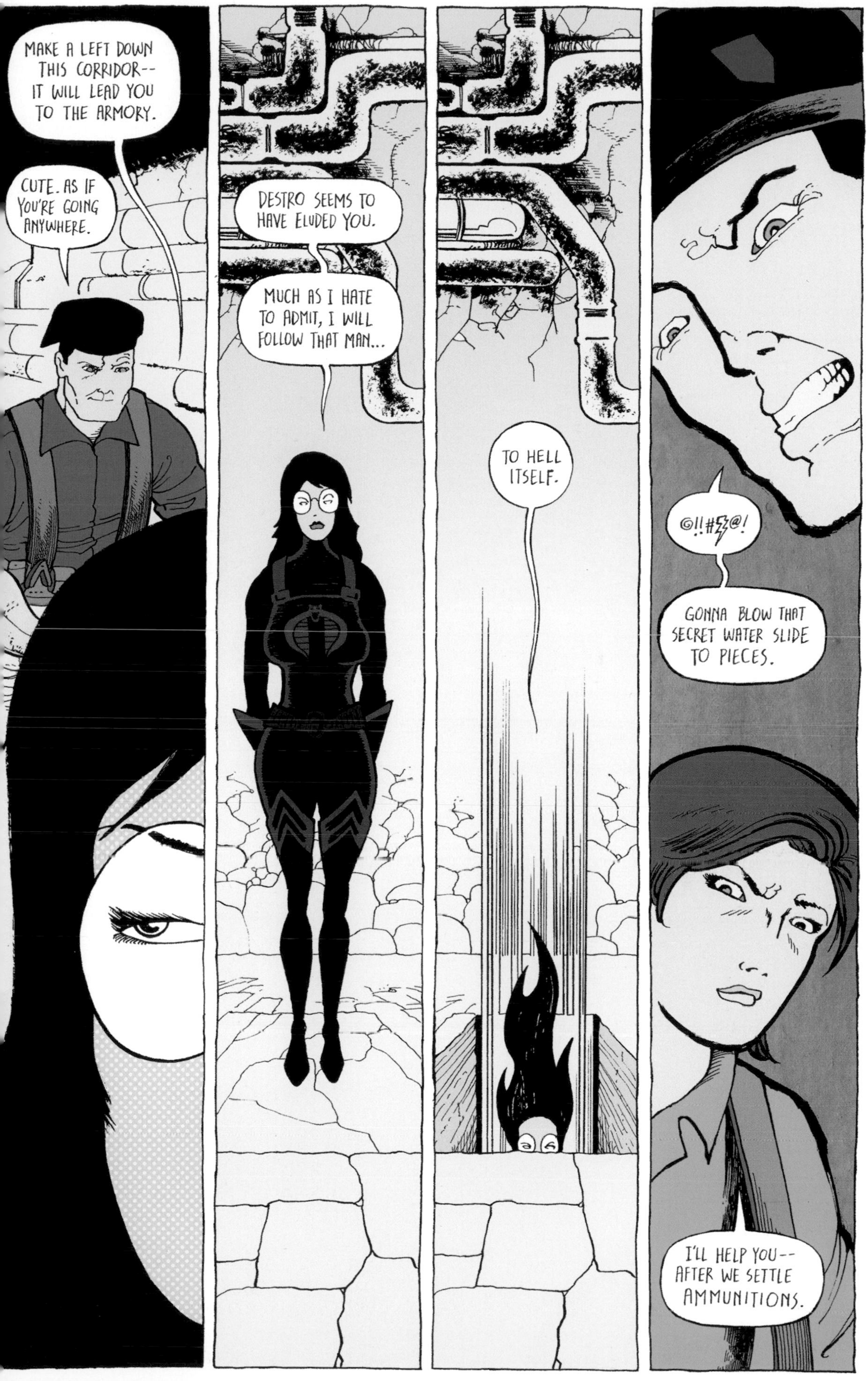
MAKE A LEFT DOWN THIS CORRIDOR-- IT WILL LEAD YOU TO THE ARMORY.
CUTE. AS IF YOU'RE GOING ANYWHERE.
DESTRO SEEMS TO HAVE ELUDED YOU.
MUCH AS I HATE TO ADMIT, I WILL FOLLOW THAT MAN...
TO HELL ITSELF.
@!!#$@!
GONNA BLOW THAT SECRET WATER SLIDE TO PIECES.
I'LL HELP YOU-- AFTER WE SETTLE AMMUNITIONS.

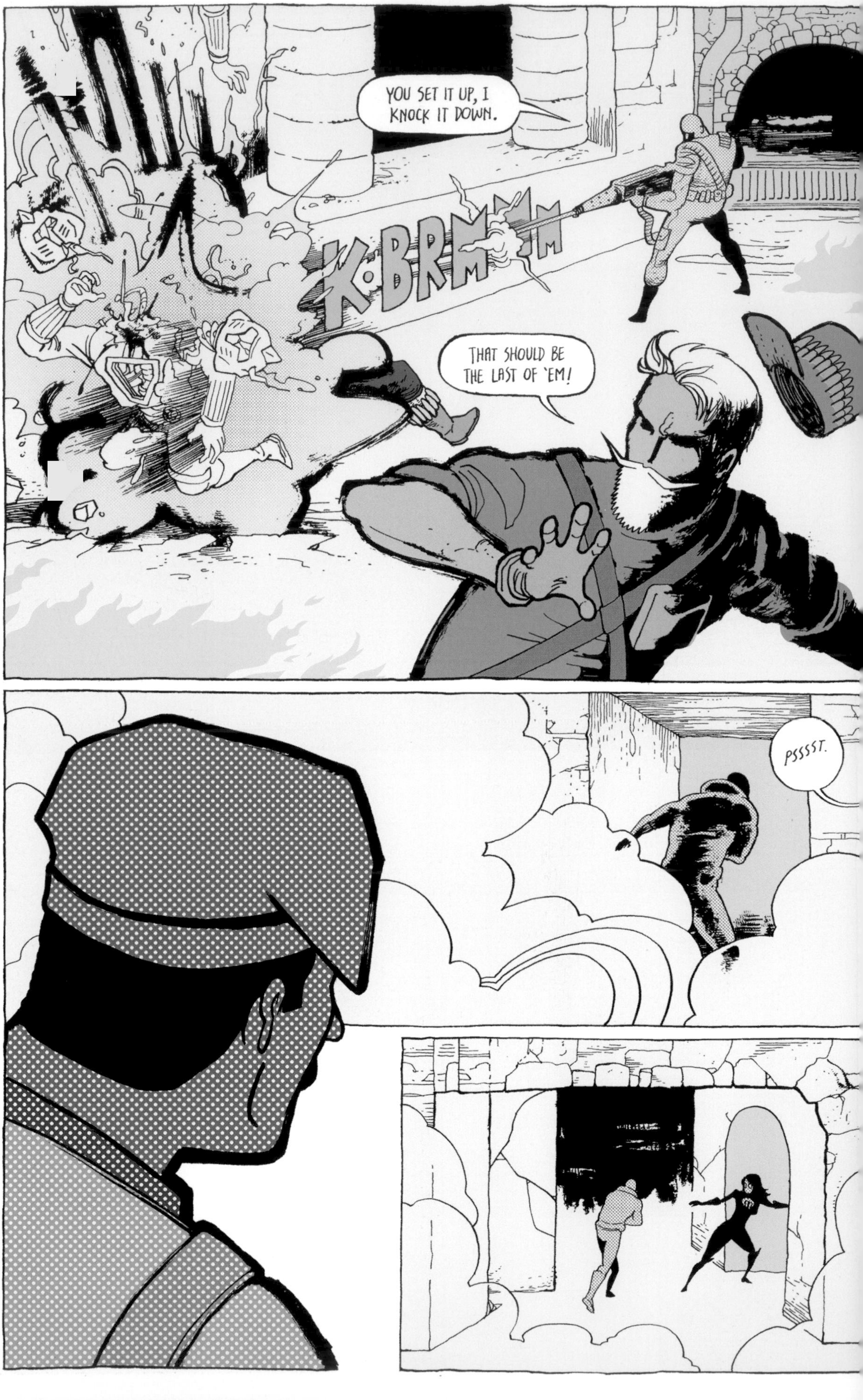
YOU SET IT UP, I KNOCK IT DOWN.
K-BRMMMM
THAT SHOULD BE THE LAST OF 'EM!
PSSSST.

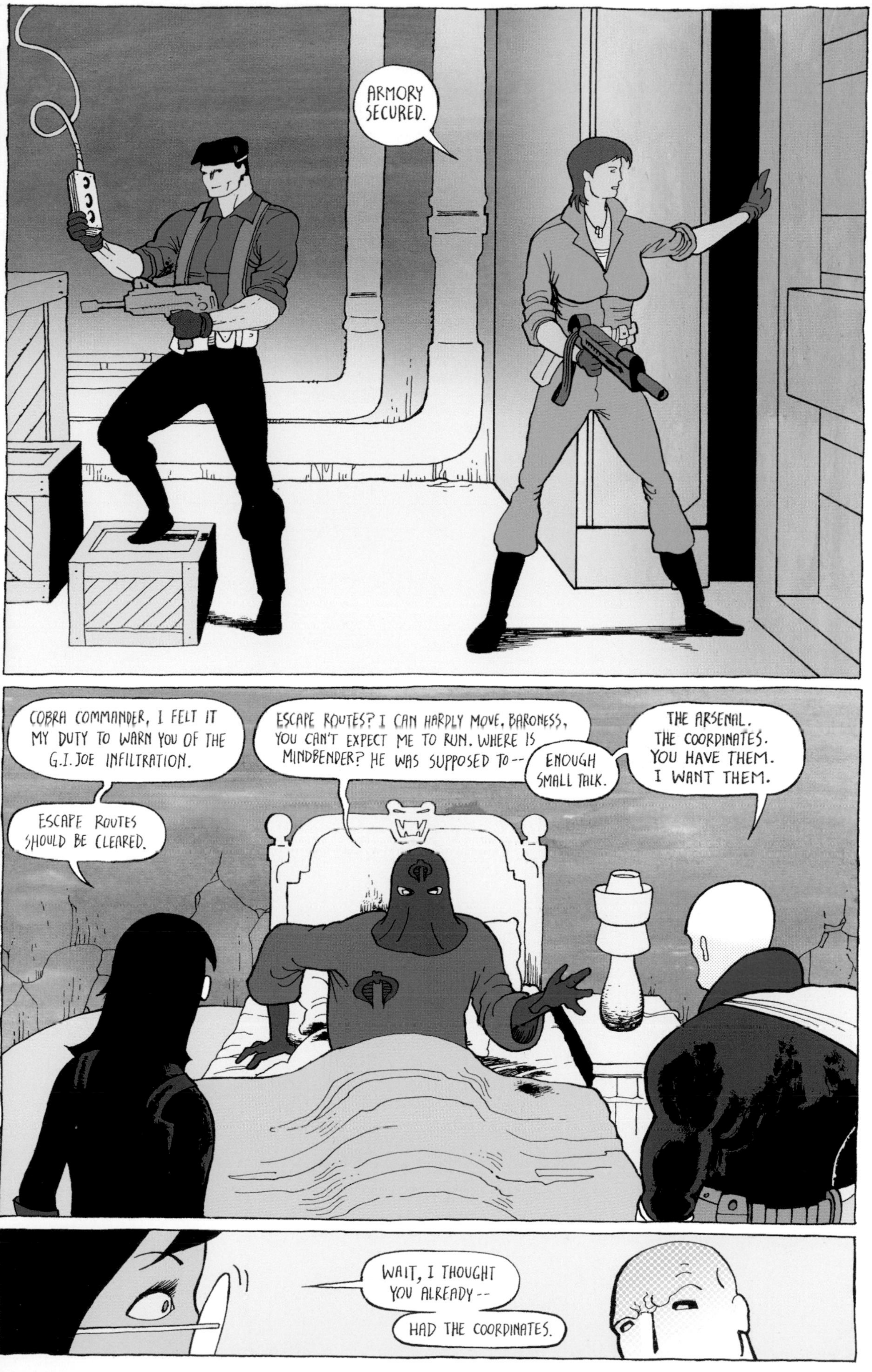
ARMORY SECURED.
COBRA COMMANDER, I FELT IT MY DUTY TO WARN YOU OF THE G.I. JOE INFILTRATION.
ESCAPE ROUTES SHOULD BE CLEARED.
ESCAPE ROUTES? I CAN HARDLY MOVE, BARONESS, YOU CAN'T EXPECT ME TO RUN. WHERE IS MINDBENDER? HE WAS SUPPOSED TO--
ENOUGH SMALL TALK.
THE ARSENAL. THE COORDINATES. YOU HAVE THEM. I WANT THEM.
WAIT, I THOUGHT YOU ALREADY--
HAD THE COORDINATES.

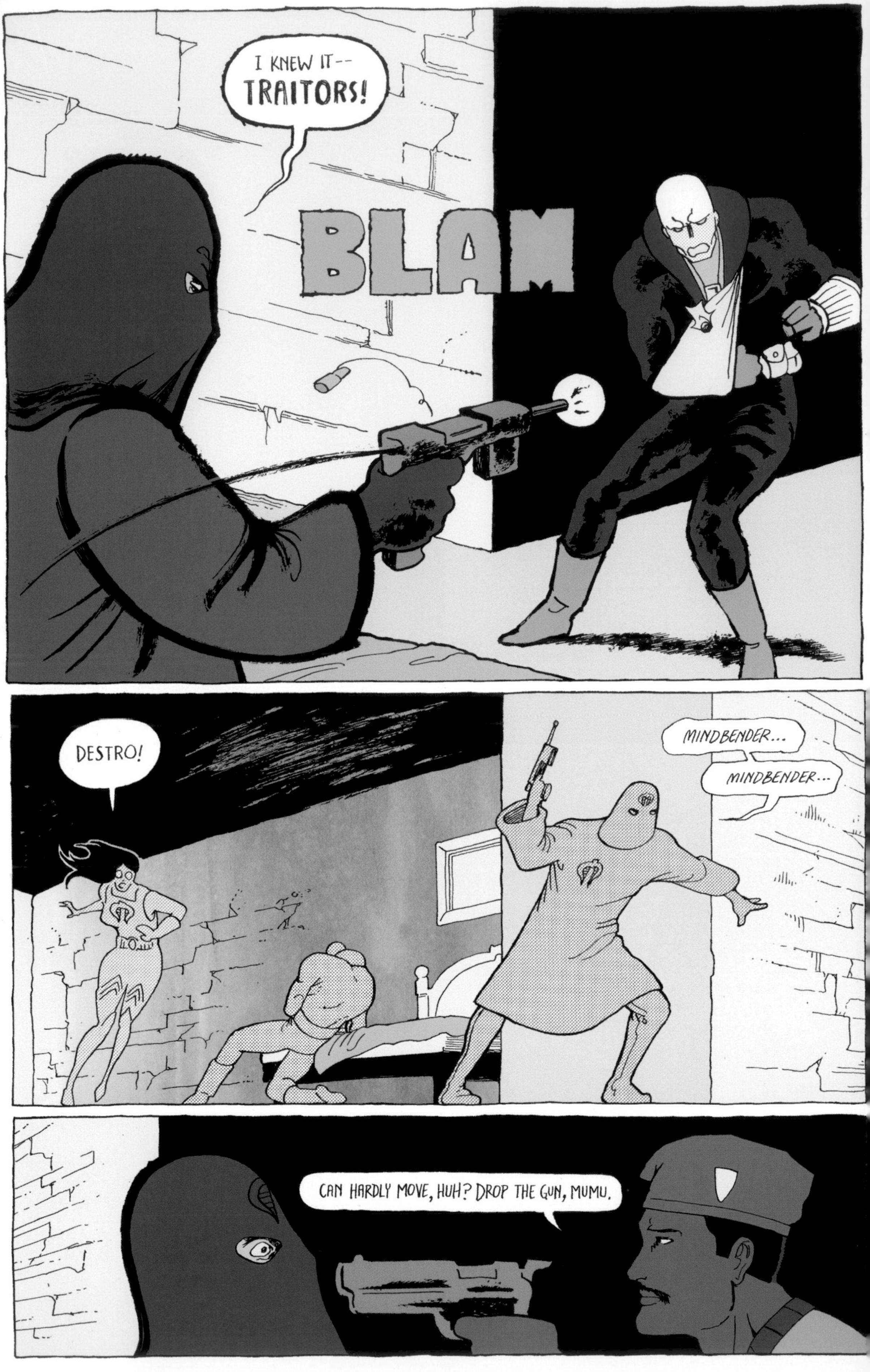
I KNEW IT-- TRAITORS!
BLAM
DESTRO!
MINDBENDER...
MINDBENDER...
CAN HARDLY MOVE, HUH? DROP THE GUN, MUMU.

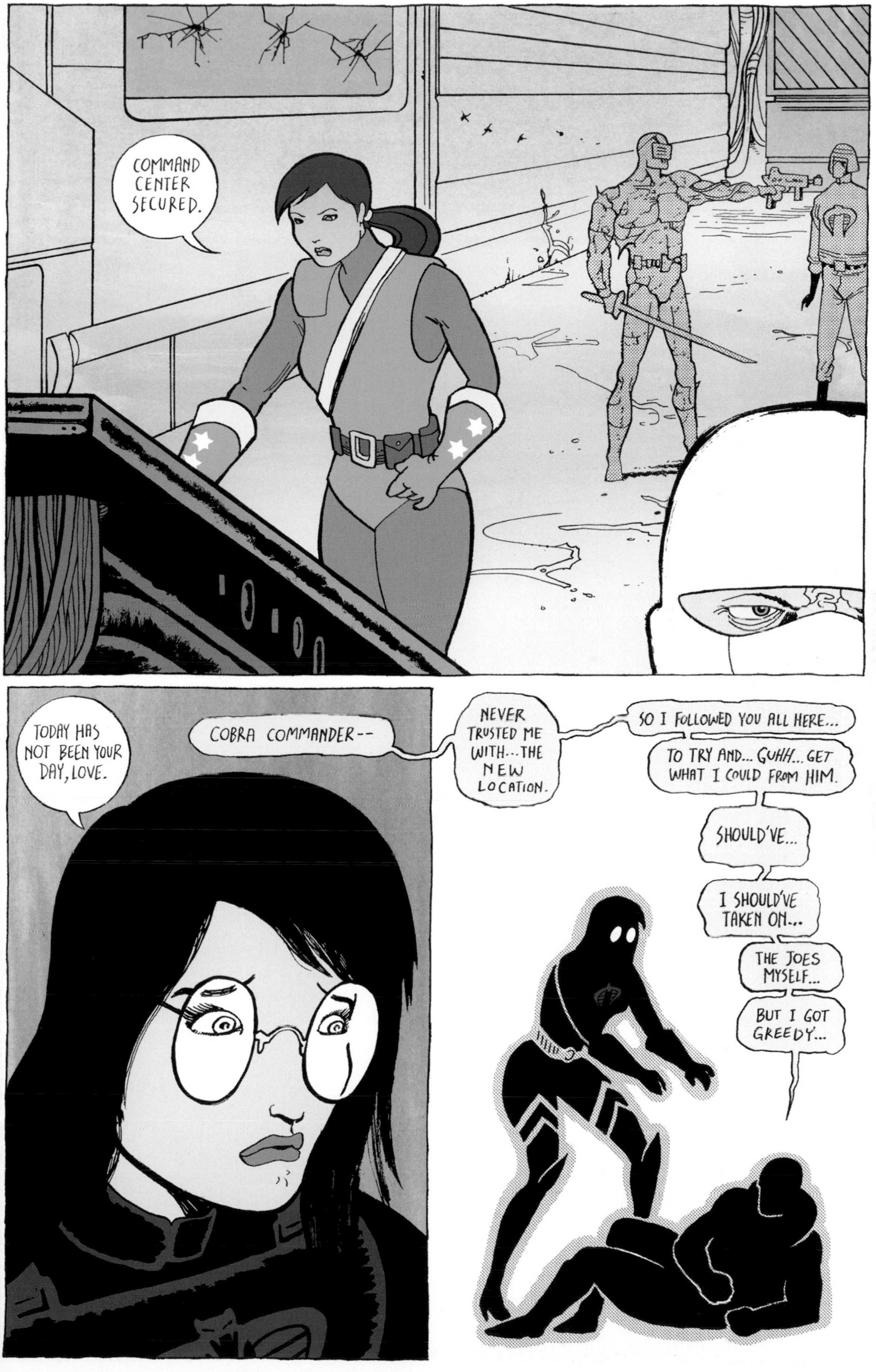
COMMAND CENTER SECURED.
TODAY HAS NOT BEEN YOUR DAY, LOVE.
COBRA COMMANDER--
NEVER TRUSTED ME WITH...THE NEW LOCATION.
SO I FOLLOWED YOU ALL HERE...
TO TRY AND... GUHH... GET WHAT I COULD FROM HIM.
SHOULD'VE...
I SHOULD'VE TAKEN ON...
THE JOES MYSELF...
BUT I GOT GREEDY...

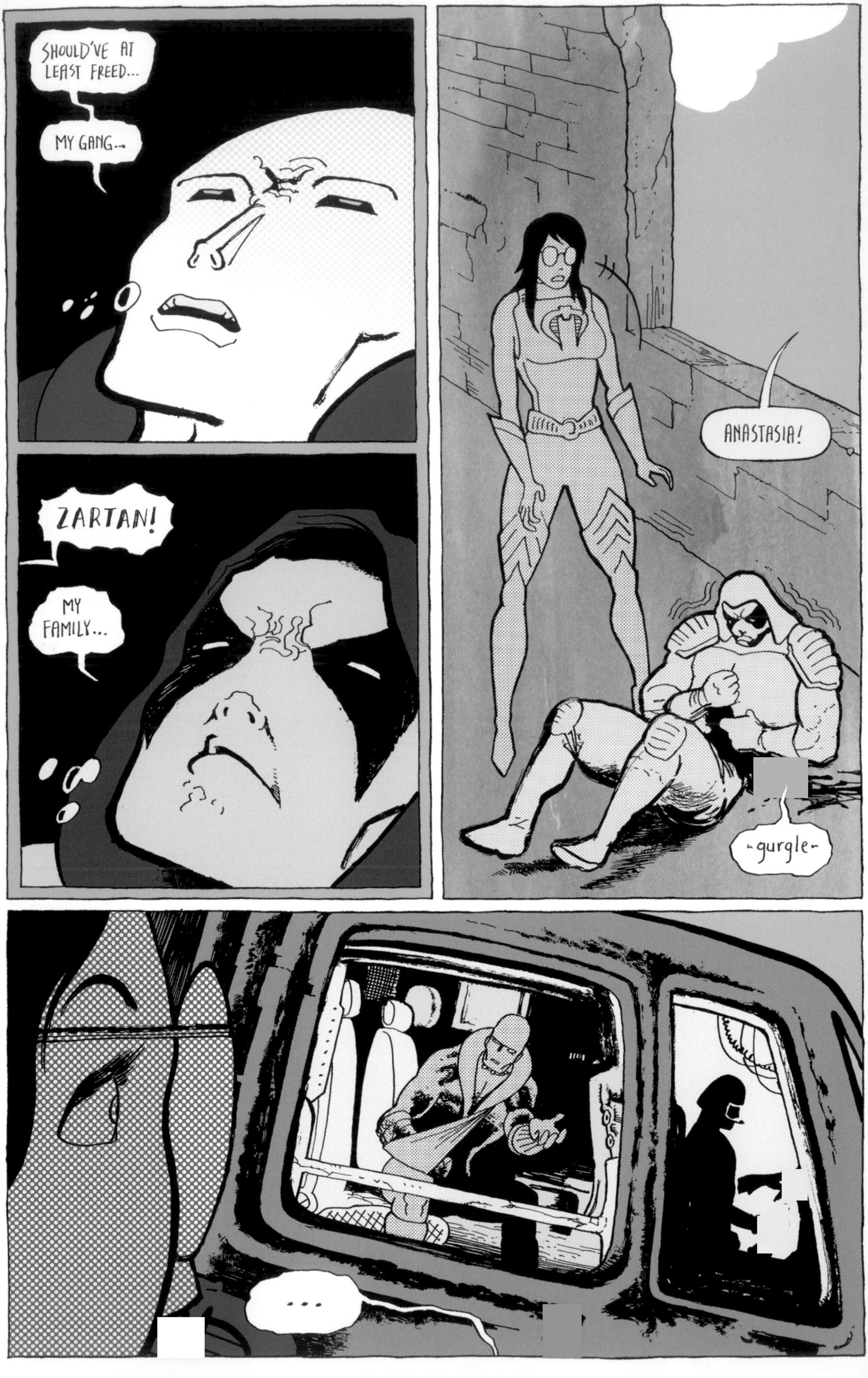
SHOULD'VE AT LEAST FREED...
MY GANG...
ZARTAN!
MY FAMILY...
ANASTASIA!
-gurgle-
...

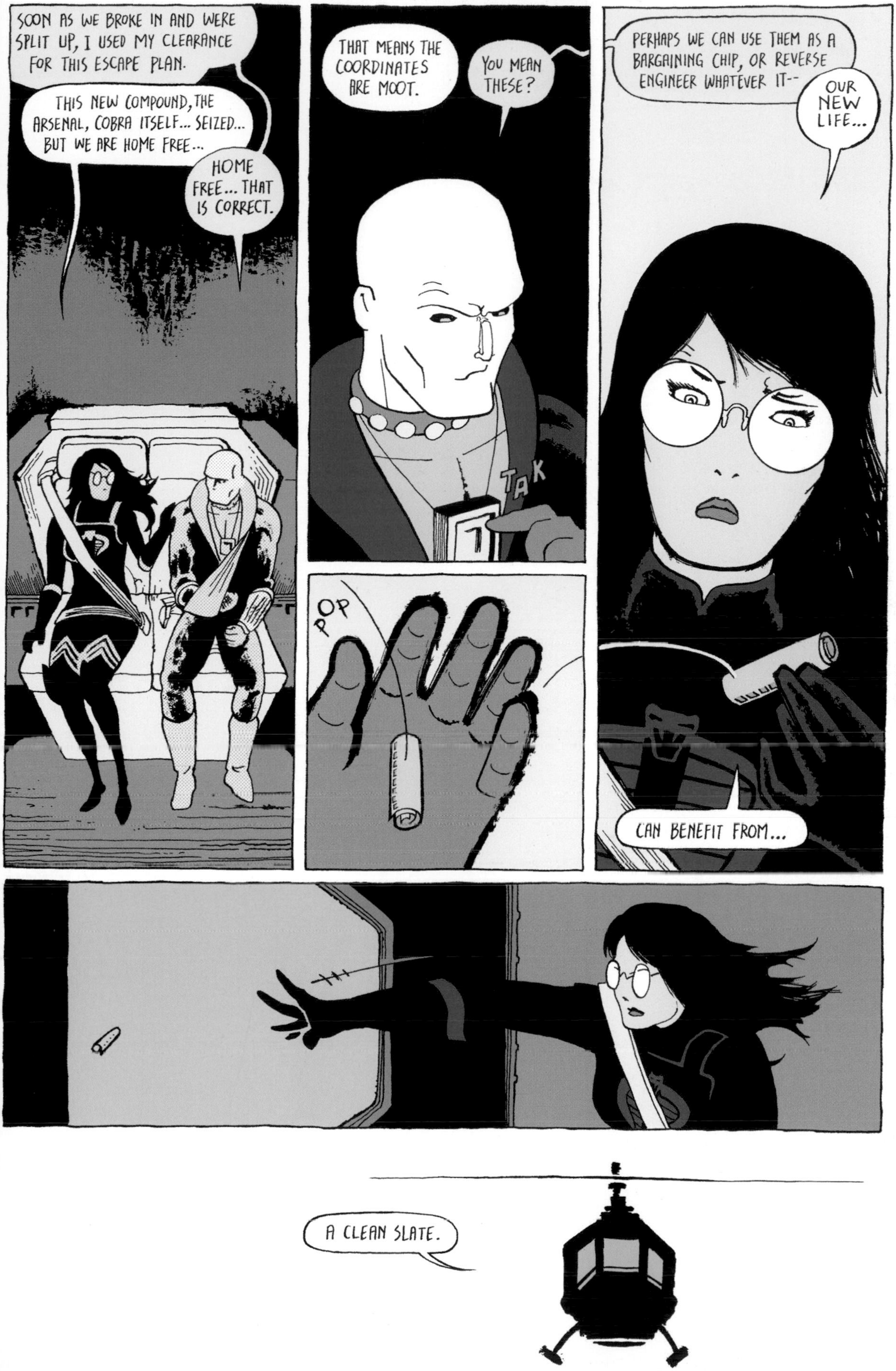
SOON AS WE BROKE IN AND WERE SPLIT UP, I USED MY CLEARANCE FOR THIS ESCAPE PLAN.
THIS NEW COMPOUND, THE ARSENAL, COBRA ITSELF... SEIZED... BUT WE ARE HOME FREE...
HOME FREE... THAT IS CORRECT.
THAT MEANS THE COORDINATES ARE MOOT.
YOU MEAN THESE?
TAK
POP
PERHAPS WE CAN USE THEM AS A BARGAINING CHIP, OR REVERSE ENGINEER WHATEVER IT--
OUR NEW LIFE...
CAN BENEFIT FROM...
A CLEAN SLATE.

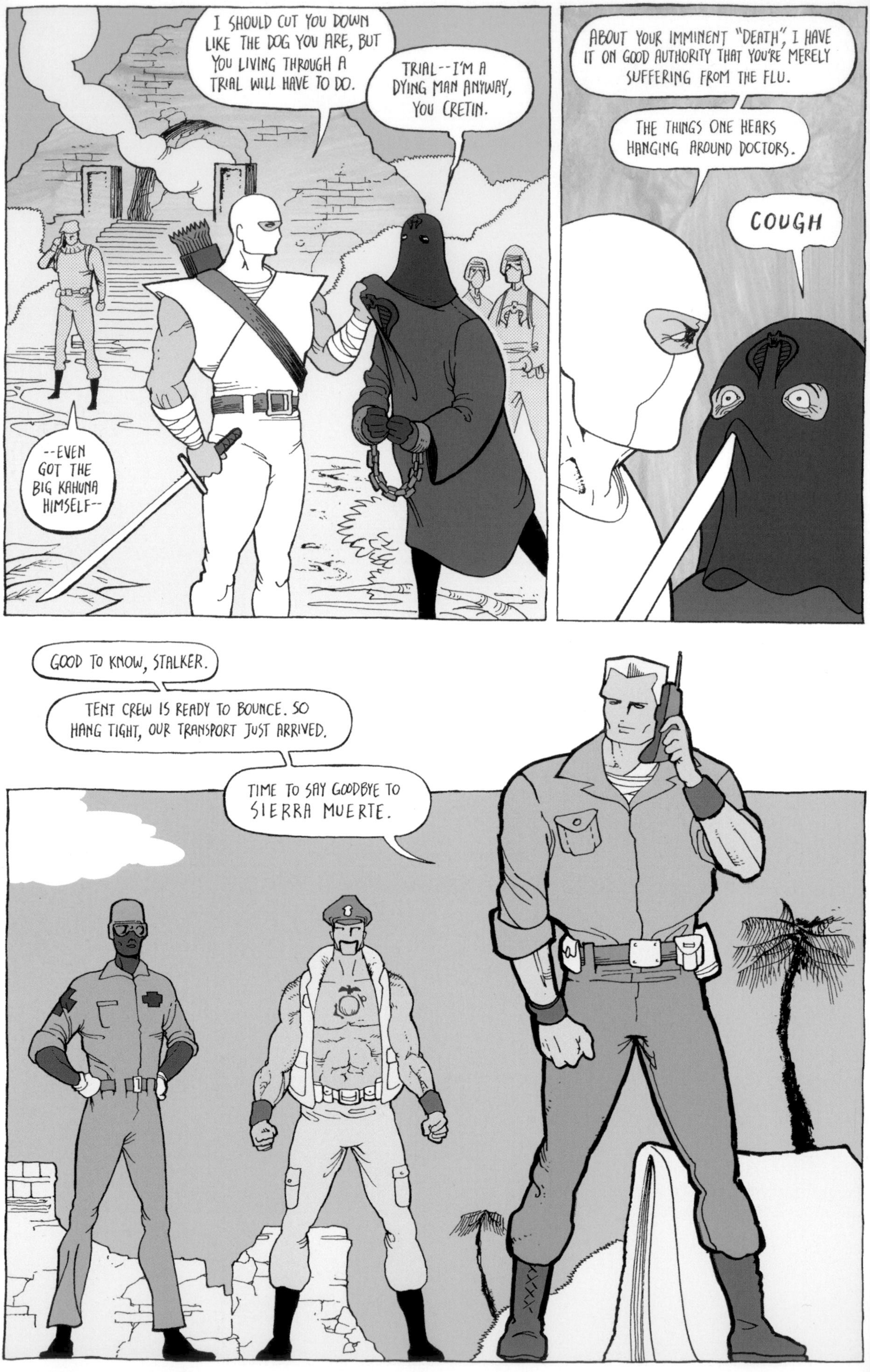
I SHOULD CUT YOU DOWN LIKE THE DOG YOU ARE, BUT YOU LIVING THROUGH A TRIAL WILL HAVE TO DO.
TRIAL--I'M A DYING MAN ANYWAY, YOU CRETIN.
--EVEN GOT THE BIG KAHUNA HIMSELF--
ABOUT YOUR IMMINENT "DEATH", I HAVE IT ON GOOD AUTHORITY THAT YOU'RE MERELY SUFFERING FROM THE FLU.
THE THINGS ONE HEARS HANGING AROUND DOCTORS.
COUGH
GOOD TO KNOW, STALKER.
TENT CREW IS READY TO BOUNCE. SO HANG TIGHT, OUR TRANSPORT JUST ARRIVED.
TIME TO SAY GOODBYE TO SIERRA MUERTE.

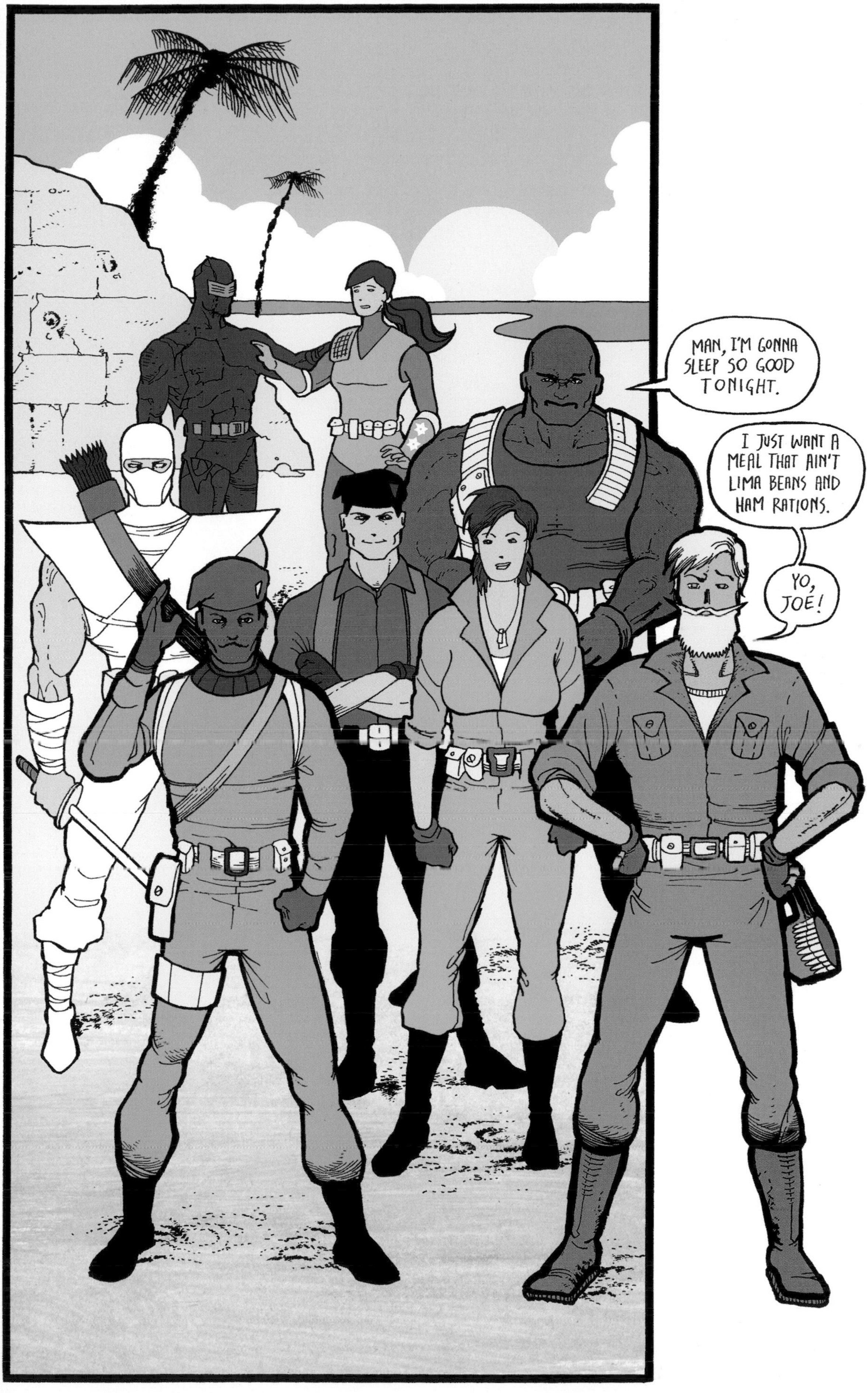
MAN, I'M GONNA SLEEP SO GOOD TONIGHT.
I JUST WANT A MEAL THAT AIN'T LIMA BEANS AND HAM RATIONS.
YO, JOE!

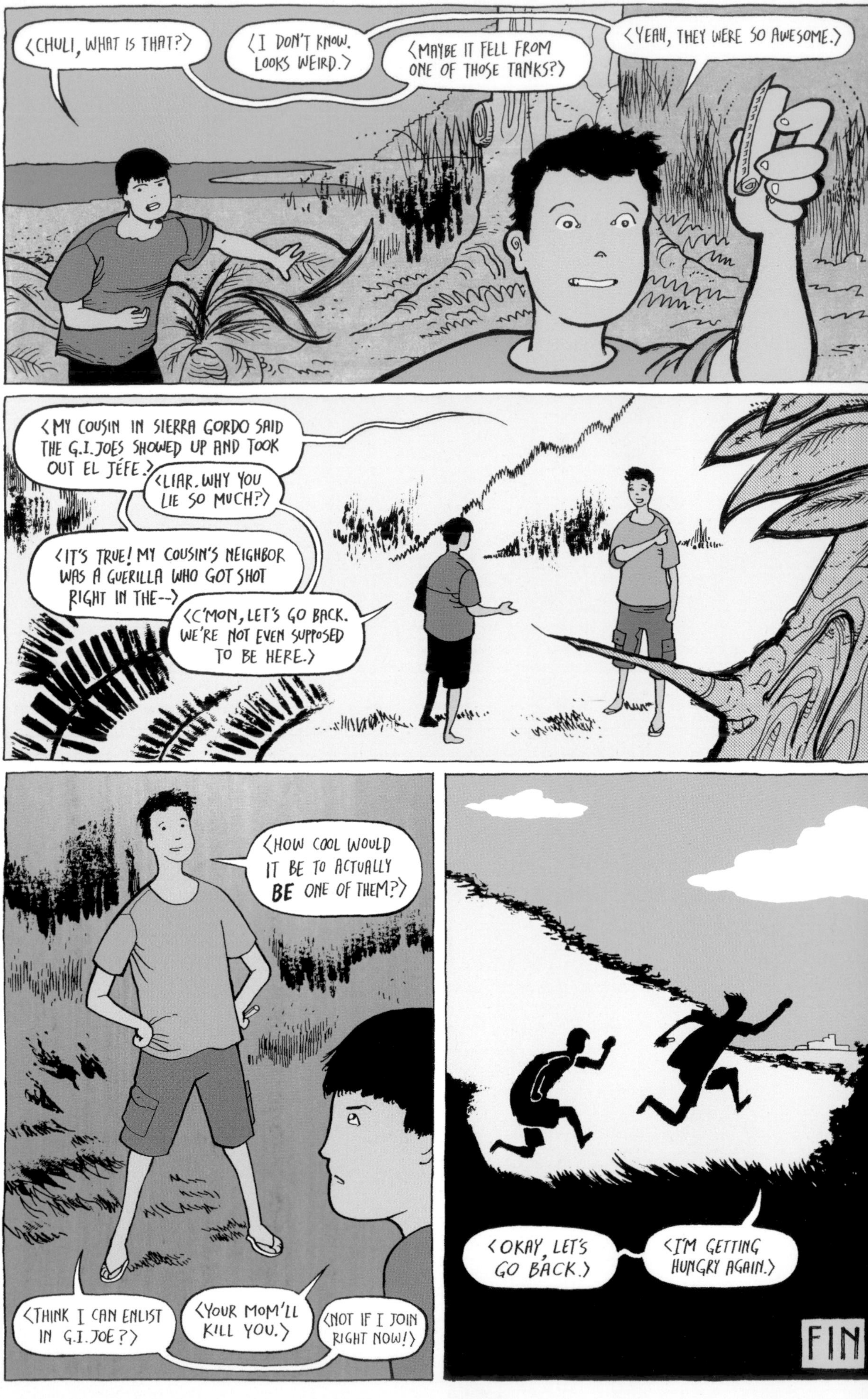

<CHULI, WHAT IS THAT?>
<I DON'T KNOW. LOOKS WEIRD.>
<MAYBE IT FELL FROM ONE OF THOSE TANKS?>
<YEAH, THEY WERE SO AWESOME.>
<MY COUSIN IN SIERRA GORDO SAID THE G.I.JOES SHOWED UP AND TOOK OUT EL JÉFE.>
<LIAR. WHY YOU LIE SO MUCH?>
<IT'S TRUE! MY COUSIN'S NEIGHBOR WAS A GUERILLA WHO GOT SHOT RIGHT IN THE-->
<C'MON, LET'S GO BACK. WE'RE NOT EVEN SUPPOSED TO BE HERE.>
<HOW COOL WOULD IT BE TO ACTUALLY **BE** ONE OF THEM?>
<THINK I CAN ENLIST IN G.I. JOE?>
<YOUR MOM'LL KILL YOU.>
<NOT IF I JOIN RIGHT NOW!>
<OKAY, LET'S GO BACK.>
<I'M GETTING HUNGRY AGAIN.>
FIN

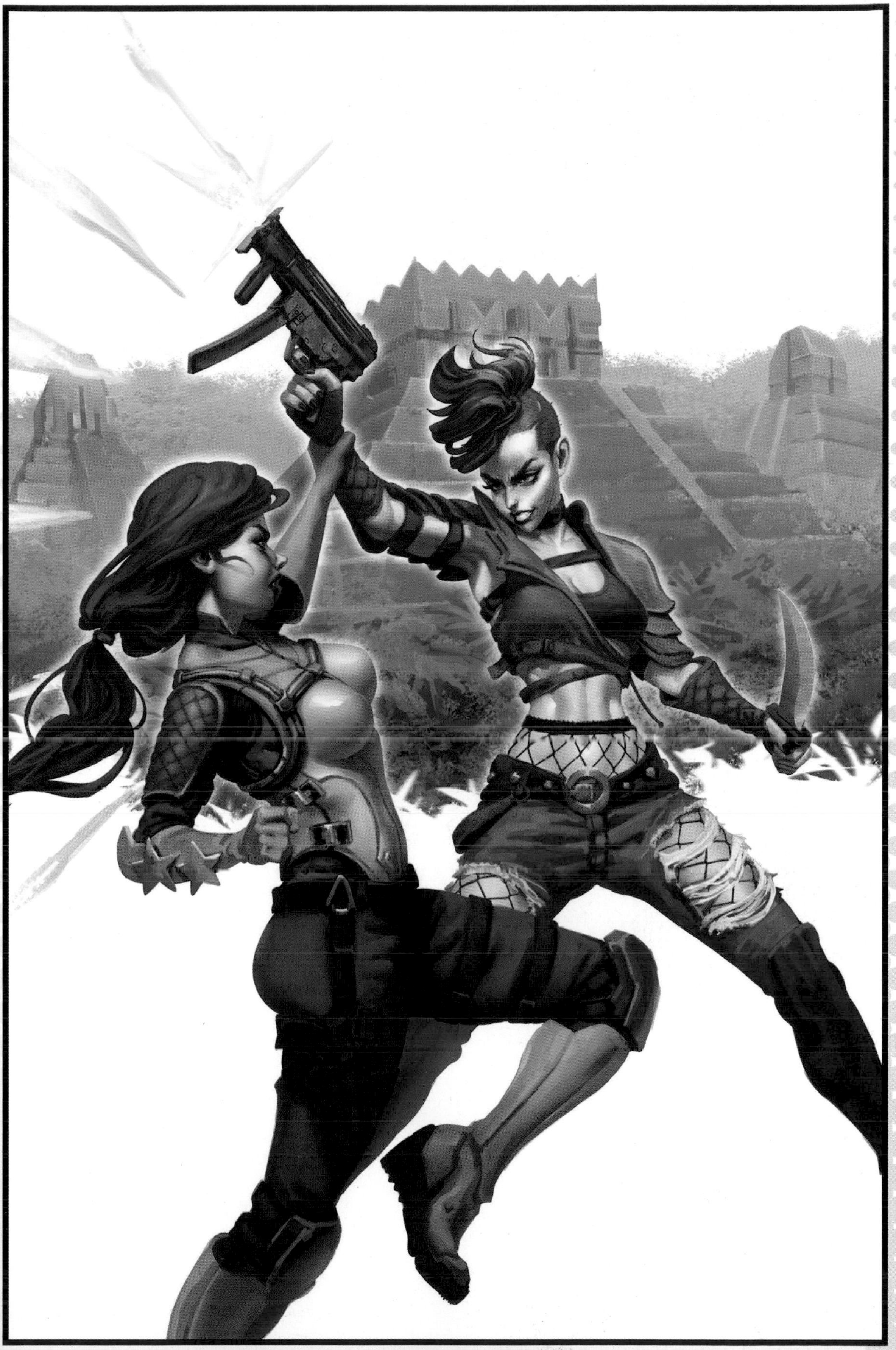

ART BY **IBRAHEM SWAID**

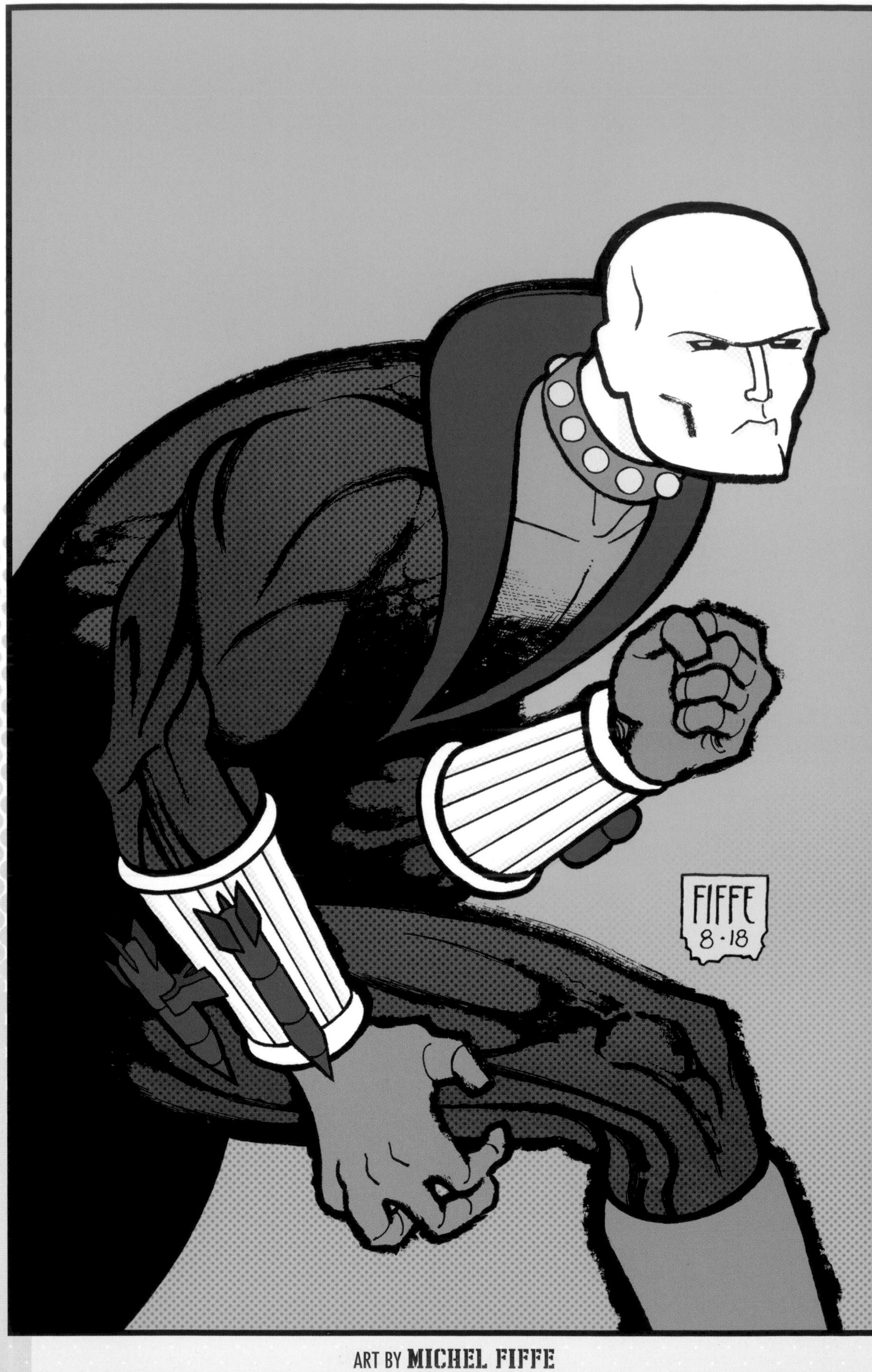
FIFFE
8-18

ART BY **MICHEL FIFFE**

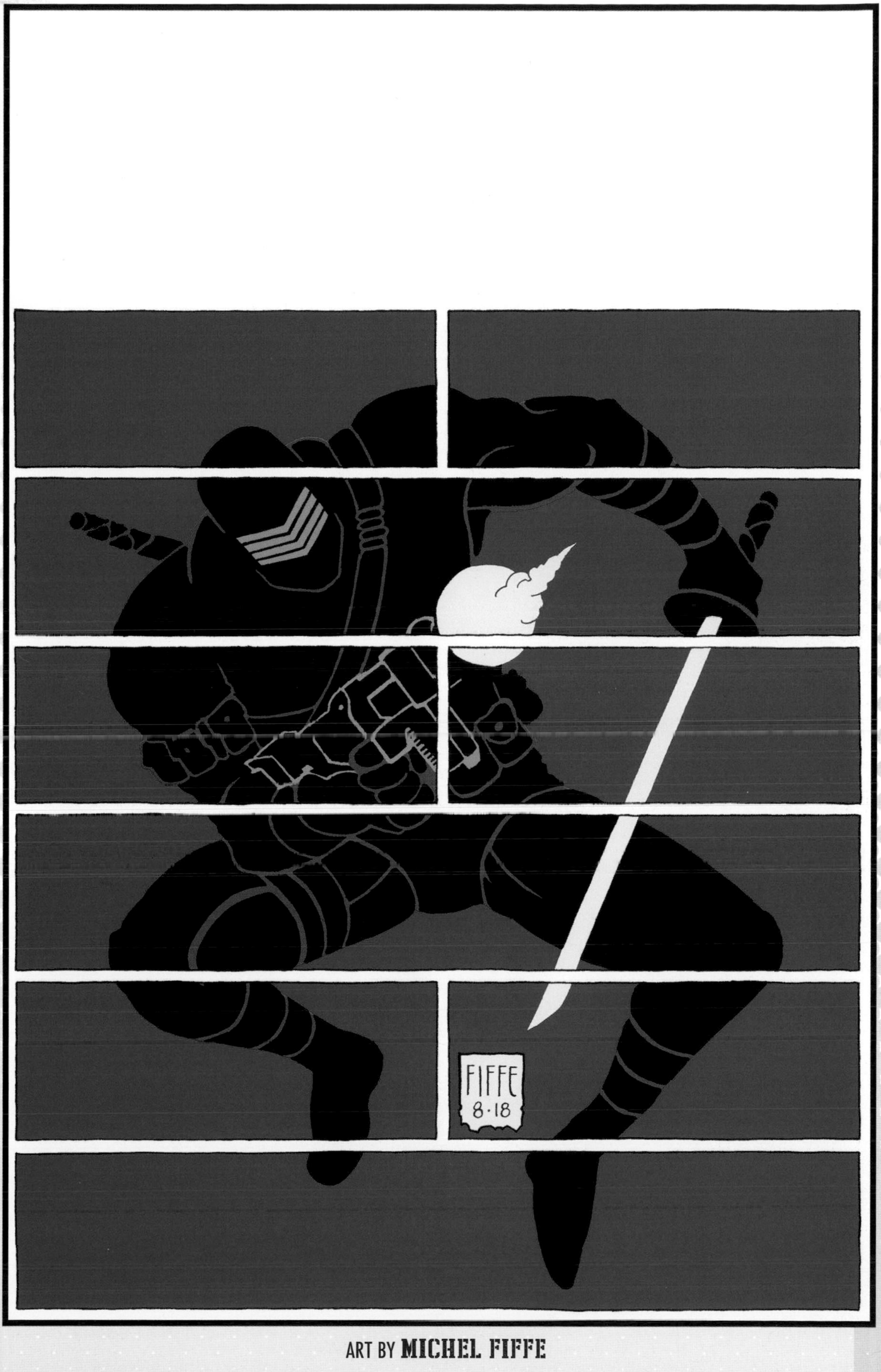
FIFFE
8·18

ART BY **MICHEL FIFFE**

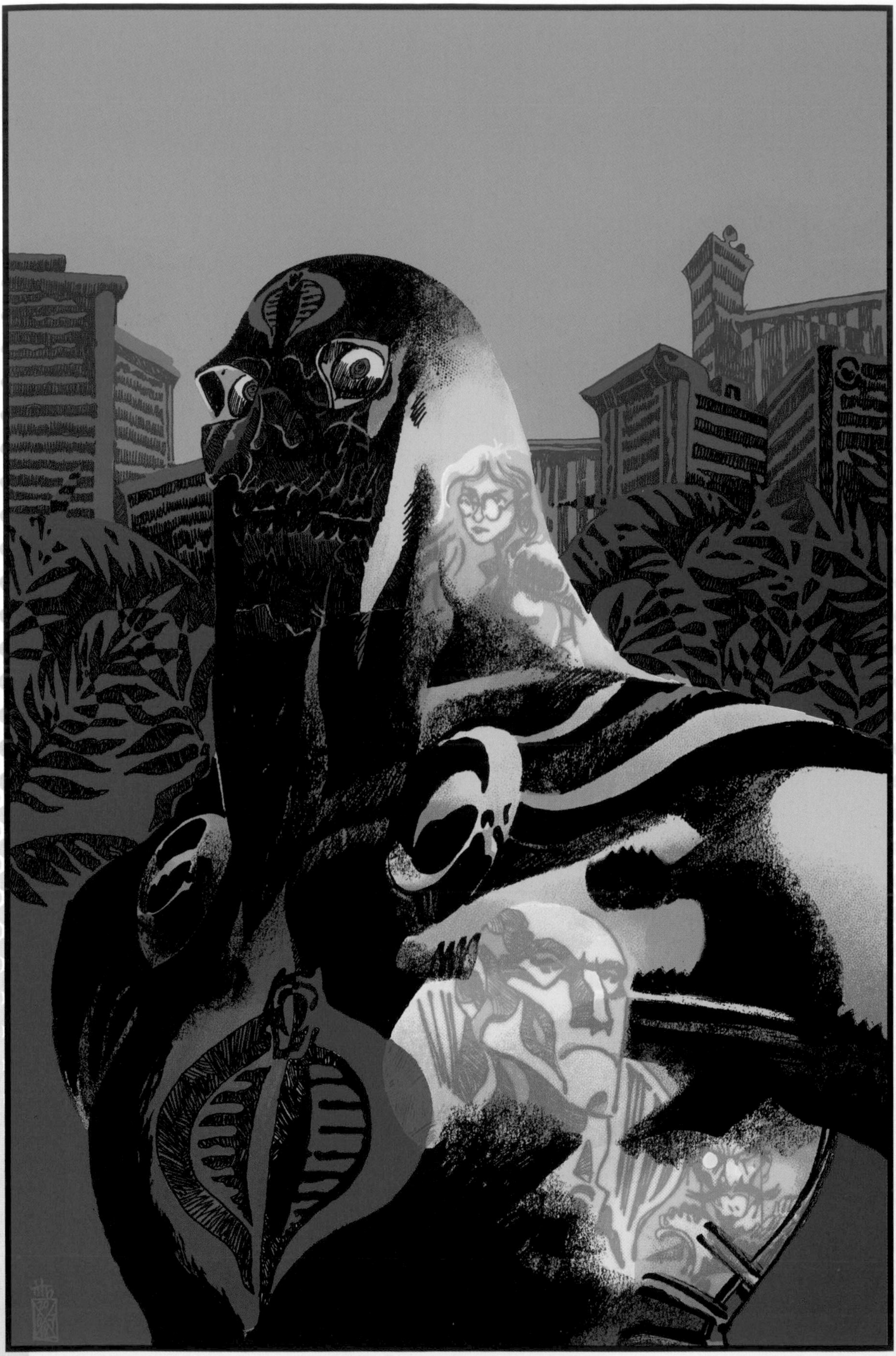

ART BY **ARTYOM TRAKHANOV**

YOU CAN'T GET THERE FROM HERE:
A Guide to the Fictional Geography of G.I. Joe
By Chad Bowers

The fight against Cobra has taken G.I. Joe all over the world, but not every place they've deployed can be found on a map.

Who, What, When, Where, and Why—The Five Ws—are the bedrock of any narrative, including the legendary G.I. Joe. Hasbro took care of "what" when they decided to reinvent the toyline in the early 1980s. Marvel Comics supplied the "who" and "why" of it all when they helped develop the brand beyond its early, somewhat eclectic premise, giving characters real names and personalities as well as introducing Cobra as the team's raison d'etre. For the new G.I. Joe to stand out from other military franchises of the day like *Sgt. Rock* and *M.A.S.H*, the property abandoned its Vietnam-era origins and cemented itself firmly in the modern aesthetic of the '80s (maybe even a little beyond it), answering the question "when." But what about "where"?

The G.I. Joe theme song—written before the line was even approved by Hasbro CEO Stephen Hassenfeld—told kids, "He'll fight for freedom wherever there's trouble." This was a start, but still pretty vague. The task of figuring out *where* the Joes fought Cobra fell into the laps of hugely talented and imaginative creators like Larry Hama and Buzz Dixon.

THE PIT

With over two hundred and fifty issues to his credit, longtime G.I. Joe scribe Larry Hama created a number of fictional places and landmarks unique to comics, and he's still going strong today! In the classic *G.I. JOE: A REAL AMERICAN HERO*(RAH), and in the pages of its modern-day return, Hama, probably more than anyone else, has expanded the mythology of G.I. Joe beyond its toy roots. He wasted no time getting started, introducing readers to the Joe's top-secret headquarters in the pages of *RAH* #1 ("Operation: Lady Doomsday," June 1982).

G.I. Joe HQ—more commonly known as The Pit—was hidden beneath the Army Chaplain's Assistant School's motor pool in Fort Wadsworth, located on Staten Island. The multi-level, underground complex boasted a combat training facility, a high-tech garage filled with V.A.M.P.s (Vehicle: Attack: Multi Purpose), M.O.B.A.T.s (Motorized Battle Tanks), H.A.L.s (Heavy Artillery Lasers), and Hawk's personal M.M.S. (Mobile Missile System), as well as comfortable living quarters for the Joes and the most advanced computer network the '80s had to offer.

Like so many of Hama's contributions to G.I. Joe, his decision to connect The Pit to the legendary military base can be traced back to his own experience in the service. "In the army, I knew a Chaplain assistant who was from Staten Island, and actually went to the school there back when it was still a thing," said Hama. "That's why I chose Fort Wadsworth. That's all I knew about it."

For a while, Fort Wadsworth served as the perfect cover, allowing the Joes to come and go as they pleased without drawing much attention to themselves or their highly classified mission.

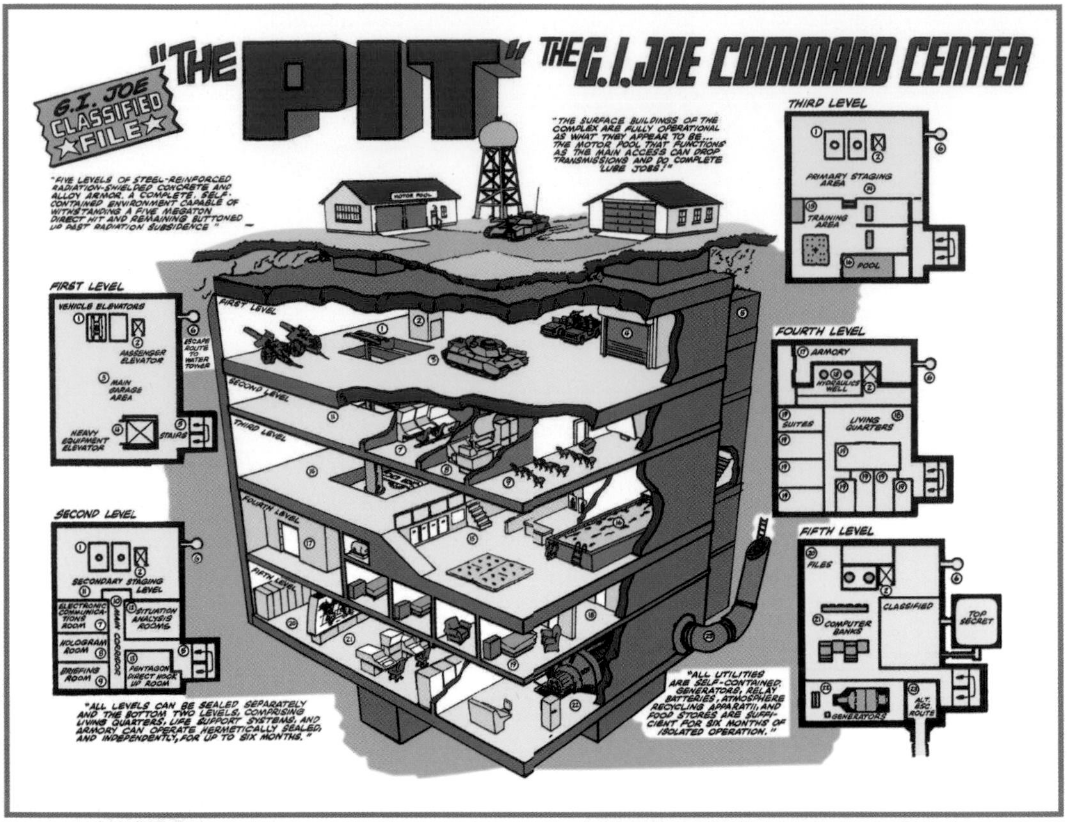

"THE PIT" THE G.I. JOE COMMAND CENTER
G.I. JOE CLASSIFIED ★FILE★
"FIVE LEVELS OF STEEL-REINFORCED RADIATION-SHIELDED CONCRETE AND ALLOY ARMOR. A COMPLETE, SELF-CONTAINED ENVIRONMENT CAPABLE OF WITHSTANDING A FIVE MEGATON DIRECT HIT AND REMAINING BUTTONED UP PAST RADIATION SUBSIDENCE."
"THE SURFACE BUILDINGS OF THE COMPLEX ARE FULLY OPERATIONAL AS WHAT THEY APPEAR TO BE... THE MOTOR POOL THAT FUNCTIONS AS THE MAIN ACCESS CAN DROP TRANSMISSIONS AND DO COMPLETE 'LUBE JOBS!'"
FIRST LEVEL
VEHICLE ELEVATORS
PASSENGER ELEVATOR
ESCAPE ROUTE TO WATER TOWER
MAIN GARAGE AREA
HEAVY EQUIPMENT ELEVATOR
STAIRS
SECOND LEVEL
SECONDARY STAGING LEVEL
ELECTRONIC COMMUNICATIONS ROOM
MAIN CORRIDOR
SITUATION ANALYSIS ROOMS
HOLOGRAM ROOM
BRIEFING ROOM
PENTAGON DIRECT HOOK UP ROOM
THIRD LEVEL
PRIMARY STAGING AREA
TRAINING AREA
POOL
FOURTH LEVEL
ARMORY
HYDRAULICS WELL
SUITES
LIVING QUARTERS
FIFTH LEVEL
FILES
CLASSIFIED
TOP SECRET
COMPUTER BANKS
GENERATORS
ALT. ESC. ROUTE
"ALL LEVELS CAN BE SEALED SEPARATELY AND THE BOTTOM TWO LEVELS, COMPRISING LIVING QUARTERS, LIFE SUPPORT SYSTEMS, AND ARMORY CAN OPERATE HERMETICALLY SEALED, AND INDEPENDENTLY, FOR UP TO SIX MONTHS."
"ALL UTILITIES ARE SELF-CONTAINED. GENERATORS, RELAY BATTERIES, ATMOSPHERE RECYCLING APPARATII, AND FOOD STORES ARE SUFFICIENT FOR SIX MONTHS OF ISOLATED OPERATION."

But The Pit's location was eventually discovered by Cobra, who destroyed much of the above ground motor pool in *RAH* #19 ("Joe Triumph," January 1984). And while the Joes successfully fended off the attack—convincing Cobra they'd got the wrong place, thanks to a hastily fabricated decoy base (because comics are awesome!)—the issue serves as a major turning point, as the team suffers its first loss when G.I. Joe commander General Flagg is killed by Major Bludd, leading to Hawk's promotion to CO and the introduction of Sgt. "Duke" Hauser as the Joe's new field leader.

Currently, the third iteration of The Pit exists in an undisclosed location somewhere in the deserts of Utah. It continues to be the most popular go-to name for G.I. Joe headquarters in comics and other media, and appeared in the 2009 motion picture, *G.I. Joe: The Rise of Cobra*.

SPRINGFIELD

After that debut issue, most of the series' first year saw the Joes facing Cobra or adjacent threats on U.S. soil and abroad, with Hama electing to stick to real world locations and often tying their struggles into current events and other geopolitical conflicts in the news. In *RAH* #4 ("Operation: Wingfield," October 1982), the team goes undercover to stop the Cobra-funded, Montana-based secret militia known as "First Strike." *RAH* #5 ("Tanks for the Memories," November 1982) features a high-speed tank chase through New York City's Central Park, while *RAH* #6 sees the Joes travel to Afghanistan to recover a downed spy plane and, for the first time, team-up with their Soviet counterparts, the Oktober Guard.

But in *RAH* #10 ("A Nice Little Town Like Ours...," April 1983), Hama starts to rethink this approach, as four Joes are kidnapped and stumble onto the existence of Springfield, a suburban paradise completely occupied by Cobra, answering the question of "where" with maybe the most disconcerting answer—"right here."

"There's a Springfield in almost every state of the union, so I thought it would be safe," said Hama. "I always liked the fantasy of a town with a secret identity or a hidden agenda. Like *Village of the Damned* or *The Stepford Wives*."

Springfield is a nice little town located somewhere in the continental U.S. It's a picturesque slice of the American dream, but, like Fort Wadsworth, Springfield has a secret. Below the perfectly paved parking lots of Springfield's busiest shopping centers is a Cobra stronghold dedicated to indoctrinating the town's population in the ways of the snake. In Springfield, every pizza parlor hides a chemical weapons reserve, every service station houses H.I.S.S. tanks, and every gun in the local arcade fires real bullets. More than the overblown and often farcical pomp of the animated takes on Cobra, or what we see of them in even Hama's earliest issues, Springfield fully sells the idea that Cobra should be feared. They're not comic book "bad guys," but a full-blown ideological movement—and they've got fangs.

Like The Pit, Springfield has carried over into other media. Shipwreck spends some time in a slightly different, albeit no less disturbing version in the G.I. Joe animated series two-parter "There's No Place Like Springfield." We're also given a glimpse of Springfield some years later in the Adult Swim animated mini-series, *G.I. Joe Resolute*. But it's in the comics that Springfield definitely carries the most weight, as over time Hama explores the concept of homegrown terrorism and the invasive nature of cultism in society. Springfield is what G.I. Joe is supposed to defend us against, and they fail—Cobra, the enemy, wins a major victory while no one's looking, and that's as frightening today as it was thirty years ago.

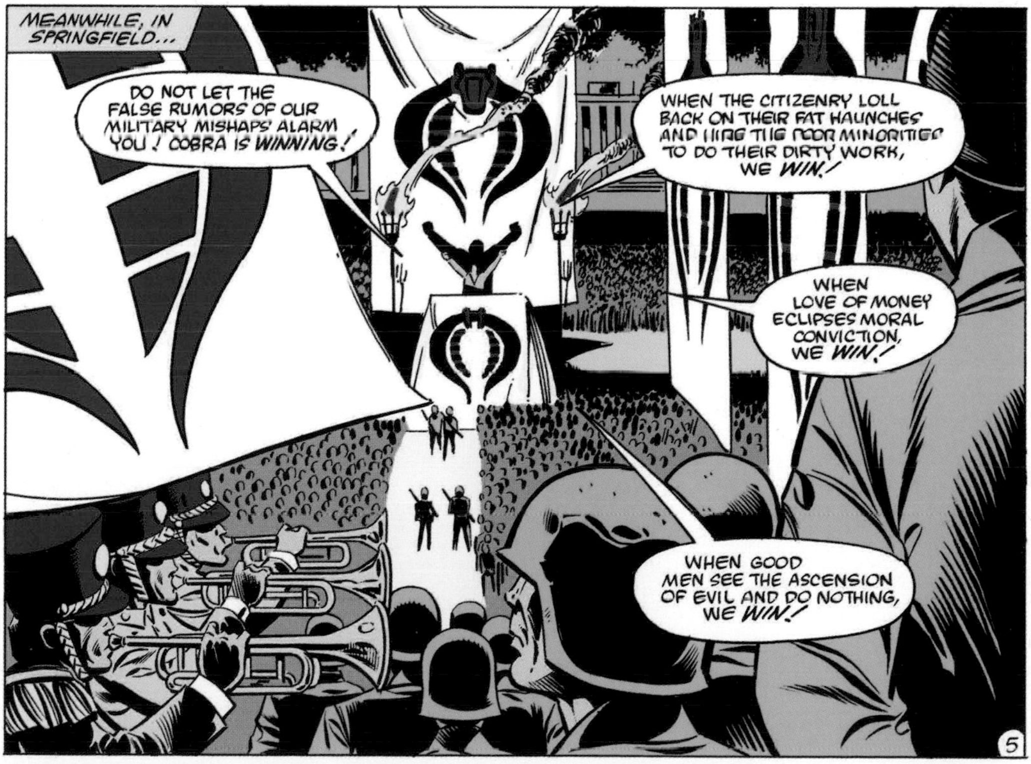
MEANWHILE, IN SPRINGFIELD...
DO NOT LET THE FALSE RUMORS OF OUR MILITARY MISHAPS ALARM YOU! COBRA IS WINNING!
WHEN THE CITIZENRY LOLL BACK ON THEIR FAT HAUNCHES AND HIRE THE POOR MINORITIES TO DO THEIR DIRTY WORK, WE WIN!
WHEN LOVE OF MONEY ECLIPSES MORAL CONVICTION, WE WIN!
WHEN GOOD MEN SEE THE ASCENSION OF EVIL AND DO NOTHING, WE WIN!
5

SIERRA GORDO

The Joes escape Springfield without learning its location and return to The Pit empty handed. But the Springfield mystery served to strengthen the ongoing nature of the series, and inspired Hama to lean into the world building even more with a focus on parts of the world outside the United States.

"Marvel always used made-up places," explained Hama. "Look at Wakanda, Madripoor, and Latveria. It seemed the best route to go rather than have people get bent out of shape because I said their country was ruled by dictators, etc. I started using fictional countries right away with Sierra Gordo."

With the Central American crisis at the center of U.S. foreign policy in the '80s, Hama took the Joes into a Latin American hotspot of his own creation—Sierra Gordo, a highly volatile jungle nation consumed by revolution and civil war. Hama uses the conflict between G.I. Joe and Cobra to mirror the tumultuous, real world relationship between the United States and Communist forces in the region. That said, the stories remain relatively neutral, with Hama taking only inspiration, never dipping into hard commentary or condemnation of any one party involved. "I tried to extrapolate off current events and go to where the next phase was instead of trying to duplicate something that was going on at the time," explained Hama.

Sierra Gordo served as the backdrop for a number of story arcs over the years. *RAH* #12 ("Three Strikes for Snake Eyes," June 1983) sees the Joes investigate a Cobra smuggling operation in Sierra Gordo, kicking off the series' first multi-part epic—the aforementioned attack of The Pit and the death of series regulars Kwinn and Dr. Venom. *RAH* #38 ("Judgements," August 1985) introduces Recondo as he joins Stalker in Sierra Gordo on a mission to rescue Dr. Adele Burkhart for the second time (Burkhart was kidnapped by Cobra back in *RAH* #1). In *RAH* #54 ("Launch Base," December 1986), G.I. Joe discovers Cobra is selling Terror Dromes to terrorists from a manufacturing hub in—you guessed it—Sierra Gordo! *RAH* #101 ("The New Guard," June 1990) featured maybe the most epic entry into the Sierra Gordo saga with the debut of the (almost) all new Oktober Guard as they join the Joes on a mission to free the battered nation from Cobra's occupation.

Sierra Gordo is surrounded by a number of smaller island nations, one of which is the setting for creator Michel Fiffe's three issue mini-series, *G.I. JOE: SIERRA MUERTE*.

"As a fan of the Sierra Gordo stories, I always noticed that their neighbor, Sierra Muerte, was mentioned but never explored," said Fiffe. "That blank canvas was perfect for the adventure I wanted to set the Joes in... a little beach action, a trip to the swamp, some city dwelling, and a place where Cobra could set up shop without too much hassle."

Muerte sees Cobra Commander move into the already troubled region and follows a group of fan-favorite Joes fighting to keep Dr. Venom's legacy out of the snakes' hands. Fiffe's *Muerte* is a worthwhile companion to Hama's original Seirra Gordo tales, and is certainly not to be missed!

COBRA ISLAND

"Where" isn't a question reserved exclusively for the Joes. From the beginning, Hama was considering the whereabouts of Cobra's own clandestine command center.

In *RAH* #1, the Joe team is briefed on a small landmass in the Caribbean, aptly named Cobra Island. Through video surveillance footage, we're treated to a bizarre, behind-the-scenes look at the inner workings of Cobra, as officers on horseback lead a battalion of soldiers carrying Cobra-emblazoned banners in a full-on parade with Cobra Commander watching. The spectacle isn't entirely out of character from what we know of Cobra, but it definitely feels more like a prototype version than what we're familiar with today. The idea of Cobra sequestered away on a tiny island, having parades celebrating themselves, feels almost antithetical and isolationist when compared to what we learn about Springfield just a few issues later.

As G.I. Joe plans their assault on Cobra Island, we're told the perimeter is protected by concertina wire, machine gun bunkers, and a number of formidable tank traps, and that a high-powered doppler radar can spot "a hang glider clear to the horizon" (hang gliders were a serious threat in the '80s), as well as a battalion of about 1200 Cobra troops stationed there, just itching for a fight. But the seemingly impregnable nature of Cobra Island doesn't stop Hawk's team from storming the outpost and sending the place up in flames by the end of the issue. And just like that, Cobra Island is introduced and destroyed in less than thirty pages.

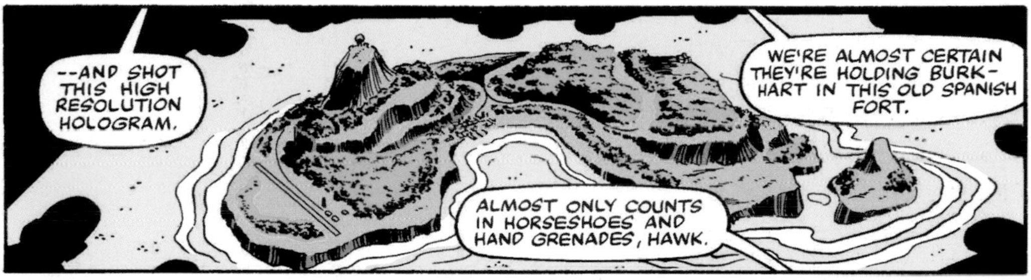
--AND SHOT THIS HIGH RESOLUTION HOLOGRAM.
WE'RE ALMOST CERTAIN THEY'RE HOLDING BURK-HART IN THIS OLD SPANISH FORT.
ALMOST ONLY COUNTS IN HORSESHOES AND HAND GRENADES, HAWK.

But never one to let a good idea (or a cool name) go to waste, Hama resurrected Cobra Island in *RAH* #41 ("Strategic Diplomacy," November 1985), and this time he swung for the bleachers. After months of toying with the Joes, Cobra dupes them into raising another landmass in the Gulf of Mexico. Then, in maybe the most over-the-top victory in all of comics, the new Cobra Island is recognized as a sovereign state, awarding Cobra recognition and protections on a global scale. It's a huge win for Cobra, one that stands in sharp contrast to what they accomplished in Springfield—a town the Joes couldn't even find. Suddenly, the whole world knows where Cobra is, and G.I. Joe can't do a thing about it.

With Cobra Island established and another new wave of action figures waiting just around the corner (including Cobra's new supreme leader, Serpentor), it was time to close out some hanging plot threads. In *RAH* #50 ("The Battle of Springfield," August 1986), Hama brings the Springfield saga to a head, with G.I. Joe invading the town, only to be outmaneuvered by a full-on Cobra evacuation that leaves no trace behind—and a lot of questions about the team's competence.

When fans and critics praise Hama's work on G.I. Joe, these are the kind of moments they point to. Like a master storyteller, Hama deftly positions Cobra as a legitimate world power and neuters our heroes for the foreseeable future. It changed the tenor of the book. It put the Joes on their heels, and Hama wasn't about to give them a break.

TRUCIAL ABYSMIA

Following the Cobra Island saga, the Joes became underdogs in their own book, and the series was never more engaging. In 1986, the success of *RAH* led to a spin-off title, *G.I. JOE: SPECIAL MISSIONS* (SM), a bi-monthly ongoing series that pitted G.I. Joe against mostly real-world threats instead of Cobra. With G.I. Joe temporarily disallowed from engaging Cobra in *RAH*, a new series with a more pragmatic mission statement made a lot of sense. But Hama still managed to work in some fictional Joe locations (Joe-cations?) here and there—most notably Trucial Abysmia.

Where Sierra Gordo was born out of the Central American crisis, Trucial's origins are found in Middle Eastern conflicts. *SM* #13 ("The Washout," September 1988) is our formal introduction to the harsh domain, and before the issue's over, at least one Joe, a rookie codenamed Mangler, lies dead. But there would be more.

A team of Joes return to Trucial Abysmia in *RAH* #108 ("Apparent Conclusions," January 1991) and quickly find themselves prisoners of Tomax and Xamot. The twins contact Cobra Commander and inform him of the Joes' capture, but the Commander is wrapped up in his own dilemma and doesn't need the headache. The unthinking Commander dismissively orders them to "get rid" of the Joes, which they erroneously interpret to mean "kill them," giving the job to particularly nasty Saw Viper. What starts as an off-kilter, almost comedic game of telephone between Cobra Commander and the Crimson Twins results in the savage deaths of six Joes—Doc, Crankcase, Thunder, Heavy Metal, Quick Kick, Crazylegs, and Breaker.

The violence inflicted on the Joes in Trucial Abysmia was more severe than anything Hama had done before, and the direct result of the complicated position he found himself in regularly—G.I. Joe was arguably the most popular toy line of all time, and new product was hitting stores just about every other quarter. And while it was great for Hasbro, it meant more Joes for Hama. "I had to get rid of characters because there were too many to keep track of," Hama revealed. "I had more characters than the Avengers, Defenders, Justice League, and Legion of Super Heroes combined. Too many characters, and Hasbro had no interest in doing new versions of them." Additionally, Hama was also writing one of the only military comics on the market during the heyday of the Gulf War. Did that have any impact on his decision? "External politics and conflicts weren't a big influence," said Hama. "I was always against 'events' for the sake of an event. Characters always came first."

COBRA-LA

Hama's influence on G.I. Joe cannot be overstated, but no conversation about the "where" of G.I. Joe would be complete without mentioning *G.I. Joe: The Movie* and the introduction of the most controversial location in the franchise's history—Cobra-La.

Sunbow Entertainment produced the G.I. Joe animated series from 1983 to 1986, and while the cartoon has a lot in common with its comics counterpart, they didn't share everything. For instance, Snake Eyes and Scarlett are romantically involved in the comics, while the animated series presented a more flirtatious, but mostly platonic friendship between Scarlett and Duke. Animated Hawk had brown hair instead of the blonde crew cut he sports in the comics. There's more stuff like that, of course, but the most notable difference between the two came in 1987's *G.I. Joe: The Movie.*

Animation writer Buzz Dixon served as a story consultant on *G.I. Joe: The Movie*, developing the film's eerie setting alongside screenwriter Ron Friedman. "I chose the organic/bio-engineered setting because I wanted the Joes to face something as different from Cobra as possible," said Dixon. "The fact they inspired Dr. Mindbender to create Serpentor by using DNA also ties in with this background."

The season preceding the film began with the five-part mini-series "Arise, Serpentor, Arise," in which Cobra's resident mad scientist Dr. Mindbender has a vision that inspires him to create Serpentor from the DNA of history's greatest leaders. Serpentor's TV origin was based on the Hama-written action figure file card, so it's no surprise he told a similar story chronicling the birth of Serpentor when it was time to introduce him in the comics. But where Hama killed the character off quickly, the animated series integrated Serpentor into the full cast, setting up a highly entertaining rivalry between him and the usurped Cobra Commander that culminated in *G.I. Joe: The Movie*.

Cobra Commander's origins in *G.I. Joe: The Movie* trace back to the Lovecraftian Cobra-La, a race of monstrous humanoids who've been hiding in the Himalayas since before the ice age. When their half-man, half-snake ruler Golobulus reveals Cobra Commander is an exile of Cobra-La and exposes him as a disfigured, blue-skinned scientist, it's a far cry from the grounded, disenfranchised car salesman created by Hama and Co. in the comics. But it's no less compelling.

Using the framework allowed by Broadcast Standards and Practices for a children's cartoon, Dixon and Friedman managed to tap into fears of terrorism by personifying it as something hideous and otherworldly, but still looming ever-present in our collective pasts. "There are several points of inspiration for this, everything from old cartoons to the *Nausicaä* anime," revealed Dixon. "Larry Niven's booster trees in his *Known Space* stories, Richard E. Geis' *One Immortal Man*, etc. I suppose we could go as far back as H.G. Wells' *Island of Dr. Moreau* as an inspiration." Cobra-La was... different from Springfield and Cobra Island. And maybe it's lessened by the fact that it comes out of left field. Still, within its own context, it works exceptionally well as a frightening reminder that we rarely know as much as we think we do about where we come from.

Beyond what's covered here, there's Trans-Carpathia, an ersatz Transylvania concealing Cobra's Silent Castle; its neighbor, Darklonia, home of Destro's equally ostentatious cousin, Darklon; Nanzhao, the now decimated capital of Cobra's narcotics empire; Borovia and Broca Beach; and even Cybertron! A comprehensive record of all the "wheres" of G.I. Joe is quickly made incomplete by talents like Hama, Dixon, and Michel Fiffe, who are continually adding new places to the tapestry! After half-a-century, the world of G.I. Joe is still growing, and with each fresh or refreshed locale, another chapter is added to the ongoing legend of America's daring, highly trained special missions force. Over land, and sea, and air, and everywhere in between—G.I. Joe is there.

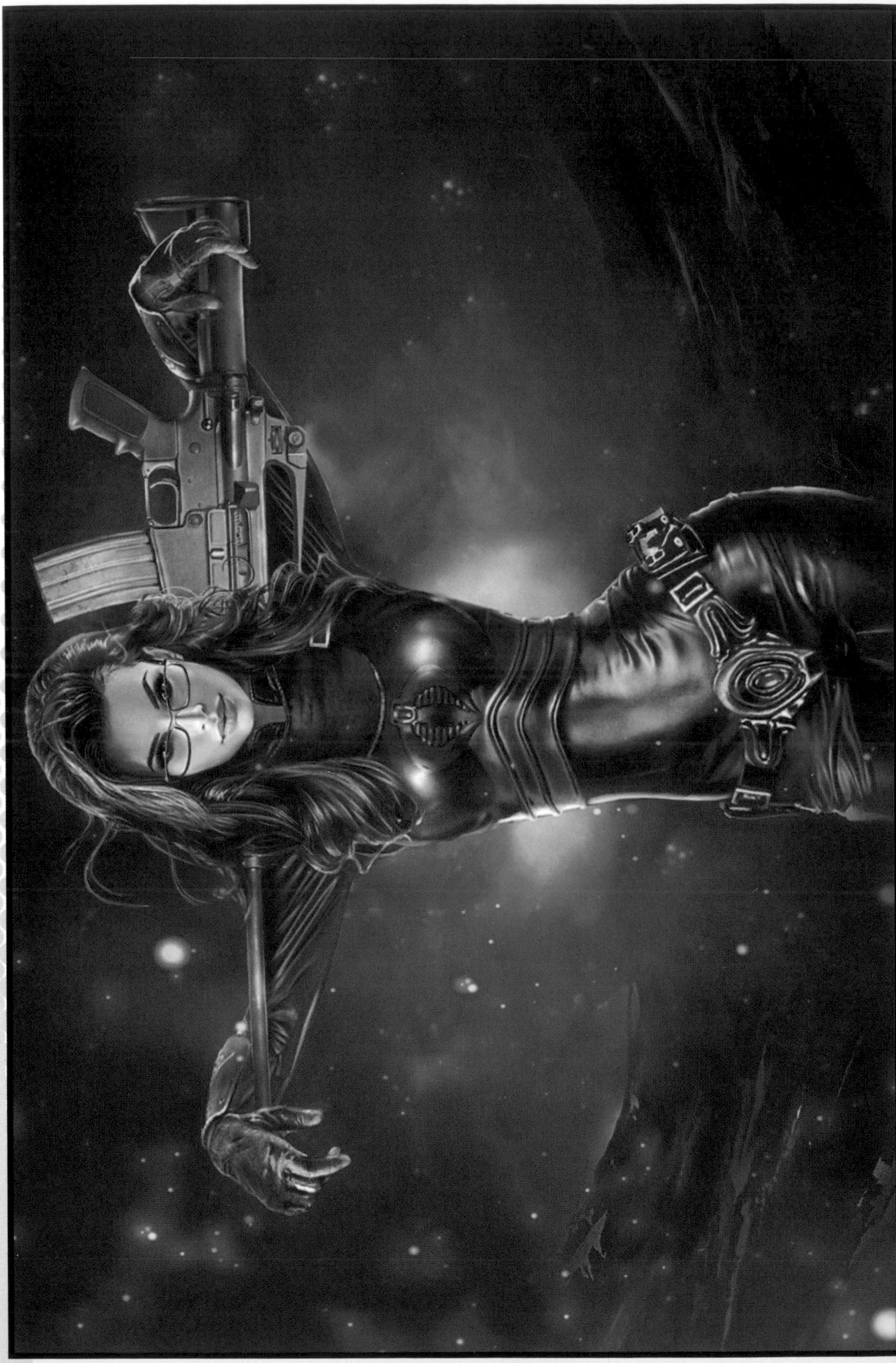

ART BY **NATALI SANDERS**

ACTION LOUDER THAN WORDS:
A Brief History of Snake Eyes
By Chad Bowers

In 1982, Hasbro reintroduced the world to G.I. Joe. Smaller than its 12" predecessor, the new Joe was scaled down to a modest 3.75" to accommodate a more versatile play experience that included vehicles, playsets, and a wider range of characters and personalities—real American heroes with codenames like "Hawk" and "Scarlett." There were thirteen Joes in the first release, twelve decked out in familiar shades of army green and one clad in all black with his face concealed underneath a balaclava. He stood out from the rest, but the front of his packaging only gave a name—"Snake Eyes"—and a quick glance on the back of the toy revealed... well, not much else.

As it turned out, the phrase "he's the best" was more than enough to hook children's imaginations. And before anyone could even pull the figure off its blister card, they were asking questions!

"What is his real name?" "What does he look like underneath the mask?" "What else is he hiding?"

In 1982, an entire generation of kids went all-in on the mystery of Snake Eyes, and there was only one place to go for answers!

SHOW DON'T TELL

Pioneering a unique marketing strategy that involved advertising comics instead of toys, Hasbro partnered with the creative minds at Marvel Comics to develop an all-new G.I. Joe comic book to help brand the revamped franchise. Editor/artist Larry Hama was selected to script the book, with Herb Trimpe and Bob McLeod on art duties. *G.I. JOE: A REAL AMERICAN HERO* (RAH) #1 debuted July 1982 with an explosive cover spotlighting Hawk, Scarlett, Stalker, Zap, Flash, the M.O.B.A.T. (Motorized Battle Tank) and its driver, Steeler. Snake Eyes was nowhere to be seen.

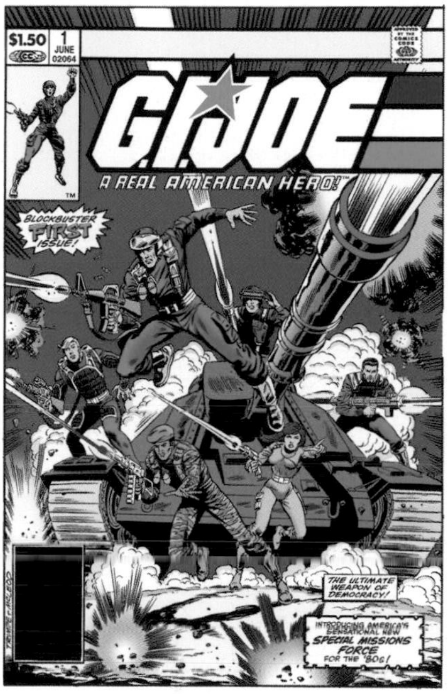
$1.50
1
JUNE
G.I. JOE
A REAL AMERICAN HERO!
BLOCKBUSTER FIRST ISSUE!
THE ULTIMATE WEAPON OF DEMOCRACY!
SPECIAL MISSIONS FORCE

In fact, Snake Eyes was anything but a leading man in those early days. *RAH* #1 ("Operation: Lady Doomsday") introduces G.I. Joe and Cobra in a perfectly paced action story that sees Cobra kidnapping a nuclear physicist and the Joes' subsequent rescue of her. But there's not much in the way of Snake Eyes mythology, unless you count Hawk's decision to pair him with Scarlett on the mission to Cobra Island, subtly hinting at the relationship to come.

He gets a little more time on the page with *RAH* #2 ("Panic at the North Pole," August 1982), accompanying Scarlett, Stalker, and Breaker on a mission to the arctic. But he's a far cry from the ninja master we know today, kicking over more tables than bad guys and even forgetting to reload his Uzi at one point. However, the issue does introduce Tracker Kwinn, a Cobra-employed mercenary who befriends Snake Eyes only to lose his life at the hands of Dr. Venom. It's the first of many character deaths that would impact Snake Eyes over the years.

RAH #4 ("Operation: Wingfield," October 1982) gives readers a direct, and rare, look into the mind of Snake Eyes through a hand-written recon report. While not the most prolific note taker around, Snake Eyes does manage to work in a few jabs at Hawk and Grunt's unconvincing efforts to infiltrate Vance Wingfield's First Strike militia, describing them as "pretending to be clumsy and slow." It's not much, but it's the first hint of Snake Eyes having an actual personality—maybe even a sense of humor—and that's more than we knew before.

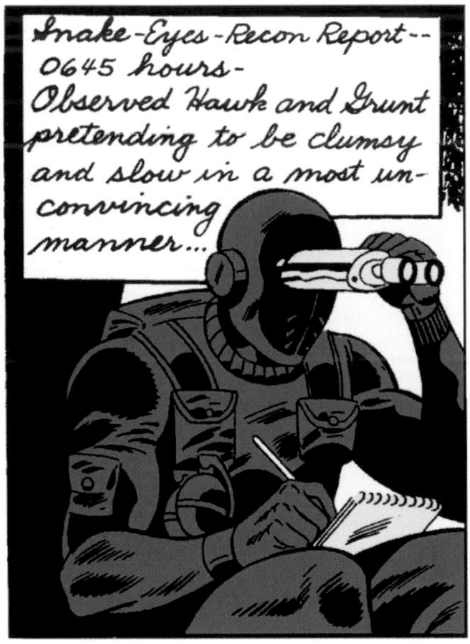

Snake-Eyes-Recon Report--
0645 hours-
Observed Hawk and Grunt pretending to be clumsy and slow in a most un-convincing manner...

Snake Eyes continued to bounce around in the pages of *RAH*, featuring prominently in both the Springfield and Sierra Gordo sagas. But Hama refrained from plunging too far into the history of the man, forcing those eager to learn more about Snake Eyes to wait patiently as he built to the next big reveal!

A new wave of figures in 1984 meant more Joes would be joining the cast. *RAH* #19 ("Joe Triumphs," January 1984) was a major turning point for the series, with Hama tying up a number of hanging plot threads to make way for the newbies. But it would be a few months before readers met the likes of Roadblock, Duke, or Spirit Iron-Knife. Instead, they would be introduced to one of the bad guys first in an issue written and drawn by Hama with Steve Leialoha providing inks. When the finished product arrived, Hama's editor couldn't help but wonder, "Where are the words?"

His response was simple: "There aren't any."

The bold decision to print the issue without dialogue thrilled G.I. Joe fans, while critics in, and outside, the world of comics praised Hama's innovative approach to storytelling and his willingness to experiment with the medium. Today, *RAH* # 21 ("Silent Interlude," March 1984) exists as the most celebrated and sought-after issue of the entire series, and with good reason.

G.I. JOE
A REAL AMERICAN HERO
60¢
21
MAR
THE MOST UNUSUAL G.I. JOE STORY EVER!!

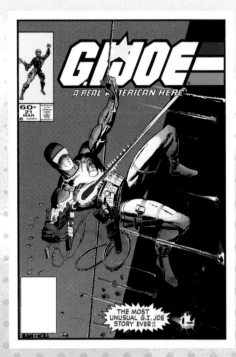

Interlude begins *in media res*, with a ninja wearing all white arriving in spectacular fashion at a secret Cobra stronghold with Scarlett in tow. Snake Eyes parachutes in soon

after, and immediately dispatches three Cobra troopers with ease. He means business.

Facing off against the mysterious and equally formidable white ninja, Snake Eyes suffers a cut to his right forearm. Having freed herself (she's no damsel in distress), Scarlett swoops in to save her would-be rescuer just as the ninja tosses his blade at her. As it misses its mark, Snake Eyes catches it (milestone moment: his first time touching a sword) before tossing it aside as he and Scarlett zoom away on a stolen Cobra C.L.A.W. (Covert Light Aerial Weapon).

Through a tear in his suit, we can see that Snake Eyes sports a curious tattoo on his right forearm—a red Hexagram from the I Ching. Atop of the castle, the white ninja watches as they go, his own forearm exposed to reveal the same mark.

And just like that, G.I. Joe went from zero to NINJA in twenty-two pages. The unnamed ninja of *Silent Interlude* is, of course, Storm Shadow. Introduced in 1984 as G.I. Joe's answer to the ninja craze of the time, Storm Shadow proved to be the spark Hama needed to propel the series over the dreaded three-year hurdle that had flattened so many licensed comics prior.

Instead of wrapping up plot threads, Hama was emboldened, diving deeper into the characters' stories than ever before. Beginning with *RAH* #24 ("The Commander Escapes," June 1984), new figures like Duke, Roadblock, Spirit, and Zartan inspired fresh concepts that took the series to sophisticated heights previously unseen in a toy comic. By the time *RAH* #26 and 27 ("Snake Eyes: The Origin," August 1984) hit stands, the book had achieved "must read" status. Fans were hungry for the next chapter in the Snake Eyes saga, and Hama, joined once again by Leialoha, intended to deliver.

G.I. JOE
A REAL AMERICAN HERO!
60¢
26
AUG
AT LAST!
THE STRANGEST SECRET OF ALL!
DODF2167
SUBJECT:
SNAKE-EYES
Family wiped out in flaming wreck

At G.I. Joe HQ, Stalker reminisces about his time in Vietnam with Snake Eyes and Storm Shadow, while a plump old man in Spanish Harlem recounts Snake Eyes' journey back to the states. Hawk takes the reigns, detailing the most tragic moment of Snake Eyes' life: there was no one waiting for him at the airport when he returned from the war. Snake Eyes' entire family—his mother, father, and his twin sister—were killed in a car accident on their way to pick him up. "The victims of a stoned-out vet," explains Hawk, before admitting he was the one who had to deliver the bad news.

After losing everything, his old friend Tommy "Storm Shadow" Arashikage offers Snake Eyes a position in "the family business." Snake Eyes accepts, finding purpose and direction in the ways of the ninja—but it all falls to pieces when Storm Shadow inexplicably murders their teacher, the Hard Master. Leaving Japan, Snake Eyes retreats into the High Sierras for a life of solitude, but it isn't meant to be—his country needs him. Scarlett's contribution to the story brings things into the present with Snake Eyes' G.I. Joe recruitment, their budding romance, and ultimately, the horrific helicopter crash that irreparably scarred his face and took his voice.

Hama ends #27 with a rematch between Snake Eyes and Storm Shadow taking place atop a speeding train in Harlem—a battle that ultimately ends in a draw when Storm Shadow declares his innocence, saying that he didn't murder the Hard Master and confessing to Snake Eyes that the only reason he's with Cobra is to smoke out the fiend who did. Storm Shadow then vanishes into the night, leaving behind Snake Eyes to ponder this new information.

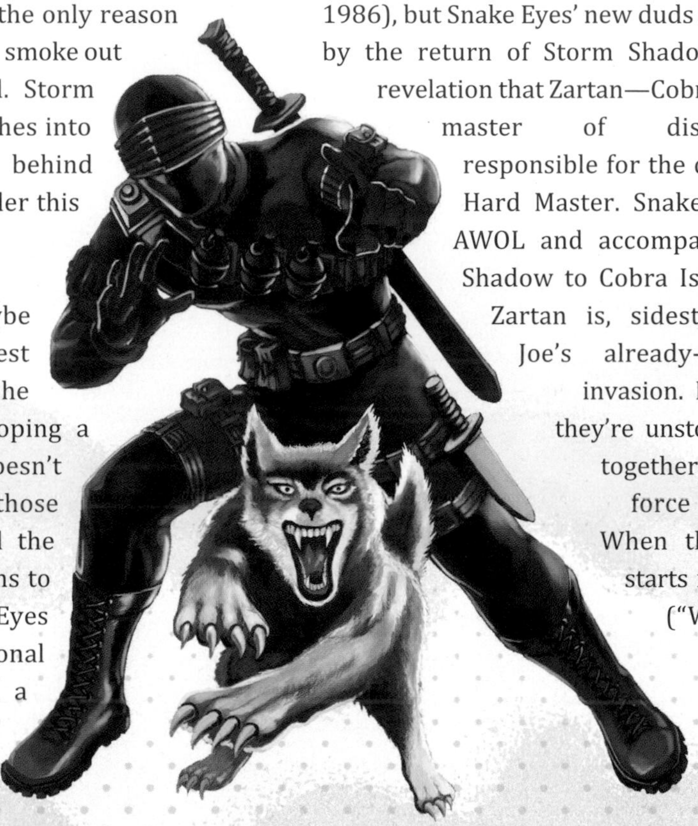

Origin is maybe Hama's strongest piece of writing, as he succeeds in developing a character who doesn't speak by letting those closest to him tell the story. He takes pains to elevate Snake Eyes beyond the traditional masked hero with a clumsy secret identity by revealing that many in G.I. Joe know who Snake Eyes is—telling us these same people have known him for years. By the end of the story, we're maybe the only ones who *don't* know him, and somehow that's okay. The conversation has changed—who Snake Eyes is doesn't matter so much anymore. All we care about is what happens next!

NO MASK, WHO DIS?

As Snake Eyes' popularity rose, so did demand for his action figure. Hasbro reissued and updated Snake Eyes for 1985's series IV, the first "version 2" figure of the line (not counting the hooded Cobra Commander, which only featured a new head). The new look Snake Eyes replaced the original's goggles with an almost medieval-inspired knight's visor, a wolf sidekick, and—for the first time—a sword. V2 Snake Eyes was a huge hit, supplanting the original as the character's most iconic version and influencing the appearance of almost every iteration since.

The updated look finds its way into comics with *RAH* #45 ("In Search of Candy," March 1986), but Snake Eyes' new duds are eclipsed by the return of Storm Shadow, and the revelation that Zartan—Cobra's resident master of disguise—was responsible for the death of the Hard Master. Snake Eyes goes AWOL and accompanies Storm Shadow to Cobra Island where Zartan is, sidestepping G.I. Joe's already-in-progress invasion. Individually, they're unstoppable, but together, they're a force of nature. When the violence starts in *RAH* #46 ("Who's Who on Cobra Island," April 1986), the contrast of Snake Eyes' black and Storm Shadow's white together creates a chaotic symphony of yin and yang—the embodiment of light and darkness—but it's hard to distinguish who's who. It's the first time we've seen real Arashikage in action, and nothing in their way has a chance at surviving.

But before they can satisfy their thirst for vengeance, the two are abruptly separated at sea. Storm Shadow's lifeless body is claimed by Dr. Mindbender, and his DNA used to give life to Serpentor, the Cobra Emperor. Robbed of his payback and believing his sword brother dead, Snake Eyes joins the Joes to defend The Pit against Cobra, only to end up captured himself, effectively vanishing from the book for almost half a year.

SILENT PARTNERS

When Snake Eyes returns in *RAH* #65 ("Shuttle Complex," November 1987), he joins Scarlett and Storm Shadow on an unsanctioned mission to Borovia to rescue Stalker. With so many disparate pieces of Snake Eyes (past, present, and future) converging in one place, this arc establishes the united front of Scarlett, Stalker, and Storm Shadow, characters who, going forward, will provide invaluable stability to Snake Eyes' life. It's a dynamic only teased at back in *RAH* #26 and 27 that solidifies here into something akin to family, creating bonds that go beyond commitments to the Arashikage, Cobra, and even G.I. Joe.

After Borovia, the ninja plot takes a backseat for a while, as Hama widens the book's scope to better accommodate the ever-expanding cast of characters and vehicles. But in *RAH* #84, he starts connecting dots again with one of the series' most monumental bombshells—the driver of the car that killed Snake Eyes' family? Cobra Commander's brother! We then learn that after his brother's death, the man-who-would-be Cobra Commander hired a mercenary (Zartan) to assassinate the last living member of the family he blamed for destroying his own. What's more, the accident was the final push the already disillusioned car salesman needed to put him on the road to becoming Cobra Commander.

And so begins the trend of connecting Snake Eyes to everything! It's no surprise, really. Not only was he the most popular character, but with a serpent-esque codename and a mask covering his entire face (traits shared with Cobra Commander), it's no wonder Hama was inspired to go full soap opera and position Snake Eyes at the center of nearly everything and everyone. Well, everyone except Destro and the Baroness... right? Not so fast.

With *RAH* #93 ("Taking the Plunge," November 1989), Hama kicks off the series' most sensational era with "The Snake Eyes Trilogy." A trip to Switzerland for reconstructive surgery leaves Scarlett in a coma and Snake Eyes in the clutches of the Baroness. The crux of the story is the Baroness' misinformed quest for revenge, as she erroneously believes Snake Eyes killed her brother in Vietnam. But as Destro explains, he was there in Vietnam, too, offering an angst-free version of events that exonerates Snake Eyes, forcing the Baroness to question everything she's ever believed in.

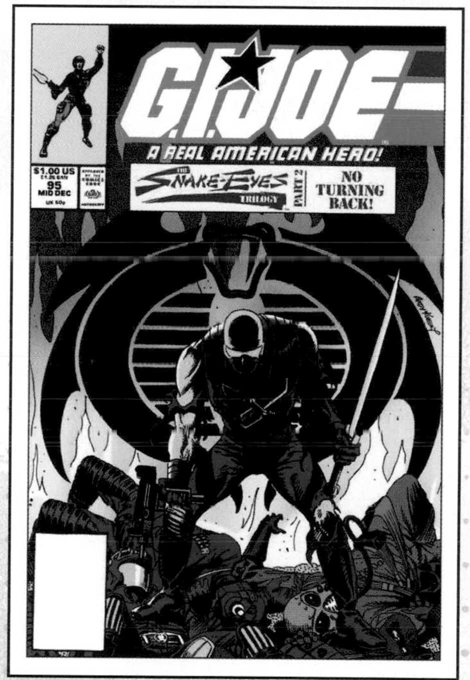
G.I. JOE
A REAL AMERICAN HERO!
$1.00 US
95
MID DEC
THE SNAKE-EYES TRILOGY
PART 2
NO TURNING BACK!

Trilogy works as something of a greatest hits story, reinforcing Snake Eyes' position as the central character in the G.I. Joe saga—this time, sharing a pre-G.I. Joe connection to both Destro and the Baroness. And it again delivers another fine example of Stalker and Storm Shadow's loyalty, having Snake Eyes' back beyond the call of duty when they attempt to rescue him from a flame-engulfed embassy.

RAH #103 ("The Amazing Welkin," August 1990), Trilogy's thematic follow-up, has Storm Shadow manipulating the Jugglers (a group of high-ranking military know-it-alls) into giving Snake Eyes a reason to leave the comatose Scarlett's bedside. A suicide mission into Borovia to save his twin sister's one-time fiancé sees Storm Shadow using the Arashikage mindset to clear Snake Eyes' mind of all distractions, including pain and remorse—"Go forth as a killing wraith and let no man deter you." It's the most violent we've seen Snake Eyes, leading Stalker to question Storm Shadow's methods and his motives. In the end, the mission forces all of them—Storm Shadow, Stalker, and the freshly awakened Scarlett—to question how far they'll go for Snake Eyes. The answer? To hell and back.

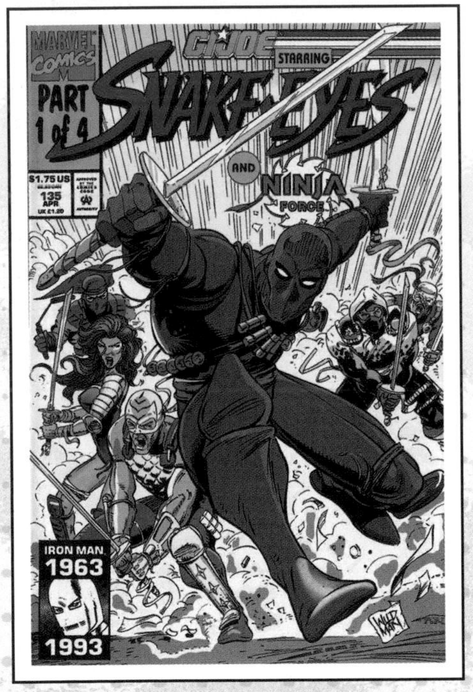
MARVEL COMICS
G.I.JOE
STARRING
SNAKE EYES
AND
NINJA FORCE
PART 1 of 4
$1.75 US
135 APR
UK £1.20
IRON MAN
1963
1993

With *RAH* moving into its final years, the title briefly became *G.I JOE: STARRING SNAKE EYES AND NINJA FORCE* (*RAH* #135 – 145). Hama manages to make the shift in title and tone work by using it as an opportunity to mold Snake Eyes into a mentor—the Silent Master! There's a newfound pride in Snake Eyes as he, Scarlett, and Storm Shadow take on apprentices and redirect the Arashikage as a force for good. Despite being surrounded by copious amounts of sword-wielding gladiators, Snake Eyes finds some semblance of peace and contentment in who he's become. And by the time *RAH* #150 ("Slam Dance In The Cyber Castle," July 1994) rolls around—the final showdown with Cobra Commander—Snake Eyes doesn't even wear a mask. It's his last costume change, but this one's not inspired by a toy. He just doesn't need to cover himself up anymore.

RAH #155 ("A Letter From Snake Eyes," December 1994) is the final issue of the original series. In it, we see our silent soldier replying to a missive from Sean Collins, the teenaged son of another of Snake Eyes' brothers from 'Nam. Sean wants to join the army against his father's protestations, so he reaches out for a bit of perspective. In what is almost certainly a callback to the recon journal seen way back in *RAH* #4, Snake Eyes sends Sean a handwritten letter filled with hard stories of war and loss—but of bravery and sacrifice as well. It's the end of Snake Eyes, and the man underneath regrets nothing. He's served his country and saved lives—his own included.

QUIET AS A GRAVE

In 2010, IDW Publishing brought back *G.I. JOE: A REAL AMERICAN HERO* with Larry Hama at the helm once again. Picking up where the classic series left off, Hama and artists Agustin Padilla and SL Gallant brought the fight against Cobra into the 21st century, introducing the property to an all new generation of fans.

Hama's enthusiasm for telling Snake Eyes stories saw him throw all manner of new and unique challenges at the Silent Master and the rest of the Joes. But his commitment to keeping things fresh took readers down an unprecedented path in 2015 with a story arc entitled "The Death of Snake Eyes" (*RAH* #s

212 – 215). True to its title, Snake Eyes gave his life to save lives, and in doing so inspired an unlikely legacy as important as the man himself. A severely scarred Sean Collins—the same kid who wrote Snake Eyes a letter way back in *RAH* #155—takes up the mantle in *RAH* #213, continuing his mentor's mission as well as inheriting no small amount of the same pain. And he wouldn't be the only one.

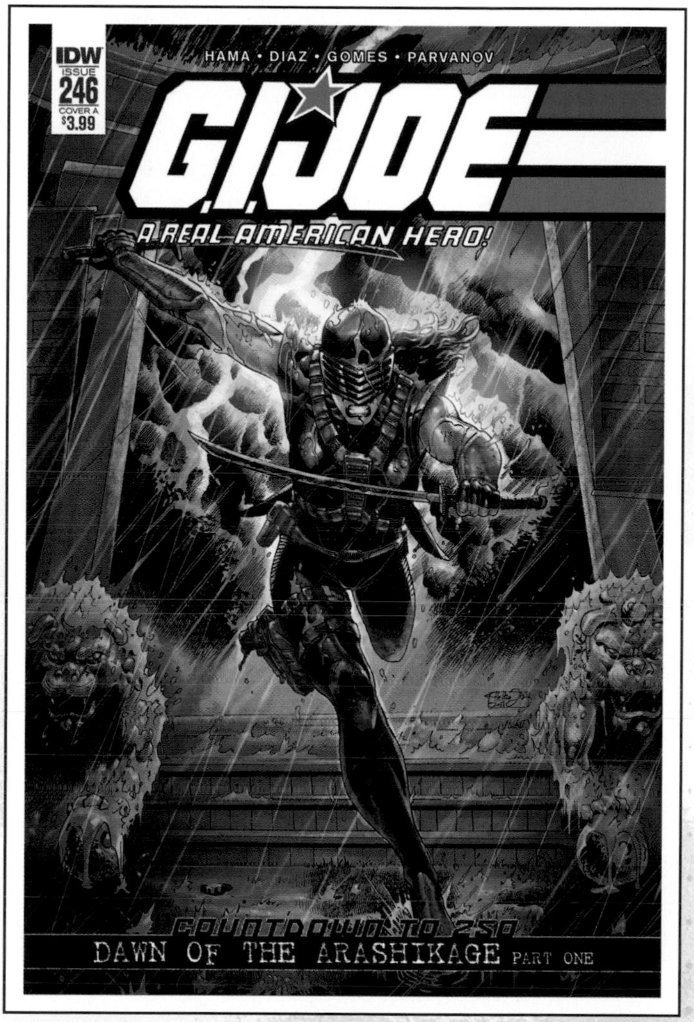
IDW
ISSUE
246
COVER A
$3.99
HAMA • DIAZ • GOMES • PARVANOV
G.I. JOE
A REAL AMERICAN HERO!
COUNTDOWN TO 250
DAWN OF THE ARASHIKAGE PART ONE

Almost a year later, in *RAH* #226 ("Cobra Nation, Part 2," April 2016), Hama introduced readers to Dawn Moreno, a Springfield High student of some interest to Cobra Commander. Over the next year, Dawn undergoes Cobra indoctrination, eventually finding herself hooked to a faulty brainwave scanner housing the memories of the original Snake Eyes. When the switch is thrown, Dawn absorbs the very essence of Snake Eyes, taking not only his name but his years of experience. Dawn wreaks havoc on Cobra, tapping into the darkest and most cold-blooded aspects of Snake Eyes' nature before taking control of the rage and finding balance of mind and body.

Even in death, Snake Eyes' comics legacy is alive and well. *RAH* is still going strong, with Dawn and Sean both inhabiting the role of Snake Eyes. 2019's *G.I. JOE: SIERRA MUERTE* by Michel Fiffe applies an auteur's pen to the comradeship of the Arashikage sword brothers. The Silent Master's story appears to be far from over.

For more than thirty years, the legend of Snake Eyes has played out in the comic pages of *G.I. JOE: A REAL AMERICAN HERO*. His journey from mystery man to G.I. Joe's most celebrated member is a Dickensian narrative filled with tragedy, revenge, redemption, and death... including his own. Still, it's hard to keep a ninja commando down, and despite a lifetime of setbacks, Snake Eyes never fails to "charlie mike"—he continues the mission, inspiring the hearts and minds of those who know him best, both in the comics and in the real world.

ART BY **JAMIE SULLIVAN** | COLORS BY **VINICIUS TOWNSEND**

Twenty Questions:
The Michel Fiffe Interview
Interview conducted by Chad Bowers

G.I. JOE: SIERRA MUERTE is the story of a compact G.I. Joe unit dropped into the Central American hotbed of Sierra Muerte to keep a legacy of mad science from falling into the hands of Cobra. More than that, it's author Michel Fiffe's striking love letter to the greatest action adventure saga of the '80s and '90s—*G.I. Joe: A Real American Hero!*—and one of the most energetic and imaginative comics you'll read this year!

Here, the critically acclaimed creator of *COPRA* and *ZEGAS* opens up about his creative process, a love for the animated G.I. Joe, and drops a few hints at what we might see in the sequel.

CHAD BOWERS: How did the project come about? What's the secret origin of *G.I. Joe: Sierra Muerte*?

MICHEL FIFFE: *I was reading some old Sierra Gordo stories and their neighboring country, Sierra Muerte, came up. I immediately called up IDW to see if there was any possible way I would be able to feature the Sierra Muerte locale. Cut to a year later (these things take*

time), and I was drawing Roadblock deep in the Muerte swamps.

CB: What is your earliest memory of *G.I. Joe*? Was it a big part of your childhood?

MF: *My childhood was dominated by comic books, but my intro to the Joes came via the cartoon. The animation was some of my favorite. The name of the studio escapes me, but it had that clean, quasi-anime style that was cooler than anything else.*

CB: The animation studio was Sunbow Entertainment, and yeah, they were brilliant! They produced the animated commercials for the Marvel book, too. Like you, I was into the animated series before I started reading the comics. When I finally started picking up *Real American Hero*, I actually thought it was like supplemental material to the show or something, even though I knew it came first. Kid logic, man.

So what's your working method on something like *Sierra Muerte*? Hama is known to be a plot-first guy, obviously, and

STALKER · SCARLETT · SNAKE EYES · FLINT · LADY JAYE

I gotta wonder if you follow a similar practice... is there a script or do you jump straight to drawing?

MF: *The dialogue goes through several drafts on handwritten notes along with the layouts. I don't usually divorce the two. It's funny because I've learned to embrace Hama's improv plotting approach in my own book,* Copra*. This being a limited series, I was hyper-aware of the narrative real estate I had. I wanted to pack as much in as possible, so I had to be on top of it.*

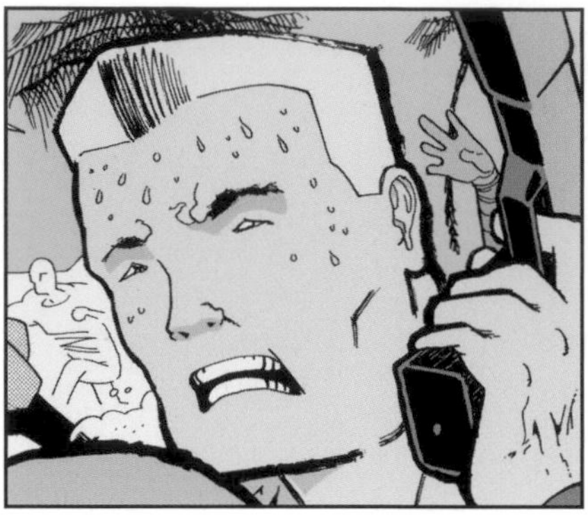

CB: How was working on *Sierra Muerte* different from the way you produce an issue of *Copra*, or something like *Bloodstrike Brutalists*?

MF: *On* Copra *I don't have to answer to anyone, so that speeds the process along.* Bloodstrike *was similar in that Rob [Liefeld, creator of* Bloodstrike*] trusted what I delivered, but I would still send him updates to prove I wasn't going off the rails.* Sierra Muerte *was much more measured in production. Every step of the way was accounted for, which was a dynamic I really appreciate because it's so what I'm not used to.*

CB: It goes without saying, but I love the title of this series. *Sierra Muerte* just reminds me of the toys, and those promotional storylines Hasbro would sometimes build into the releases. "Mission: Brazil," "Cobra Island," etc... It's perfectly reminiscent of things like that for me. Did you ever consider going with another title or setting it in a different location?

MF: *I was spanning the world in my early notes, but I found myself getting more excited for the Sierra Muerte parts. My instinct told me to zero in on this basically uncharted land. The story opened up itself once I did that.*

CB: In the first issue you dive headfirst into Hama country, and treat us with a reference to Dr. Venom right there on page one, panel one! What kind of time did you spend with the Marvel and IDW-published material going into *Sierra Muerte*?

MF: *Ha, Dr. Venom was a nod for all the heads out there. I've read Hama's stuff for years, but I took a deep refresher course just to get juiced up for the project. I was pleasantly surprised at Hama's return, with the original numbering at that. Before legacy numbering became trendy, too.*

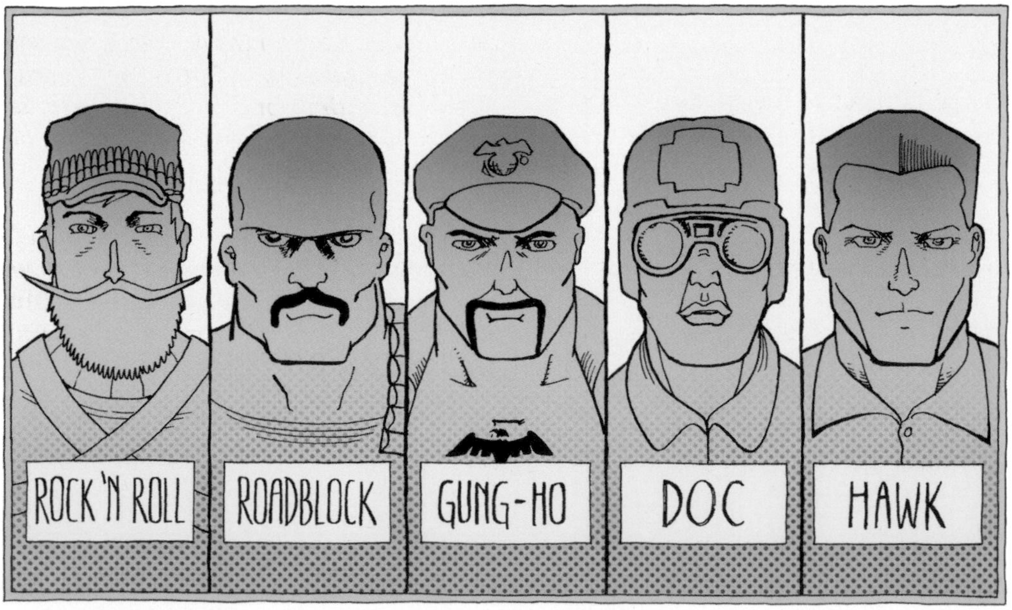
ROCK 'N ROLL
ROADBLOCK
GUNG-HO
DOC
HAWK

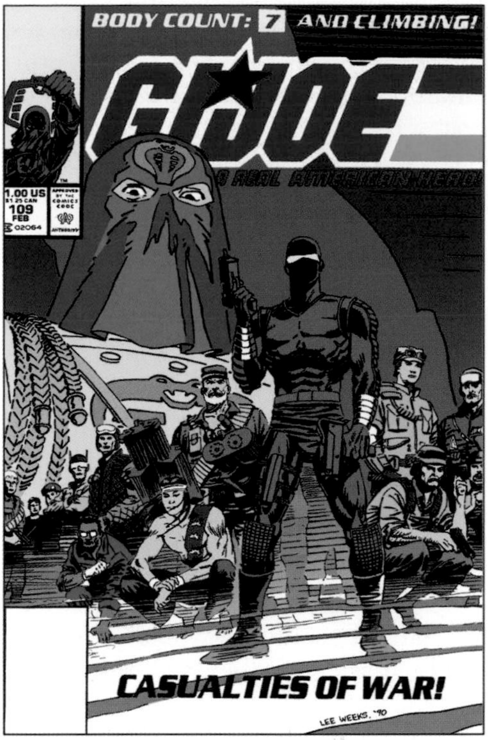
BODY COUNT: 7 AND CLIMBING!
G.I. JOE
1.00 US
109
FEB
CASUALTIES OF WAR!
LEE WEEKS, '90

CB: There's that gorgeous two-page spread in *Sierra Muerte* #1—the title page, with the Joes dropping down onto Cobra, guns blazing, swords drawn! It's genuinely inspired, and like nothing I've seen before in a Joe comic. I absolutely loved it. Do I detect shades of the animated series, maybe?

MF: *You nailed it. I mean, that is the visual cue I'm going on. It's clean, sharp, nothing fussy about it. It helped give this story the direct tone it required.*

CB: There's a lot of sweat in this comic, Michel. And not that I'm complaining, because I love sweaty Hawk's exasperated face! But it's a really innovative way of reminding us it's hot and miserable as hell in Sierra Muerte. Anyway.

Let's talk a little about this killer cast of Joes and Cobras. How did you decide which characters you were going to use? Was there a specific Joe you couldn't wait to get your hands on?

MF: *Snake Eyes was the one I couldn't believe I was drawing. Picking a cast was a combination of who would function best in my story and who would be most fun to draw. Simple as that.*

CB: Your Joes get shot, and your Cobras get shot by each other. Let's talk about violence for a quick sec, and how there's traditionally not a lot of bloodshed in *G.I. Joe* (despite being directly tied to themes of war and the military). When I was little, I kind of filled in the blanks, you know? Until *RAH* #109 , and those hardcore (but still bloodless) deaths in Trucial Abysmia. I've seen you point to that arc as a favorite, so what's your take on those issues, and the depiction of violence in *G.I. Joe* in general?

MF: *It's such a tricky, delicate balance that even the cartoon had to reckon with. Y'know, lots of lasers that never land. Hama was essentially doing a war book aimed at kids; you don't want to underserve the reality of violence in these stories, but you don't want to go overboard, either. He pulled it off.*

CB: Do you have a favorite story from the Marvel era? Mine's the Snake Eyes Trilogy, and the subsequent Borovia mission.

MF: *That's a good one. I recently made a personal top ten Joe stories but an honorable mention goes to the Cobra Commander's origin story, the one where he and Destro are trapped underground but eventually escape and go on a road trip in disguise. It stands out for being so emotional. It's such a rarity.*

CB: I love that you include a few vehicles! Your designs feel very toyetic without getting too specific. Is that on purpose?

MF: *Totally. I drew my own version of some established vehicles. It has to be a natural extension of the world I draw, though, so I always put my own spin on things. Not only vehicles, but everything, every project.*

CB: You do a spectacular job working in the iconic Cobra Commander outfits. Do you have a favorite look for the ol' Blue-Hooded Hell Raiser? (That's what the NES video game ad called him, and man... I wish it would've stuck.)

MF: *I remember that ad! That reminds me that I used to play the Nintendo game, too. I remember it being hypnotic, but maybe it was the great soundtrack. But yeah, Cobra Commander. I'm a fan of the hooded version all the way. It's just creepier. I drew both versions, of course.*

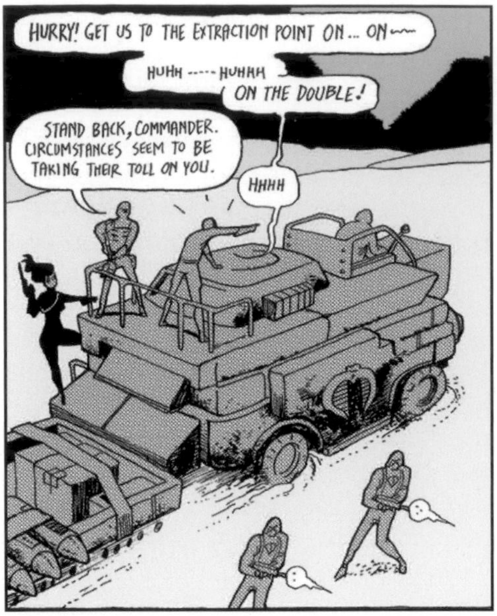
HURRY! GET US TO THE EXTRACTION POINT ON... ON~~
HUHH ----- HUHHH
ON THE DOUBLE!
STAND BACK, COMMANDER. CIRCUMSTANCES SEEM TO BE TAKING THEIR TOLL ON YOU.
HHHH

CB: I'm interested in hearing what inspired the color choices in *Sierra Muerte*, and how you accomplish the signature Fiffe look. Did your color choices vary from issue to issue?

MF: *It goes back to being inspired by the '80s cartoon. And that isn't my comfort zone, either—I usually do a lot of hand coloring. So I went for a combination, but I definitely tried to keep the characters sharp-looking and classic, even when they're all sweaty and bloody.*

CB: As a ride-or-die Snake Eyes guy, I put Red Snake Eyes in the top five visuals of the whole series. What are your favorite scenes and moments for the series? What are you most proud of?

MF: *Oh, that's awesome to hear. I gotta say that the reason I made Snake Eyes red was so that when he was battle damaged, he would somewhat resemble the ultra rare Cobra Mortal figure. Having him and Storm Shadow square off in a silent chunk of the story was a kick, but just as good. Writing Baroness and Destro's back-and-forth was also a high point for me.*

CB: The Destro and Baroness scenes are amazing! Like Scarlett and Snake Eyes, or Flint and Lady Jaye, the Baroness and Destro's weird, grand romance is absolutely one of my favorite things about *G.I. Joe*, and you handled it beautifully!

I'm curious, was there any piece of *G.I. Joe* you felt obligated to include? And was there anything juicy left on the cutting room floor you wish you could've worked in?

MF: *I wanted to incorporate Serpentor, but had no natural room for it to work. I seeded him, though, so I would love to tackle him and bring in Cobra-La. I would love to draw every single last one of them.*

CB: I say go for it! Cobra-La gets such a bad rap, man. I feel like once you accept Destro, Zartan, and Raptor as part of the story, you're a step away from snakemen in the Himalayas already, so why not just roll with it?

All right, last one. How have your feelings or opinions about *G.I. Joe,* changed over the course of the series?

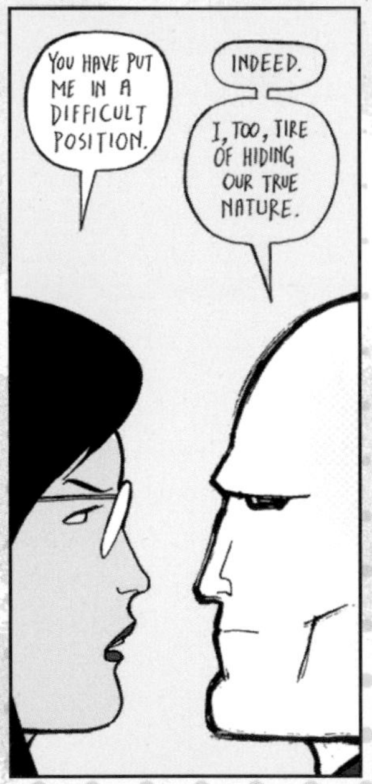
YOU HAVE PUT ME IN A DIFFICULT POSITION.
INDEED.
I, TOO, TIRE OF HIDING OUR TRUE NATURE.

MF: *By nature of working on the characters so intensely, I can't help but feel connected to all of them in a deeper way than when I was solely a reader. I'm just fortunate to have taken a crack at them. Maybe next time I'll even include a Fred.*

Chad Bowers is a writer from South Carolina. His credits include the fan-favorite Marvel Comics series X-MEN '92, INFINITY COUNTDOWN DARKHAWK, and the original graphic novel DEADPOOL: BAD BLOOD. He's worked for Oni Press, Dynamite Entertainment, IDW, BOOM Studios, and is currently writing INFINITY WARS: SLEEPWALKER (Marvel), YOUNGBLOOD: BLOOD WARS (Image Comics), and some other stuff that doesn't have "WARS" in the title.